A bird in the hand . . .

"What a fine mind you have, my Persian woman," the duke purred in a manner Persys instantly mistrusted.

Yet when he reached out a hand to touch her cheek with a gentle finger, she made no move to evade him. Like a mesmerized bird, she stood gazing up at him, her breath suspended, waiting. She had not long.

He was careful not to startle her, treating her like the timid bird she felt. With the odd sensation that this had been fated, she felt his lips touch hers, igniting a fire within her such as she had never known before. It was impossible not to respond. Strangely enough she felt no displeasure, no fear of him, no feeling of revulsion whatsoever. Rather, she welcomed his lips, their warm touch on hers, with the feeling that she had longed for his kiss. . . .

Miss Timothy Perseveres

Emily Hendrickson

A SIGNET BOOK

SIGNET
Published by the Penguin Group
Penguin Putnam Inc., 375 Hudson Street,
New York, New York 10014, U.S.A.
Penguin Books Ltd, 27 Wrights Lane,
London W8 5TZ, England
Penguin Books Australia Ltd,
Ringwood, Victoria, Australia
Penguin Books Canada Ltd, 10 Alcorn Avenue,
Toronto, Ontario, Canada M4V 3B2
Penguin Books (N.Z.) Ltd, 182–190 Wairau Road,
Auckland 10, New Zealand

Penguin Books Ltd, Registered Offices:
Harmondsworth, Middlesex, England

First published by Signet, an imprint of Dutton NAL,
a member of Penguin Putnam Inc.

First Printing, February, 1999
10 9 8 7 6 5 4 3 2 1

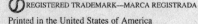REGISTERED TRADEMARK—MARCA REGISTRADA

Printed in the United States of America

Chapter One

The lush fragrance of late spring flowers mingling with the pungent scent of burning candles drifted over the assembled guests seated in the elegant vastness of St. George's, Hanover Square. What was assuredly the wedding of the year was in progress and Society had come forth en masse to view the union of the beautiful and well-dowered Miss Katherine Talbot to the wealthy, highly eligible Marquess of Torrington. Beautiful blooms graced the altar; the groomsmen and the bridal attendants were exquisitely garbed and the ladies in particular were suitably demure. All was as it ought to be.

The urbane and fashionable gentleman seated prominently near the front crossed his arms across his chest while he surveyed the pair at the altar. They were well matched, both in looks and fortune. It was a good marriage, one of which he highly approved, being nominal head of the family. His gaze shifted from the pair to the maid of honor—Torrington's sister Lady Jocelyn, then to the bridal attendant.

He'd been informed she was a cousin of the bride. Miss Timothy, he believed. The Honorable Miss Persys Timothy, although one who looked less like a Persian woman he could not imagine. She far more resembled an exotic waif with her delicate features and faintly slanted eyes. The wreath of pink rosebuds perched on her ash-brown hair added to her piquancy. She intrigued him. As he watched her while the vows were concluded, he caught a swift look of anguish cross her face. Why such a pretty young woman should know pain at the wedding of her cousin he couldn't imagine. Jealousy? Possibly. On the other hand, perhaps it was but a momentary twinge. He resolved to take note of her behavior at the breakfast to follow.

Persys clutched her small posy with determined hands. She would endure this ordeal. She would. And, she vowed, no one would ever know that her heart was shattered into a hundred tiny pieces, never to be repaired. The very sight of the handsome groom smiling down at his bride cut her into ribbons of pain. Oh, that she might exchange places with her cousin!

The final words of the ceremony rolled forth from the severe and rather daunting bishop. In a flurry of slight confusion the happy couple retired to sign the register. Persys reluctantly followed, knowing she must appear as happy as she ought.

There was to be a sumptuous breakfast following the wedding. Persys wondered if she would survive the ordeal intact. Surely she could conceal her feelings for another few hours? After that, nothing really mattered, did it?

There was a slight breeze once they reached the outside. Dust swirled about the bridal party while they laughingly gathered on the sidewalk, then entered the awaiting carriages. Persys nodded politely when spoken to and smiled in reply to the groomsman's light chatter. He was Torrington's younger brother, Lord Charles, and a shadow of his handsome sibling.

Chin up, that's what was required.

The spacious rooms where Aunt Talbot had organized the breakfast fairly bloomed with flowers. An incredible array of foods graced the tables. An epergne overflowing with exotic flowers and fruits was centered between her prized silver candleholders and surrounded by bowls and dishes that vied in an extravagant display to tempt any jaded palate.

Persys could not eat a bite but she pretended, pushing a small selection of food around and around on her plate.

"I should have thought you would be hungry after all that business," a well-modulated and highly cultured voice said dryly for Persys alone to hear. "I'll wager you scarcely ate earlier this morning. Are you sure you feel quite all right?"

Surprised at the note of concern she detected in his tone, Persys turned her head to look at the speaker. Heavens above, it was none other than the man she had been cautioned not to approach, the noble Duke of Eddington.

"Indeed, Your Grace, while what you say is true, I find I am not interested in food at the moment. Nerves, perhaps?" She gave him a polite smile, turning away and taking one step when he spoke again, halting her in her flight.

"I have no one with whom to speak." He managed to sound wistful and lonely, which had to be errant nonsense. Yet he appealed to something deep within, and ignoring her instructions she paused to look at him. "Stay and keep me company. I would avoid those toad-eaters who edge close in hopes of snaring a bit of conversation with a duke and those who would invite me to some event I really don't wish to attend. It's a devil of a coil to be polite when not desired."

Startled, Persys half-smiled and nodded. "I can see that would be a dilemma. I am fortunate not to worry about that."

"But something is worrying you, is it not?" he gently queried while guiding her across the room to a somewhat sheltered spot blessedly obscured from her aunt's view. Potted palms conveniently offered rather whimsical refuge. Persys doubted if her aunt was the least concerned about her reputation, but it would not do to be found speaking to the most important guest, one her aunt hoped to parade before her friends as proof of the groom's excellent connections in the unlikely event they didn't know of them already.

Her back to the cool comfort of the wall, Persys faced him, her puzzlement at his interest unconcealed. "I cannot think why you should be concerned, Your Grace. I am quite pleased at my cousin's most excellent marriage and happy to have been of help to her during the time of her come-out. If I seem a trifle blue-deviled it is merely that I shall miss her excellent company." Persys studied the elegant gentleman before her to see if he accepted her remarks without question.

"You have been her companion?" he asked, his rich voice revealing nothing more than polite interest.

"Indeed, Your Grace. Upon the death of my parents Aunt Talbot graciously invited me to live with them, later to keep Katherine company until such time as she married."

"And now?" he persisted gently, not seeming greatly interested. Yet there was a quality about him that made Persys reply honestly, without evasion.

"Now? I do not know what will happen. Perhaps my aunt will take me as her companion. While I have a modest dowry, it is scarcely sufficient to tempt anyone of merit. Besides, I have no interest in becoming married," she concluded with a hint of defiance and a peek at the man of her dreams, the . . . dashing Marquess of Torrington, her cousin's new husband.

"Curious," he commented. "I thought all young women were interested in marriage. After all, what else is there?"

"True," she replied almost bitterly, in her melancholy state far more open than she normally was. "But then, I have the disadvantage of three and twenty years on my plate. I am quite on the shelf, I suspect."

"Indeed, I had not thought you to be so elderly," he replied with a teasing smile. The duke appeared to lose interest in their admittedly uninspiring conversation and turned to gaze at the overladen table. "Your aunt and uncle have certainly done well by their daughter."

"Their only daughter, Your Grace. That does make a difference." Persys gave him a wry smile.

"They'd not do the same for you, their niece?" He gave her a knowing look. She elected not to answer.

"Excuse me. I have no doubt there is something my aunt wishes me to do. There usually is." With a polite curtsy, she whisked herself around him to seek her aunt. She suspected her relative actually would think of some duty for Persys to perform. It seemed to irk Aunt Talbot if Persys were not continually kept busy at something or other.

"There you are," her stout and vastly overdressed aunt declared as Persys slipped into place in the receiving line.

"I felt in need of a restorative, dear aunt." Persys responded mildly. "Knowing how concerned you are for the health of all who live here, I felt certain you'd not mind. I am scarcely required at the moment."

"Now that you mention it, there is a matter of some import we must discuss, Persys," her aunt began, only to be interrupted by a guest.

Left to wonder precisely what it might be that her aunt sought to discuss, Persys automatically greeted the various guests entering the house with her customary cool charm.

From his position in the haven of potted palms, the duke watched the much-too-slim girl converse with her aunt. There was little doubt in his mind that she possessed good breeding. She carried herself with an elegance that could only come from a proper background. She was a brave young thing, unless he missed his guess. She also possessed a most amazing pair of violet eyes— large, thickly lashed, and most expressive. He wondered how she would fare with her aunt. Something told him that she had little to hope for from that quarter. Lady Talbot possessed a hard look about her, without the least sign of softness, not even when she glanced at her daughter. Only when she looked at her son, a rather weak-eyed creature of dandyfied perfection, did she appear to unbend, and then only slightly. But then, David Talbot was the sort who could only inspire warm thoughts in the heart of his mother.

"Ha? There you are!" The duke's good friend and sometimes companion Ninian Hervey appeared at his side, carrying a plate heaped with delicacies. It always amazed the duke that Ninian could eat such prodigious quantities and never gain a pound.

"As you see," the duke replied wryly. "I gather you are enjoying the repast at any rate. Any comments on the affair?" A grin flashed briefly before he added, "Do you know any of them?"

"Know Torrington fairly well. Met his bride—the fair Katherine—at numerous balls and so forth. You know how it is. Fellow don't dare spend much time with any female, else he finds himself leg-shackled." Ninian forked a morsel of crab cake into his mouth, then added, "Not ready for that, myself."

"Most of us prefer the unmarried state until that fatal moment when we meet the one we cannot live without," the duke said lightly. His gaze strayed to the slim elegance of Miss Timothy as she bent an ear to listen to her aunt. Whatever she heard was evidently not pleasing for she started with alarm, her usual pallor increasing. He wondered what the old biddy had to say that produced such an effect.

Across the room Persys trembled at her aunt's words.

"You must see that it is time for you to leave," Aunt Talbot said firmly. "It is not that you have been idle while here, child. It is simply that you are no longer needed. I feel certain that you will find a suitable position in no time at all. There are any number of governess openings, I fancy. You would be capable of such. Or perhaps you may prefer to be a companion to a lady of quality? You are three and twenty now, and ought to be either married or in a suitable occupation."

Persys swallowed carefully. To be bluntly informed while in the midst of a large gathering of Society that she was to leave as soon as possible was something only her thoughtless aunt could manage. There was little Persys might do but nod gracefully as though her aunt had not uttered such dreadful words, and retreat. She turned to escape.

"Persys," her aunt demanded.

Persys pretended not to hear. She needed a moment to herself, to consider her options. Of course, in the very back of her mind she had known this was coming. She merely had not expected it to happen quite so soon and without the slightest warning.

"Miss Timothy," someone said nearby as she slipped through the throng. Again she pretended not to hear the voice. There was such a crowd it was quite possible. She was not conscious of the duke's gaze. Nor would she have cared in the least that anyone observed her in her flight. She only knew that she must leave this house and soon, and however was she to do it? Where could she go? Did one find positions listed in the newspaper? Or perhaps one went to an agency? She must ask.

She entered the hall and hurried along until she reached the library to find sanctuary there. Moments later her peace ended. Intruding footsteps brought her whirling about to face the one who entered her refuge. "You!"

"I trust I am not unwelcome. I shall leave the door open to still any gossiping tongues." The duke pushed the tall mahogany door back as far as it would go, then sauntered forward. "Although I must add that most of the throng seems intent upon the food and the conversation, not in refuge, nor in books." He gave her a cool smile. " 'Tis unlikely we shall be disturbed."

"How lovely," she replied tartly, wrapping her slender arms about her as though to ward off a chill. She gave him a curious look, then walked slowly around the room, glancing at the shelves lined with books, most of them unread.

"I believe you have a problem. May I help?" He didn't know what had prompted him to leave the gathering to follow the distressed young woman. Nor did he understand what it was that now urged him to offer his assistance. The chit clearly wished him to the devil—or at the very least far away.

"I seriously doubt if there is a thing you can do—unless you can conjure a position for me on a moment's notice. My dear aunt informed me just now that I must leave—the sooner, the better. I confess I had not expected to be put out quite so promptly." She tossed him a hurt look. "This is the only home I can remember and as such I had thought to remain a little longer. But it appears I have no choice."

"It seems rather heartless," he commented, crossing to lean against the fireplace mantel. A fitful fire burned to ward off any chill that might dare invade the splendid interior of the Talbot mansion. He glanced at the flames that licked at the sole log and handful of coal then added, "You have no one else?"

"Not a soul," Persys admitted. "No grandmother to welcome me to her bosom, no other aunts that I know of; certainly none have stepped forward to offer me a place beneath her roof. It would seem I am quite, quite alone in this world. What a pity I have such a small dowry."

"Why do you say that?" He nudged the lone log with a polished shoe and a few sparks shot up.

"Why, so a gallant gentleman would whisk me off to Gretna Green and perhaps a not unpleasant fate." She gave him a scornful look, then shrugged her shoulders as though acknowledging the futility of her words. "It is a damnable position to be in!" she whispered fiercely. Surely her aunt wouldn't push her out the door until she had a place to go? Or would she? Lady Talbot was quite capable of ordering Persys to leave, then taking herself and her docile husband off to some spa after giving instructions to the staff that Persys was to be gone immediately.

"But you told me not minutes ago you had no desire to marry. Have circumstances altered your determination?" He flicked her a casual look that saw far too much. "You would do well to team up with Ninian Hervey—he is of like opinion."

"This is no joking matter, Your Grace," she said, stiff with indignation.

"No, I don't suppose it is," he replied quietly. "Never having been in such a position I scarcely know, do I? I suffer from the opposite. I am always in demand and seldom for my own charming self. Rather it is my title they desire. Rather humbling, you know," he concluded meekly.

She laughed at that bit of nonsense. "You hardly strike me as the humble sort, Your Grace. But I suppose it can be annoying, having to suspect the motives of every person you meet. Well, you needn't suspect mine. I am far more concerned about a roof over my head than your title, however impressive it might be. Am I a heretic? I fear I often annoy my aunt with my little irreverences."

"What shall you do?" he persisted.

"I have money—nothing much by your standards, I imagine, but enough to live on if I am not too demanding. However, I am not permitted to live alone and there's the rub. I have sufficient for myself but not an establishment such as would be deemed proper." She mocked, not him but the dictates of Society.

"Perhaps you would allow me to make inquiries among my female acquaintances? Surely something can be found." He moved away from the fireplace, restlessly pacing along the perimeter of the Persian rug.

"I haven't the least notion as to why you would want to help me, but I shan't cavil at the offer. While I might wish to be independent, I am all too aware of the difficulties in such behavior. It simply will not do for a gently bred woman to reject help— particularly yours."

"I am well and truly put in my place," he said with an air of humility that returned a faint smile to her lips.

Harry—as known to his family and closest friends—noted that in spite of her slim figure her mouth was full and ripe. Enticing. And although she was slender, she still possessed womanly curves in all the right places. He turned his gaze to a particularly repellent painting of a dead pheasant draped across a platter with suitable garnish around it. He studied the oil a moment, then turned to her. "Let me think on it awhile. Something is bound to occur to me."

Persys nodded, then urged, "You had best go from here before someone chances to see you. The last thing you can wish is to have gossip heaped on your head." She made shooing motions with slender, well-gloved hands and as he strolled from the library the thought occurred to him that Miss Timothy was an amazing young woman in more ways than one.

Persys gave up her seclusion, knowing full well that did she not return to the gathering, someone was bound to seek her out and ask questions she might not wish to answer.

"Persys . . . there you are!" Katherine cried, walking swiftly to her in a flurry of cream silk. "It is time for me to change and I would that you join me. I am so happy I wish to share it."

"Of course." Persys wondered if her smile looked as strained as it felt.

They made their way up the stairs and to the luxurious room that had been the bride's. While Katherine bubbled joyously about her bridal trip, Persys and Lady Jocelyn assisted her with the changes of clothing. The maid of honor appeared as reflective and absent-minded as did Persys. Perhaps she also wondered what would befall her once her brother and his bride returned to the only home she knew. Weddings! It was surprising how they could upset so many plans and people.

"I hope it will not be long before you find the man you wish to marry, Persys," Katherine caroled, her eyes twinkling. Nothing was said about Lady Jocelyn, for it was known that she had no desire to wed, as she was still mourning the fiancé who had perished in the war.

"It is unlikely," Persys replied. "I fear you have captured the cream of the crop. Find me one such as he and perhaps I shall reconsider."

"There are few like my brother, Miss Timothy," Lady Jocelyn murmured.

Persys blinked and nodded, quite determined she would not turn into a watering pot.

"Now let us finish with the last of the buttons so Katherine may join her impatient husband," Lady Jocelyn said with a glance at Persys.

"She is the most lovely bride the Season has seen, I declare," Persys announced brightly.

They stood at the top of the stairs, watching as Katherine sped down and into the swift embrace of her new husband.

"You may not think so at this moment, but life does go on, you know," Lady Jocelyn said with an abruptness that startled Persys.

"I do not know what you mean, my lady—" Persys began, only to be stopped by a wave of the other's hand.

"I rather think you do. I have seen you look at my brother when you thought no one was watching. Dear girl! Never mind, one with your looks will marry. Perhaps not as soon as you would like, but it is inevitable. Those violet eyes, you know."

"I scarcely know what to say," Persys whispered, utterly undone that her secret had been uncovered.

"You might well wonder how I can be such an expert in matrimony and love when I am single at such an age. Christopher teases me with it, said I ought to get away and find my own life once again. Now I fear I must. I would not intrude on their happiness." With a resigned smile, Lady Jocelyn walked regally down the stairs to be followed by a very thoughtful Persys.

It took quite some time for the assembled guests to leave. Lady Talbot was in alt that her little wedding breakfast had drawn the very cream of Society, particularly the elegant and reserved Duke of Eddington. Naturally, he might have felt compelled to attend the ceremony, but to spend such a long time at the breakfast was certainly a feather in her cap. She cast frequent, rather fatuous smiles his way.

Persys stood near the door, smiling until she thought her face would freeze and shaking hands until hers felt numb. She watched the duke approach with a sinking heart. He had promised to help her and not another word had been uttered since then. Well, it was not so surprising that he would change his mind. He must be overwhelmed with requests and demands from near-strangers. Small wonder he would forget about a woman dimly related by marriage.

His hand engulfed hers gently, drawing a reluctant smile to her lips. "I saw you wince at that last hand clasp. I'll not add to your woe."

"I trust you enjoyed the wedding, Your Grace," she replied, ever mindful of her aunt's proximity. It would not do to appear on friendly terms with this man.

He glanced about them, then said in a barely heard voice. "Meet me at five in Green Park tomorrow. I shall have my carriage and we can discuss matters then."

The shock she felt must have shown in her eyes. But then, nothing mattered now but to get away. Almost anything he suggested would be welcome. He gave her hand a faint tightening of reassurance, then left the house.

"Now there's a man for you," her aunt mused. "I confess that not even my new son-in-law can touch him for elegance."

Persys wanted to deny such heresy. She had considered the Marquess of Torrington the height of masculine perfection. That Katherine's mother would say such words seemed perfectly dreadful. As soon as might be Persys excused herself and hurried to the security of her room.

Not for her the elegance of the daughter of the house. She had a simple little chamber on an upper floor. But it had been hers all these years and she hated to leave it.

"Fetch some cases for me, will you, Libby?" she asked of her maid when she entered the room.

"Going somewhere?" Libby said in surprise.

"I do not know where, but I had best be prepared to leave as soon as may be," Persys grimly replied.

The next afternoon found Persys—feeling rather much the fool—strolling through Green Park at the fashionable hour of five.

Her aunt had expressed sarcasm at the notion of such a walk. Persys had calmly pointed out that she might make some useful connection while there, which had the effect of silencing her aunt completely.

"Libby, it is possible I may see someone who was at the wedding," Persys said with care. "Should someone wish to speak with me, you will tactfully retire and be careful to say nothing to anyone at the house. Promise?"

Intrigued at this most unusual behavior of her proper mistress, Libby nodded hastily.

It was some time before Persys saw the duke. His carriage was notable for its simplicity, the elegance of design, and lack of ostentation. Much like the man, she reflected.

He drew his perfectly matched chestnuts to a halt, then handed the reins to his groom. He stepped down to join her on the path, bowing most correctly. "Good afternoon, Miss Timothy. This must be a pleasant diversion for you after the bustle of the wedding."

Persys dipped a graceful curtsy while nodding in agreement. "Indeed, Your Grace. The weather is most agreeable this time of year."

"I would speak with you. Would you join me in my carriage?"

Persys met his gaze and held out her hand. "Of course." She gave Libby a significant look, then entered the carriage with a feeling that her future had appeared.

Libby remained with the groom while His Grace tooled the carriage expertly along the park road.

The silence broke when Persys ventured into speech. "You had something to tell me?"

"Indeed. I have been wondering how to approach the matter. I would not have you misunderstand my offer."

"Your offer?" she echoed faintly, somewhat alarmed at the sound of it.

"Quite simple, actually."

For something simple, he had a peculiar way of telling her about it. "And?" she encouraged.

"My mother has injured her knee rather badly and is all but

helpless. What she needs is a companion to amuse her—something her maid is scarcely able to do."

"I see." Persys thought she had a glimmer.

"I should like you to travel to my country home and reside there with her until such time as she can manage on her own. Normally she is a very active woman, certainly not sedentary as she must be now. She finds her situation most vexing." His mouth tightened as he considered the scene to which he was treated on his last trip. "I should warn you that she is inclined to be capricious. She has many interests and is curious regarding a great many things."

"It seems almost too good to be true," Persys said slowly. "You are not inventing this position merely from the goodness of your heart, feeling sorry for a spinster who must make her way in a cold world?"

"Truly, I am not that considerate. I fear you will earn every penny you are paid." He then mentioned a sum that seemed princely to Persys. She had managed to live on her meager allowance for years. To have an added sum would be delightful. It would mean that she would have new clothes and perhaps set a bit aside for the inevitable rainy day.

"I will be more than happy to help your mother. If she is an active woman I can see where it would indeed vex her to be still for long."

"How soon can you leave?"

Persys looked up at the duke, then darted her gaze about as she thought. "Whenever you wish to leave."

"Admirable woman!" he exclaimed. "The day after tomorrow. And best say nothing to your aunt. While not a malicious person, she does love to gossip. I'd not have you put to the blush with innuendos."

At this bit of plain speaking Persys did indeed blush, and delightfully so, to the duke's point of view.

"I shall be ready early in the morning two days hence, Your Grace. You will send a traveling carriage, I fancy?" Persys wondered precisely what manner of equipage the duke elected to use for travel. She suspected it would be elegant and in excellent repair. She also expected it would have a telltale crest on the doors.

As though he guessed her thoughts, he said, "I imagine your aunt will not be up at that hour of the day, will she? I suppose you will say your good-bye the evening before?"

"Indeed."

"I shall see you early the morning after next, then."

Chapter Two

The following day, Persys and Libby managed to pack her meager belongings in spite of the many demands made on her time by her aunt. Libby had declared she'd not remain without Persys and so packed a modest valise for herself, determined to go with her mistress come what may.

"Her ladyship will set me to upstairs maiding again," Libby explained when Persys questioned her decision.

"I do not know what Her Grace will think when I bring a maid with me," Persys mused.

"She will think you a proper young lady who has come to give her a bit of cheer, miss," Libby pronounced with a nod.

Had she not known better, Persys would have believed Aunt Talbot had learned that Persys planned to leave shortly and wished to wring every ounce of help from her before she left.

There were flowers to see to, replacement of furniture to supervise. Naturally, Aunt could do nothing; she retreated to her bedroom with a sick headache. Indeed, Persys decided, it was actually better for Aunt to be out of the way, for it meant fewer orders and counterorders tossed at the beleaguered servants.

And while Persys bustled about the house, her serviceable apron protecting her muslin day dress, her thoughts kept returning to the puzzle that plagued her. Why had the duke offered to help her? She had never heard a word about him—other than that he was handsome, elusive, and a rather dashing man about London. Why in the world had a man who obviously had a magnificent share of the world's blessings decided to help such an undistinguished person as herself? The daughter of the late Baron Timothy was scarcely in the same category as a duke, although her father *had* distinguished himself as a collector of rare plants. Persys had been most pleased to learn that his heir, her cousin, continued this interest. It was as though something of her father yet lived.

All the while she hurried through her day her heart ached for her lost love. Not that she had ever been in the way for his attentions. She had earned a few smiles from him, a few dances before the betrothal to her cousin, and in turn tumbled into love. It was seeing him wed to her cousin that had torn her to bits and pieces. She could still feel that twisting anguish inside that flashed over her when she knew—really accepted—that he was once and for all beyond her. She was quite certain she could never love another; for where was there another so fine and good? So she had best resolve to be a spinster.

Perhaps in due time, with careful management of her money, she could set up a modest establishment on her own with Libby to serve her and perhaps another female to keep her company. The notion gave her comfort while she went about her tasks, then retreated to her room after dinner to check her belongings and make certain everything she valued had been packed. She had little enough. Aunt had never given her a thing, reminding Persys time and again that she should be grateful for a roof over her head and food on the table. She'd acquired Libby to maid her by means of her own allowance, for her aunt had made it plain the maids in the house were to wait upon Katherine and herself. Persys had to look to her own needs.

By the end of the day Persys and Libby were prepared and packed. Indeed, Libby appeared most anxious to depart.

"If we can get out of here without her ladyship demanding you do another thing, it will be a miracle," Libby grumbled.

She helped Persys carry vases of flowers to the room off the kitchen where a small stone sink could be used for dumping water and rearranging flowers. Persys found this to be an agreeable task. One good thing about living in the country was that there would be flowers to enjoy. She had inherited her father's love for plants.

Privately, Persys agreed with Libby regarding her aunt, but she prudently said nothing.

That evening she informed her aunt she would be moving elsewhere.

"And where do you go? What have you found to do?" her aunt demanded without a great deal of interest, pausing on her way out to a dinner party to which Persys, of course, had not been invited.

"I met a friend who told me about a lady who needs a companion. She lives in the country. I must go to her at once." Persys had thought long and hard about what she would say to Aunt Talbot. She wanted to be as vague as possible without actually prevaricating.

"A lady, do you say? Well, and I suppose it will do. It is as I said, a companion's job will work out well for you. Do you leave an address should you be needed?"

Her aunt was admiring the lace trim on her sleeve and didn't see Persys dart a look at the butler. "I doubt there will be mail for me, but should any come, I feel certain it can be forwarded." Persys doubted that any other reason might occur for which her presence might be required.

Not particularly interested, Lady Talbot shrugged and bid her niece a cool good night, never mentioning the years Persys had spent with the Talbot family, nor all she had done to assist in that time. As the door closed behind Lady Talbot, Persys exchanged a wordless look with the butler. He had her new direction and had been told to keep it a secret unless dire circumstances demanded it.

Thus it was that very early the next morning—long before her ladyship opened her eyes—Persys, followed by an anxious Libby, left the house. A steady rain pounded on the cobblestones, puddles forming everywhere. The treeless square before the house was utterly still. Few ventured into this sort of weather and Persys suspected they would have the roads pretty much to themselves.

An elegant traveling coach pulled up with dispatch to the front of the house. The groom jumped down and within minutes had helped them into the coach, Libby to sit facing the rear and Persys opposite next to the duke. It was but a brief time before their few valises and cases were loaded and they were off.

She didn't know quite what she had expected, but it wasn't the duke's company. And yet it made sense; she could scarcely present herself at the gates of Eddington Park without someone to recommend her.

"Good morning, Your Grace. What a dismal rain we have in which to travel." She offered a polite smile to find he did not so much as look at her.

"Indeed," he murmured, while staring out of the window.

This did not seem like a very propitious beginning to a trip. She made another effort. "Is it very far to your home in the country?"

"Unless we encounter bad road conditions we ought to be there by late afternoon." At which he drew forth some papers from a pocket. "Excuse me, please. My steward sent these for me to read and I've scarce had time in which to attend them."

"Of course," Persys said hastily. Reading papers might be considered by some to be bad manners, but she could hardly cavil at his lack of interest in her. She didn't want his attention. He was merely a means of finding employment when she badly needed such.

Her aunt's lack of interest in Persys's future had hurt, although Persys ought to know better than to expect otherwise. Lady Talbot had stood in place of a mother since Persys could remember, but there had been little affection in that guardianship. If Persys ever took in an orphaned child, she would make certain that child felt welcome and cuddle the poor creature should it cry at night. As to clothes, it was a blessing Persys had a modest allowance of her own that enabled her to buy a decent, if smallish, wardrobe. She would never set the Thames on fire with her looks or garb, but she was properly covered and thought she appeared well enough.

She exchanged a look with Libby and then with resignation surveyed the scene out of the window. The rain abated some as they crossed a bridge beyond the first tollgate. Perhaps they would be lucky and enjoy a bit of sun. She peeked at the man so silent at her side. He couldn't make it any plainer that he had not the slightest interest in her. Well, she could hardly blame him for that. She was simply a means to an end. His mother needed someone to entertain her and he discovered Persys needed a roof over her head. It had been a simple matter of matching the two.

She didn't think she liked him much—not that her liking or disliking made a difference to anyone, least of all him. Most likely he would introduce her to his dear injured mother, then leave. He would be happy to return to London and all the enticing amusements to be found there. And Persys decided she would be glad to see him go, even if he had shown kindness to her when she badly needed some. She found him faintly disturbing to her peace. He was too aloof. Of course, she supposed a duke was naturally that way. It probably helped fend off all those toad-eaters he mentioned.

"Are there many of them?" she wondered aloud before she realized she had given voice to her thoughts.

"I beg your pardon?" he inquired in a cool voice.

"Excuse me. I was merely wondering if you are often plagued by toad-eaters. It must be a great nuisance," she reflected.

A glimmer of a smile flashed across his face before he turned to gaze at her. "Indeed. One learns to ignore them after a time, however."

"I suspect you do rather well at that sort of thing—depressing encroaching people."

He placed the papers on his lap, giving her a curious frown. "And how is that?"

"Well," said an intrepid Persys, "you have that wonderful self-possession about you. It would probably freeze a mushroom in his tracks." And then she realized what she had said and to whom.

For a moment she sat in horrified silence, fearful that once again she had overstepped herself. Then he nodded, bestowing a somewhat frosty smile on her.

"Indeed, it is as you say, Miss Timothy."

Thankful he hadn't booted her out of the coach, Persys glanced at Libby, who looked quite mortified, and then continued an intense concentration on the scenery. Her fingers shook just a trifle as she smoothed her gloved hands over the fine kerseymere of her pelisse.

The rustle of papers at her side indicated that he had resumed his reading.

The coach pulled off the road to halt before a sizable inn. Since her breakfast had been sketchy at best, Persys was hopeful they would have time for more than a cup of tea.

"I doubt you took time for a proper meal before you left," he said, putting his papers back in the pocket. "Will you join me for a light repast now—even if I am aloof? I promise you I shan't freeze you."

"But then," the irrepressible Persys shot back, "I'm not a toad-eater." She gave him a serene smile before gracefully exiting the coach with the help of an admiring groom.

All had been arranged for them in advance. The host of the inn greeted His Grace with pleasant deference and ushered the two to a small dining room. Persys looked back to see Libby going down the hall with His Grace's groom.

It looked more like a feast than a light repast. Roast beef and browned potatoes, egg and bacon pie, scones; a great variety of foods enough to tempt the most jaded of palates. Persys pulled off her gloves and determined she would enjoy the good food.

"I am glad to see that you are not a timid miss, nor afraid to make a decent meal."

Persys looked up from her plate to find him watching her. Thinking that perhaps she had displeased him in some manner, she placed her fork on the plate. "Well, I'll confess that I have had a good many interrupted meals over the years. I learned to concentrate on my food when I had the chance. Besides, I truly did not think you wished conversation, Your Grace."

"Was I being more aloof than usual, then?" His quizzical smile nearly undid her poise.

Chagrined at his words, she shook her head.

He began to chat about London and her relatives. Before she knew it he had drawn a great deal of her background from her with Persys scarcely aware of all she revealed.

She knew better now than to comment on his friendliness. She picked up her fork to complete her meal, answering his gentle queries with serene amiability. It was a good thing she didn't realize just how much she had divulged or she would have been embarrassed clear into the next week. As it was, she returned to the coach satisfied and content.

They settled into the vehicle with little conversation and Persys was disheartened to see that he had the papers out once more and had totally immersed himself in the contents. She might not particularly like the man, but she would have welcomed a bit of conversation to pass the time. As it was, she hesitated to chat with Libby, as she might have done if they had been alone. She had no desire to annoy the duke.

With a stifled sigh, she resumed her inspection of the passing landscape. Unbidden, thoughts of the marquess crept into her mind, memories of fleeting smiles, exquisite dances. In all fairness she had to confess he had not encouraged her love. Indeed, she believed him unaware of it. In such a brief time she had loved and lost, for who could compete with the beautiful and wealthy Katherine? Not Persys.

She could see prosperous villages and well-tended estates. Had she a copy of *Patterson's Roads* she could have noted whose these were. The rain had completely stopped, yet heavy clouds hung over the green fields. She hoped it was not an omen of her future. The miles passed in continued silence with a pause for a cup of tea in the middle of the afternoon.

"We are almost there," he said at long last into the tranquility that hovered in the coach.

Persys looked about with increased interest. The road ran along a high stone fence, over which she could see tall oak trees. The sound of the horn to alert the gatekeeper echoed in the late afternoon air. Shortly, they reached a massive stone gateway with intricate wrought iron gates held open by a man wearing a green coat and top hat.

"You have attentive workers here," Persys observed.

"I pay them well," the duke answered with a wry touch in his voice.

Persys looked at him and smiled a trifle. "There is a difference, though. I have noted that a good employer is far more readily obeyed."

"I suppose that is better than being termed aloof."

"Perhaps you would be so good as to forget I said that. I'm sorry if you'd prefer a different description. I shall try to think of one." She slanted a look at him, her violet eyes holding a mischievous gleam.

"By all means. Perhaps I can think of a sobriquet for you. It will be something unusual to go with your unusual eyes," he said with an abrupt laugh that startled a dozing Libby to wakefulness.

The avenue leading to the main house was long, tree-lined, and well maintained. There was a vast green off to one side that was beautifully scythed, the sculptured hill rolling gently to a lovely lake.

"My late father had Capability Brown in to perfect the grounds," the duke said when he observed Persys's interest.

Then the house came into view and Persys could not restrain a gasp of delight at the sheer beauty of the place. Although it was far too enormous for ordinary mortals, it somehow seemed just right for the man at her side. He had the rather lordly air that such a magnificent house would demand of its owner.

"Home," he said softly with such a sound of pleasure that Persys knew her thought had been right. No matter the place was huge—it was his home.

"It is most impressive," she said quietly.

"Father had Kent in to remodel the house save for the front. That, he left be, thank goodness."

Whatever else might have been shared about the history of the building was left unsaid as the excellent traveling coach stopped precisely before the steps leading to the oversized front door that stared out at the world from beneath a massive pediment. Looking up, Persys counted the rows of windows, thinking it must take a vast army of servants to tend so great a house.

The door opened and several footmen hurried forth to open the door to the coach, remove baggage, and in general make themselves useful. At the top of the stairs an imposing man stood in the garb Persys recognized as that of a very superior butler. Libby would be awed into total silence.

"Portman," the duke said politely but distantly, "see that Mrs.

Biddle settles Miss Timothy in a room close to my mother's." The duke strolled into the house and Persys bravely followed him. She had been in great houses before, but nothing so grand as this.

Upon entering, her steps slowed and finally came to a halt. The expanse of pale gray marble accented by squares of black was broken only by a large table with an appropriately large vase of flowers. Enormous paintings of horses hung on the walls, apparently favorites of the previous duke to judge by the costumes worn by the riders and handlers.

She was not allowed to linger in the study, for a plump, comfortable-looking woman with a great bunch of keys dangling from her chatelaine hurried forth to greet them.

"This is Miss Timothy, come to attend my mother," the duke said, then murmured a few words to the lady before turning to Persys, looking as remote as if he had been anointed king. "Mrs. Biddle will see you settled first, then be so good as to come to the yellow drawing room to meet my mother."

Persys curtsied deeply, then followed the housekeeper up an oak staircase. On the first floor they turned and Persys began to fully appreciate the complexity of the house for at the landing she could see various doors that must lead, not to rooms, but to wings which in turn would lead to rooms. Mrs. Biddle opened one of these doors and Persys found a long hall stretching out before them. It was broad and carpeted with a fine Persian woven in shades of blue and buttery yellow. The very thought of maintaining all of this gave her momentary pause.

"Her Grace's suite is through this door," the housekeeper said, speaking in soft country accents. "And I shall put you in here." She opened the next door down the hall.

Persys entered her assigned room with violet eyes at their widest. It was grand, as might be expected. Furnished in dainty Hepplewhite with hangings of pale violet and white, the room had to be every young woman's dream.

"Thank you, Mrs. Biddle," Persys said properly. "Send my maid, Libby, please." It would never do, Persys supposed, to tell Mrs. Biddle how impressive the room was. "How very well you keep things here."

A slight smile crossed the housekeeper's face. She paused at the door and said, "When you have changed out of your traveling clothes, ring and I'll send a footman to guide you to the yellow drawing room. The house is large and a mite confusing for newcomers. You will learn soon enough."

At that, Persys bestowed a warm smile on the lady. The slightest sign of friendliness was to be accepted with gratitude. "Indeed, Mrs. Biddle, I shall do as you suggest."

When Libby entered the room she stared wide-eyed at the decor, then looked at Persys with a shake of the head. "We're very grand here, I'd say."

"Very grand, indeed," Persys responded. "Come, we must find a suitable gown for me to wear to meet the duchess. Do you think there is one that is not wrinkled beyond hope?"

Rather than reply, Libby delved into the case she had carried up with her. She was in the process of holding up a sadly wrinkled dress when a scratch on the door heralded the arrival of the remaining baggage. Dropping the much-creased dress on the bed, Libby hurried to inspect the contents of one of the other cases. "Here, Miss Persys. The very thing."

Within minutes Persys stood before the elegant looking glass garbed in a simple butter-yellow gown of poplin trimmed with rows of tucks at the hem and more tucks on the puffed sleeves. It was a vastly becoming color and design, the simplicity of which revealed that it was expensive without being pretentious.

"A shawl, miss," Libby murmured while dipping into the corner of a valise to pull forth a pretty wisp of a shawl that complemented the gown perfectly. "You look just as you ought—a proper young lady and not some drudge," the maid pronounced.

"I doubt you would ever allow me to look that," Persys admitted with a chuckle.

It took fortitude to tug the bellpull, then follow the middle-aged footman to the floor below. She studied the things they passed— exquisite furniture, marvelous paintings of past Russells, and the details of the house itself.

He paused before a set of double doors, glancing at her, then opening one of them. "Here you are, miss," he said softly.

At his retreat Persys felt exceedingly alone, then bravely stepped forward to enter the charmingly decorated room. Butter-yellow and vibrant blue muted by touches of ivory and black met her eyes. Then she focused on the elegant white-haired woman stretched out on a chaise longue near tall windows that overlooked a vast expanse of gardens and lawn. Concealed by a silken cover-ing, her injured knee could scarce be noticed. Her blue eyes a warmer shade of her son's, she wore a look of severely tried pa-tience.

Persys crossed the room to stand before the duchess, curtsying deeply as she had been taught proper and remaining silent, as was also proper. Never speak until spoken to first, her aunt insisted.

"Welcome to Eddington Park, my dear. How fortunate that you have need of me just when I have need of you. I believe we shall do quite well together." Turning to her son she added, "You are right, Harry, they are violet. I had not thought it possible."

Persys gave the duke a confused look, then guessed *he* had men-tioned her eye color. Perhaps it was a trifle unusual but she had grown accustomed to it.

The duchess gestured to a chair close to where she reclined. "Sit here, my dear, and we shall become acquainted. Why do you not tend something, Harry? I suspect you and your steward have reams of papers to study."

He bestowed a wry and surprisingly fond look on his mother and bowed. "Of course."

Persys watched him leave with a sigh of relief. If only he was not so intimidating she could like him better, perhaps. Although why liking him should be desirable she didn't stop to think.

"Now, we shall get conversant with each other and learn each other's little foibles."

The following conversation revealed a great deal about Persys to the duchess; all that Persys learned was that her new employer adored doing the unusual, loved her flowers, and wanted things done precisely as she wished.

"I am an exceedingly curious person, you see," the duchess con-fided. "I wish to know so many things. Are you curious as well? And will you assist me when there is something I want to know?"

Persys swallowed with care, wondering precisely what she was letting herself in for and said, "Indeed, Your Grace. I enjoy investigating matters very much. I should find it most agreeable to assist you."

"Good." The duchess leaned back on her chaise and rang a silver bell. When the footman paused in the doorway, she commanded ever so nicely, "Tea, Robbins. We are parched."

A few minutes later the duke strolled into the drawing room, looking about him with an approving eye. Then his gaze rested upon Persys and she would have sworn that he suddenly acquired a mischievous gleam in those blue eyes of his.

"Ah, my dear Persian woman! How do you get along with my mother?"

"Your mother? Very well, indeed. Why do you call me a Persian woman, Your Grace?" she asked warily.

He grinned then, a delightful change to his usually austere countenance. His eyes positively twinkled as he replied, "I said I would find a sobriquet for you and I have. I looked up your name, you see, and discovered that it means 'Persian woman.' Henceforth you are to be known as my Persian woman."

"Stuff and nonsense," she snapped back roundly. "I am not yours and shan't be. Nor am I Persian for all that I have that ridiculous name. I believe my father was interested in some Persian flowers at the time I was born—a type of tulip unless I am much mistaken. So you see, *your* name does not apply." She sat back in her chair with the triumphant attitude of one who has won the battle.

The duchess gazed with wide-eyed amazement at the repartee between her son and her new companion. A gleam lit her eyes that was hastily suppressed.

The duke leaned against the top of her chair so that Persys was compelled to half turn to look up at him.

"If I say you are my Persian woman, then you are, and that is that," he pronounced much as a king might decree.

Persys laughed while thinking that perhaps he was a king here on his own land and in this magnificent home certainly worthy of a king. "I shan't answer that," she said with a serene smile.

"But all will know who it is when I demand my Persian woman," he said with that grin again.

Fortunately, the butler, followed by a footman, entered just then with trays bearing tea and an assortment of delicacies to tempt the duchess. She had not been eating well: boredom did not agree with her.

"I believe this will be a most agreeable healing period." She gave her son a pert glance, settling back against the chaise with teacup and saucer in hand.

The duke gave his mother a thoughtful look, then glanced at Persys. "I agree, let us hope this will prove to be a healing period." If he had other healing in mind he did not reveal it.

Persys, her head bent over her cup of tea did not look up to meet his gaze, but she did wonder at his words. He could only be referring to his mother, surely? What could he know of her problems or her need of healing her wounded heart?

His Grace, the Duke of Eddington, smiled to himself, drank his tea, and plotted. He had been spoiled, always being allowed his way. He fully intended to have it now. It might take time, but of that he had sufficient. There was little doubt that ultimately he would win. He hoped.

Chapter Three

"*H*ow shall I amuse Her Grace, Libby?" Persys asked several days after she had arrived at Eddington Park. "She enjoys flowers, but how can she be in the garden? And I am not very good at card games." Persys sighed, perceiving that entertaining the lady of the house was not to be a simple task. "And tell me—why does His Grace not leave for London? I felt certain he would be gone by now. What a vexing gentleman!"

"Yes, miss," her maid murmured, intent upon securing a stand of long hair into the complicated arrangement atop her mistress's head.

"I am tempted to cut my hair," Persys said while she surveyed Libby's efforts. "Think how simple it would be; just a quick brush and off I could go. I am hungry," she concluded plaintively.

Libby stepped back from the dressing table, pins and brush in her hands. "Never say such a thing, Miss Persys. You have lovely hair. Soft and silky, 'tis like a fine cloud on your head. Many is the time I have seen gentlemen admire it."

"I wish it was darker rather than this insipid ash. Ah, well, there is little I can do about it—or am willing to try," she ended, mindful of Libby's offer to color it with walnut extract.

Persys rose from the little stool that sat so neatly before the splendid dressing table in her room. As she looked around she considered how easy it was to become accustomed to luxury. This was so much finer than anything she had known while at the Talbots'. The canopied bed's splendid pale violet covering echoed that of a chair. The silk-hung walls displayed several charming paintings, the sort to appeal to a young woman. There was a still life, a landscape of the grounds of the Park, and a portrait of a very pretty woman with flowers cascading from her arms.

"I wonder who that is?" Persys said as she prepared to leave her sanctuary.

"Looks like Her Grace," Libby commented, pausing in the act of making up the bed.

Thinking that possible, Persys slipped from her room to halt briefly before Her Grace's suite door; hearing no sound she continued down to the small breakfast room. Here she consumed her small meal in silence, contemplating alternately the view from the window and her plans for the day. Her peace was soon broken.

"Here you are," the duke said, quite as though he had been looking for her and she had been hard to locate.

"I am enjoying a very nice breakfast," she said tartly, placing her cup on its saucer with a clink. "Have you had yours?" she dared to inquire. Libby had learned that the duke rose early.

"Some time ago. I shall have coffee while we discuss a small matter." He motioned the maid to pour him a steaming cup of fragrant brew, while seating himself at the table next to Persys. "You are settling in well?"

"Quite well, Your Grace. My room is everything a woman might wish for—quite comfortable. Not enough to do, however."

"I fear I shall put an end to that," he said after a swallow of his coffee. "Mother, you see," he added when Persys darted an alarmed look at him. "She is dreadfully confined in the house and I have devised a way for her to be out-of-doors. When you have finished eating, I will show you." He looked at her nearly empty plate with a raised brow that effectively dampened any appetite Persys might have retained.

Placing her crisp linen napkin alongside her plate, she took one last sip of the excellent tea and pushed her chair back from the rosewood table. "I expect now is as good a time as any."

It was amusing to see how pleased he was to show her whatever he had contrived for his mother. Persys walked at his side through the main drawing room out to the terrace by way of large double

French doors. Shortly they reached the edge of the terrace where a strange contraption sat.

"It is somewhere between a barrow and a bath chair," he explained with obvious pride, placing a possessive hand on the top of the back. "Now Mother can be wheeled wherever she wishes to go and you can be with her." He glanced at Persys, her soft hair shining in the morning sun. "With a proper bonnet on, of course."

Her hand flew up to rest on her head and she gave him a look to wither a lesser person.

"What a dreadful man you are, indeed, to remind me that I lack a bonnet when you scarcely gave me a moment to fetch one," she snapped. Then she realized what her impetuous tongue had done. "Oh, I *am* sorry. I ought not speak like that to you, only I do tend to forget who you are, you see." Her eyes lit with an earnest smile.

He did not smile at her, but she thought she detected a glimmer of amusement in his eyes. That penetrating blue seemed warmer, less frosty. "I do not find that reprehensible, my dear Persian woman."

Persys gave him an irate glance. "I cannot think why you find that name amusing, Your Grace."

"Nor can I think why you believe me to be aloof," he replied, sounding rather injured. "I am the most amiable of good fellows."

Persys studied him, thinking that he wouldn't understand how his imposing manner affected more ordinary mortals. "If you say so," she murmured for something of an answer, since he seemed to expect one.

"Well, I shall bring this contraption to the door where Mother can easily be placed in it. James can push her into the garden or wherever she might wish to go. Have you explored any of the gardens yet?" he said diffidently, knowing full well that she had not had a time for any such thing.

"Indeed not, Your Grace. I have scarce had a moment in which to explore anything, except my own room," she responded swiftly. Really, the man was impossible. What did he think she was?

"Come. I shall give you an abbreviated tour."

The next hour was one of sheer delight as the duke conducted Persys from the rose garden to the herb garden, then through the topiary, from which they entered the greenhouse. Here, Persys viewed exotic orchids, delicate fuchsias, and seedlings of plants the head gardener hoped to develop.

"I am overwhelmed with beauty," she whispered as she sniffed the luscious scent of a lavender orchid.

"Indeed," the duke said, his eyes focused on her violet eyes and not the flower. "Come, let us find my mother; she ought to be down about now." He turned to lead the way back to the house, setting a brisk pace.

Persys wondered what she might have done to upset him, for all at once he had retreated into that austere man again. Remote, aloof—yet, she suspected that beneath that formidable exterior existed a warm and sympathetic heart. Witness his concern for his mother. What a pity he concealed it so well.

When they entered the small drawing room it was to find the duchess reclining on her chaise longue, reading a letter she tossed aside as they entered. "I am bored, quite bored," she began, toying idly with the fringe on a shawl.

"I have a surprise that I hope will please you. Come," he beckoned a footman. Apparently the fellow was the James mentioned earlier, for a strapping young man with the most bland face Persys had ever seen, stepped forward. "Carry Her Grace to the terrace if you will."

The duke went ahead, opening doors and setting the odd chair close to the French door most convenient.

"What is this, Harry? Do you intend to place me in the refuse heap? The compost pile?" the duchess cried when she caught sight of the admittedly strange chair.

"James shall trundle you to the gardens whenever you please to go and my Persian woman will garden as you wish. Is that not right, Miss Timothy?"

Ignoring his reference to her as his Persian woman, Persys nodded dutifully. She had her doubts as to how this scheme would work, but she certainly was willing to try it. She flashed him a look of rebuke for his use of that silly name he had devised, then turned to the duchess. "Indeed, Your Grace, it promises to be a fine day and with our bonnets and parasols we should enjoy it prodigiously. I think," she added when she viewed the tilt of that regal head.

"Well, I shall give it a try. But James had best have help. I'll not have this limb of mine jostled about. It yet pains me."

Her son gave her a caressing pat on her shoulder, then nodded to the footman. Together the two men managed to lift the awkward chair to carry it to the lawn. James headed in the direction of the rose garden.

"I'll send Tessa to you at once, Mama," the duke said before striding off to the house.

Persys wondered how Tessa, just as imperious as her mistress, would take to being sent with the bonnet and parasol. Perhaps she would delegate the task to a lesser being? From Libby's comments, the abigail was very mindful of her position.

"He means well," the duchess murmured as she adjusted one of the shawls over her legs. "I truly would not have him otherwise, you know. He is precisely as he ought to be."

Persys found this a confusing remark and elected to ignore it. The duchess might find her son just as she wished. Persys found him more than a little daunting.

In less time than Persys would have believed possible, Tessa bustled from the great house with a large white parasol and two bonnets, one of exquisitely fine straw trimmed in large white roses and the other a bonnet Persys recognized immediately—her own modest straw quite suitable for gardening.

Soon the duchess wore the elegant bonnet and twirled the parasol above her head while craning her neck to see this way and that. "How pleased my husband would have been to see how well these do," she said at last, having inspected what she could from her portable chair.

"Shall we change your position, Your Grace?" Persys inquired, hoping she could maneuver the unwieldy chair.

"Please. I would go there," Her Grace instructed, pointing to a place on the opposite side of the rose garden.

With great trepidation, Persys carefully pushed the large-wheeled chair across the close-clipped grass, wincing at every bump encountered until they reached the exact spot the duchess wished.

"There, that was not half so bad as I anticipated."

Persys let out a sigh of relief, then obeyed the imperious commands issued nonstop by a lady who truly knew something about gardening.

The duchess enjoyed her nuncheon in the herb garden, inhaling the pungent scents with obvious pleasure while partaking in her customary light noon meal.

Persys made a point of eating every morsel on her plate, wondering if she would be able to hold her weight if this was to be her fare. Dainty and insubstantial might be well for an invalid, but hardly sustaining for a working girl. And work she did, dividing clumps of sweet basil, thinning the dill, gathering a sizable cluster of peppermint—for the duchess complained of a slight digestive ailment, no doubt from the shrimp bisque she had eaten.

The lavender had already been picked, but the chamomile was just right to be gathered for tea.

"If the peppermint does not help me, the chamomile will," the duchess explained while Persys sorted the herbs on the worktable at the end of the herb garden.

"We have rosemary here," the duchess said with more enthusiasm than heretofore revealed as she pointed to a raised bed on the opposite side. "It is so beneficial for headaches. If you have sore muscles you must send your maid for a bottle of the oil."

"Indeed, Your Grace," Persys murmured, quite ready to admit that she was likely to suffer from aching muscles. But at least she scarcely noticed her aching heart. She didn't have time. The duchess demanded her attention every moment with conversation about the herbs and their use.

It was mid-afternoon when the duchess insisted she be returned to the house. "I am tired and my knee bothers me some. I would have Tessa look at it. Being an invalid does not suit me in the least," she declared.

Persys would have heartily seconded that observation had her tongue not been glued to the top of her mouth, so dry was she.

Once the duchess had been whisked away to her room, Persys

sought a cup of tea and anything else that might be found for nour-
ishment. Portman came from the back of the house to inquire what
she desired. When he was so informed, Persys was soon enjoying
not only her tea, but also biscuits, tiny cakes, and thin slices of
bread and butter while seated in the shade of the terrace. She had
consumed quite a bit when she heard footsteps in the house.
Within moments the duke came out on the terrace.

"There you are. You had no difficulty pushing Mother's chair
over the grass, I take it? No calamity was reported at any rate."

Odious creature! Even if he is a duke, Persys thought. "None,
Your Grace. The gardens are beautiful."

"I'll wager she had you picking and snipping herbs, sorting and
gathering what she wanted to use. Am I right?"

"I believe I shall be grateful for some rosemary oil, if those
aching muscles she cautioned me might occur do come about. She
says rosemary is most helpful in that event."

He reached over to sample a biscuit, rose from the bench on
which he had lounged, and strolled back and forth. Persys watched
his restless pacing.

"Come, finish that tea and we shall take a walk. There are gardens other than the ones you saw. She created a wild garden and
there is a flower garden under her window—you can see it as well
from your room. In addition, Mother designed a grotto. She is most
creative, you know."

"A grotto? How clever." Persys hadn't seen one. Whenever the
Talbot family had visited a truly interesting estate, she had remained at home for one reason or another.

"You shall see it now, if you please." He paused in his rambling
to fix her with a look.

Persys placed her teacup on the tray, rose and brushed a few
crumbs from her gown, then accepted his arm before descending
the steps to the graveled path. It was obvious that here Capability
Brown had left his mark. Not that she was an expert, but she had
read articles regarding the search for the picturesque in landscaping. If this splendid view was an example, she thought it was a
rather fine thing.

"The lake was Brown's, of course," the duke said as they skirted the placid water. A squirrel scolded them from the limb of an oak while birds darted through the trees in bewildering patterns. Not familiar with such wildlife, Persys looked about her with great curiosity.

"City girl?" the duke quietly inquired.

"For the most part. Botany is considered proper for a young lady, but I confess my cousin had little interest in it. Nor did she care overmuch for learning about the various animals in the wild."

"And so you learned something else?"

Suddenly shy, Persys nodded her agreement, saying nothing more on her education or lack of it.

They passed a small replica of a Grecian temple, then rounded the far end of the lake to see the grotto Her Grace had designed.

The first impression Persys had was of darkness and damp. She shivered after the warmth of this sun. Water gushed forth from a spring, splashing over rocks and ultimately past a sculpted male figure.

"Mother says this is Neptune. The sculptor told me he intended it to be Zeus. I think the poor chap looks like he's freezing. Portman chills wine down here as this water is as cold as you can find." The duke stood aside while Persys explored the interior of the large grotto.

There were shells in abundance plastered everywhere on the walls and imbedded in the floor. Other statues were tucked into recesses and Persys thought they too looked very cold and rather forbidding. She wrapped her arms about her, for even though the day was pleasant, it was chilly in the grotto. More than chilly, it was not a place one would wish to linger.

"Shall we go?" the duke inquired, perceptive to her feelings.

"Please," Persys said gratefully. The sun felt deliciously good. Even with her garden bonnet on, Persys could sense heat and relished it after the chill of the grotto.

"What did you think of that, Miss Timothy?"

She gave him a cautious look, then said, "If your mother is pleased, that is what matters."

"And?"

"I found it cold." And so she had, not only in temperature but in feelings; all those shells and rocks and marble.

"It is not a place where I shall find you when you wish to hide, then?"

"Shall I wish to hide, Your Grace? Hide from what, may I ask?" Persys inquired with trepidation. Was there a side of his mother concealed from her?

"Only you could answer that, and I doubt you will just now."

Thinking it a very strange conversation, Persys left his side to stand by the edge of the artificial lake. It was large and of an irregular shape. A great variety of trees and shrubs grew in wild profusion. She recognized rhododendrons and expected there would be a splendid display of blooms come spring—not that she would be there to see them. His mother would be healed and walking long before then. For some reason this was not a pleasant thought and Persys walked along the lake a bit farther. Between the trees she could glimpse the upper part of the house. It seemed as though they were a far distance from anyone and very alone.

"Your grounds are quite extensive," she said to break the silence that had stretched on far too long.

"Indeed."

At that moment a workman came hurrying along the path toward where they stood, apparently intent upon reaching the duke.

"Excuse me," he murmured and left her, going to meet the man. He listened to whatever message was given, then returned to Persys with a vexed expression on his face. "I must go back. Will you come with me or return on your own? Mother is unlikely to want you for some time yet. You are at leisure for the moment."

"Go ahead, please. I feel certain you will be faster without me to slow you. I shall wander back on my own." She watched him hurry back the way they had come, avoiding the grotto by skirting around the outside of it. Within minutes he was a small figure on the far side of the lake and disappearing rapidly.

As intimidating as he might be, he was company and she felt rather lonely without him, odd as it might seem. She would have thought it would be better on her own, but it wasn't. How could she miss a man so aloof? Deciding it was a puzzle quite beyond her capabilities, she continued on the path until she heard a faint cry, a pathetic little meow.

It took a fair bit of searching until she found the cat. It was tattered and far too thin. "Poor creature, you look much as I have felt in the past." She ventured closer and the animal allowed her to pick it up, cringing just a little. It was but a bag of bones, she thought. Pathetic and neglected, it was a wonder it was still alive.

"Come on, Moggy. I shall take you back to the house and smuggle you to my room, if possible." Portman or Mrs. Biddle might object, but only if they chanced to see her. On the other hand, the housekeeper might not mind if Persys promised to take care of the little creature.

Conscious that the afternoon was fading and she would be required at the dinner table before too long, Persys hurried on her way. The cat, seeming to sense a friend, snuggled in her arms and looked as pleased as a too thin and tattered cat might.

As luck would have it Mrs. Biddle chanced to be in the hall when Persys entered the house.

"And what have you there?"

Thinking the housekeeper didn't seem terribly disapproving, Persys allowed the woman to see her little creature.

"Ah, poor beast. Come along to the kitchen and we will fix it a bowl of something nourishing. Found him on your walk, did you?"

Persys nodded and wondered how it was that servants always seemed to know everything you did, even when you thought you were alone. Within minutes she realized she had nothing to fear from the housekeeper. That good woman stirred a bit of bread and milk in a dish and offered it to the cat, who gulped it in a flash.

"If you will leave him here I'll see to it he has a bath and looks a might more fit before he comes to you again."

"Will His Grace mind if I have a pet, do you think?" Persys inquired anxiously while the cat licked the dish as clean as might be.

"Heavens, no. I recollect that as a boy he brought home everything from toads to hurt rabbits. He'll not cavil at a mere puss." The housekeeper walked with Persys back to the hall where they encountered the very man of whom they had spoken.

"Is something wrong?" he asked at the combined look of the two.

"Not in the least, Your Grace. Miss Timothy found a poor cat and brought it back to the house for care. It needs feeding and a bath and then she can have the beast in her room. It won't be the first time an animal has found its way to a bedchamber in this house. And I'll wager you still miss your dog, poor old fellow."

The housekeeper bustled off toward the kitchen while Persys edged her way to the staircase. Any thoughts she had of cleaning herself after holding the dirty cat were set aside until she could escape from the duke.

"You had a pleasant walk, then? Do you make a habit of rescuing animals, Miss Timothy?" He stared down that imposing nose at her and she wanted to slink away and hide from him, the way he looked at her.

Being made of sterner stuff, Persys tilted her chin and said, "I could not walk past the poor little thing and leave it to suffer and die. Could you?" she dared to challenge.

It was a distinct relief when he smiled—a faint smile it was true, but a smile nonetheless.

"Indeed I could not. I am glad you have a soft heart, Miss Timothy, my Persian woman. I'd not have you any other way." With that strange remark he turned and walked down the hall toward the library.

Glad of her reprieve, Persys dashed up the stairs to her room, closing each door as she went as though escaping from something, she knew not what.

Libby scolded her for the near-ruin of a good muslin dress. But when all was explained, the maid agreed that the damage had been for a good cause; besides, some of the soil likely occurred while Persys was in the garden doing for the duchess.

"How soon is dinner?" Persys demanded in a rush, fearing she had dawdled too long. The duke had been dressed for the evening and she looked a fright.

The faithful Libby had set out a pretty, though by no means new, gown for Persys. It did not take long for the change to be made. Libby untangled the hair that had been squashed beneath the bonnet during the session in the garden. When the maid deemed Persys was fit to be seen by anyone—meaning the duke—she was allowed to leave.

Pausing before the duchess's suite, the door opened and Tessa greeted Persys with a terse, "Come in. She's wanting you."

"Your Grace? There is something you wish?"

"I hear you found a cat. Is it an agreeable animal?"

"What an efficient grapevine you have. Indeed, I found a pathetic creature while walking around the lake. Who knows where he came from. Do you mind? May I keep him? It seems cruel to save him only to toss him out again, if you see what I mean."

"My son was forever bringing strays home. I shan't mind as long as he is kept to your room and not allowed to wander the house."

"I shall do my best, Your Grace."

"Good. We shall go down for dinner now."

The stalwart footman, the good James, plus another appeared when summoned and carried Her Grace down to the main floor. Persys noticed they treated the duchess as though she was made of fragile eggs likely to break at the least bump.

"Mother, just as I was about to go looking for you," the duke exclaimed from the door of the small drawing room.

Once settled on her chaise longue the duchess arranged her shawls and leaned against her pillows with an air of fragility that Persys suspected was all fraud. She'd wager the duchess was as tough as could be.

"I had a letter today, did I tell you?" she asked her son in a somewhat arch manner.

"No, but I imagine you will. From whom?" The duke crossed to lean against the fireplace mantel, a place Persys had noted that most men seemed to favor.

"Your cousin Charlotte. Poor girl. She says she is bored with Town and wishes to visit us."

Persys heard a question in her voice, although she didn't ask such. The duke said nothing for a few moments, then gave his mother a half-smile. "I suppose you have already written her to come and want only my frank before the letter is sent?"

"Do you mind so very much? It may take her some time before George is ready to travel with her."

"Ah, yes, dear cousin George. The young ladies in London will miss him, I fancy."

Persys could not miss the irony in his voice and wondered at this cousin. She wondered at both, actually. Why did they wish to intrude when the duchess was recovering from her accident? Surely they must know? Nothing was revealed and so Persys was left in the dark. She presumed that one of these days she would learn all and trusted it would not be too unpleasant. Although, come to think on it, she didn't know why she felt it would be that, rather than agreeable.

At that moment Portman appeared to announce dinner and the duchess was carried into the dining room with all the pomp of a queen.

She was like royalty, Persys reflected as she looked about her once seated at the table. The pale cream walls served as background for enormous gilt-framed paintings of previous dukes and duchesses garbed in splendid costumes fit for royalty. The sideboard, chairs, and likely the table all looked to have come from the workshop of Thomas Sheraton. The highly polished mahogany gleamed in the candlelight.

Persys looked at the duke and knew an immense satisfaction and couldn't explain it in the least. She did know that she would not wish herself elsewhere, even if he were elusive and imposing. There was a warm heart buried inside him, she was now certain of that.

The duchess claimed her attention and Persys set aside her

thoughts. But the image of the man Persys was certain she loved faded some and she was less able to recall his features that night when she went to bed.

Chapter Four

This must have been how Noah felt when the rain continued to come down in torrents for weeks and weeks, thought Persys. After a week of beautiful weather came this rain—and what rain!

"Is there any sign of blue sky at all?" the duchess asked with resignation in her voice.

"If anything, it is more gray than ever, Your Grace," Persys replied, wondering what the duke found to keep him well occupied. She had seen little or nothing of him for several days and she found she missed him. Undoubtedly it was that abrasive teasing she missed—such as a brother might have given. Yet she did not think of him as the brother she had never had, nor like her obnoxious cousin, David Talbot. She could *never* think of him as Harry, as the duchess delighted in calling him. Odd, the duke irritated her, yet she felt strangely comforted when he appeared to take control of everything.

Pity he didn't control the weather.

"What shall we do?" the duchess queried, a near-petulant sound in her voice. She stared out of the window at the seemingly eternal gray—dull, unrelieved, and exceedingly watery.

Persys couldn't blame her for being vexed. Unless one wanted to read or play cards, there was little to do inside, especially for one who enjoyed her garden, as did the duchess. Were it fall or winter the garden and plant catalogs could be perused. Instead it was a soggy summer.

Persys cuddled Moggy close to her while she considered options. Stroking the soft, furry head she admired the cat. He had grown a bit plumper and his fur looked splendid after a bath to which he had objected vociferously. It was now thick and a fine misty gray. He blinked dark green eyes as though he understood she regarded him with affection. Oddly enough for a near-grown cat he adored playing games, chasing crumpled paper, stalking a piece of trailed string like his distant relative, the tiger. "Silly beast," she said fondly.

"He has turned out amazingly well for a stray," Her Grace said, watching Persys with the cat.

"Indeed, madam," Persys replied before putting the cat down. "A handsome animal for one abandoned."

"Abandoned creatures often turn out better than expected," Her Grace said with a darted glance at Persys. Then she sighed rather dramatically. "Think of something, else I die of boredom," the duchess cried, her vexation clear.

"Excuse me, Your Grace," Mrs. Biddle said from the doorway to the yellow drawing room, "there is the linen to do. You told me to remind you the next rainy day. It be most rainy today." The housekeeper rightly calculated that by this time even a disliked chore would be welcome.

"Anything!" the duchess said firmly. "Although I do not see how I am to go through stacks of tablecloths and napkins while so confined to this chaise. You shall help me, Persys." Her Grace's eyes gleamed with the notion of her work shared, particularly a task she disliked.

"Indeed, Your Grace, I performed that duty a number of times for my aunt. Merely tell me how you want them done and I shall sort them all out and bring the questionable ones to you."

"No," the duchess decided. "I shall be carried to the linen closet and we shall work there."

Thinking the hall might be rather drafty, for in her experience linen closets were small spaces, Persys kept her opinion to herself and followed the trio who led the way along a passage to the rear of the house until the duchess instructed Persys to open a door.

Inside was a room about the size of the chamber Persys had occupied at the Talbot house. On the shelves that encircled the room were neat stacks of sheets, pillow slips, tablecloths, and napkins, not to mention piles of fine linen towels and even thick Turkish towels the likes of which Persys had never seen before. It was an awesome sight for a young woman accustomed to seeing far less.

"Now to the table linens," Her Grace said crisply, all sign of indolence gone.

Within short order Persys had orderly piles of nearly new, slightly worn, and those cloths requiring a bit of mending. The napkins met with the same treatment.

"I have an idea," the duchess said thoughtfully. "There are a great number of odd napkins that look dull and yellowed. Rather than whiten them, I believe I should like them tinted."

"Colored linens, Your Grace?" Persys asked, hoping she did not sound shocked. Aunt Talbot said no one *ever* had colored linens, they were quite déclassé.

"It would be amusing. Do you know anything about dyeing fabrics, Persys? If not, we shall learn."

Persys rightly interpreted this to mean that Persys would learn and do the dyeing. The duchess would simply claim the idea as hers.

With a wave of the hand, the duchess ordered the footman to carry her from the linen room. Meanwhile, Persys gathered the linen napkins and small towels used for wiping hands into a manageable pile, clutched them to her bosom and left the room in Her Grace's wake.

"I shall inquire of Mrs. Biddle as to the best way to proceed, Your Grace."

"Excellent notion, my dear Persys. I shall take a nap while you find out all you need to know."

It proved to be far simpler than Persys had expected.

"Her Grace likes that buttery yellow. Easy way to tint those linens that color is to use a strong infusion of chamomile tea. Let me explain what has to be done."

So Persys listened and wondered how she was to accomplish the task, given the weather.

When she reported to the duchess all she had learned, the dear lady waxed most enthusiastic about the notion.

"With any luck at all tomorrow will be better and we can proceed with our plan. Come now and read to me. I believe that would be very soothing."

Selecting an interesting book gave Persys something to do. The remainder of the afternoon was spent in reading a novel by "A Lady," whoever that might be. Persys thought the book title very descriptive: one young woman was most sensible, the other overflowing with excessive sensibility.

"I must say this is an entertaining book. Fancy dear Harry buying this for me," the duchess said with evident pleasure.

Persys suspected there were a lot of things the duke did for his mother that she knew nothing about.

He joined them at dinner, of course. What he had been doing during the day was not discussed so Persys didn't learn a thing about what occupied him. Why she was so curious, she didn't pause to examine. She scarcely realized he absorbed more and more of her idle thoughts. His chair was at the far end of the table and while exceedingly polite he said little to Persys. Perhaps he was engrossed in a problem regarding this vast estate. If so, it was likely to do with the rain. She felt somewhat neglected, although she had no right to claim a moment of his time. She completely forgot she'd wished him back in London.

"I should think that if the rain does not stop soon, we might have to build ourselves an ark," she said, putting her earlier thoughts into words.

"An ark? How droll," the duchess said with a laugh. "Do you know, Harry, Persys has agreed to color some linens for me. She says all that is needed is chamomile tea. Goodness knows I have an ample supply of that."

"You find enough to do with Persys, Mother?" the duke asked absently, his gaze on his plate. "You keep entertained?"

"Indeed. She is reading me a book she found in the library, something about sensible and insensible or like that." The duchess held her wineglass in the air, while creasing her brow in concentration. While the most amiable of creatures, Persys considered the duke must have inherited his brains from his father, for his mother seemed to have a great deal of nonsense about her.

"*Sense and Sensibility*, Your Grace," Persys murmured.

"By a Lady, so she says." The duchess gave her son an arch look. "Do you suppose a lady actually sits down to write books?"

"I daresay one could. I imagine that if one set one's mind to it, one could do almost anything. Is that not so, Miss Timothy?"

"No, Your Grace. I cannot agree. I might like to fly like a bird and try very hard, but that does not mean I shall. I should like to set up my own establishment, but the dictates of society prevent that. And I quite believe I could not write a book." She placed her fork carefully on her plate, not looking at him.

"What about a book where the heroine is in love—or thinks she is—with a married man?" he asked idly, toying with his glass, now empty of wine.

Persys darted an alarmed look at him but said nothing for the moment. He wore no expression on his face and she could not begin to guess what motivated his comment. He did not seem to be the sort of man who spoke without reason, at least he had not done so to date. She prudently ignored his little jibes about her being *his* Persian woman. *That* she would likely never understand.

"Scandalous!" the duchess pronounced. "It would be a sensation, however. Society adores books about forbidden love." She gave her son a sly little smile, then glanced at Persys to see her reaction.

"Let me see, would she pine away to die of love? Or does she persevere with her life?" the duke persisted.

"I should think that since her love is hopeless she would persevere, quite sensibly so. And I doubt one dies for love," Persys ventured to say. "I have no patience with girls seething with excess sensibility. For example, I believe Marianne Dashwood a silly little twit. She rejects a worthy suitor for one who lies and betrays the love she believes they share. I think he treats her abominably."

"Tell me, does she eventually come to love her worthy suitor?" the duke asked, his fork suspended over his plate as he waited for her reply. The butler hovered at his elbow with the bottle of wine, prepared to fill the empty glass.

"Indeed—although, I do wonder how he feels about her, for he knows of her prior attachment to Mr. Willoughby. Can the colonel ever feel certain he has her complete regard? I pity Colonel Brandon. Will he be satisfied with crumbs? Or in the remainder of the book can he persuade her to transfer her passion for the worthless Willoughby to a sensible man like himself?"

For Persys, this was a lot to say on the subject of a book. But to have an intelligent discussion on something other than the latest scandal or the design of a gown was such a novelty she could not resist.

"I should think it would be difficult to feign love. What do you say to the subject, Mother?"

"*True* love is impossible to pretend and is deep, contrary to an infatuation, which is merely a surface thing and goes as quickly as it comes. I believe you know if your love is returned. Certainly I never feigned my regard for your father, nor he for me. I still miss him dreadfully, you know." The duchess dropped her gaze to her plate for some moments before briskly changing the topic and regaling her son with the steps involved in dyeing the linen napkins. The meal concluded without another reference to the topic of love or novels.

"How does your cat get along, Miss Timothy?" the duke inquired as they left the dining room sometime later.

"Moggy? He does well enough, I believe. Her Grace likes to play with him, tossing crumpled paper for him to chase." She darted an amused glance at the duchess, who was being conveyed to her chaise longue.

"I suspect that is where yesterday's newspaper went, in that event." The duke didn't smile but Persys sensed a dryness in his tone that told her he was not truly angry.

"Oh, dear, I am sorry," Persys said, looking ahead to where the duchess entered the yellow drawing room between the two stalwart footmen. "How long has it been since her injury?"

"Five or six weeks, I should say. She is much improved and the doctor says it is a matter of keeping her quiet until the injury is well healed. It is difficult for such an active woman to remain quiet. She has such a passion for living, for doing things. I appreciate your patience with her, my Persian woman. But then, I would expect nothing less."

Persys gave him a wordless look, not quite sure what he meant by the last remark. "It will not be long before I am no longer needed by her, then?"

"That is true." He bowed and walked briskly down the hall in the direction of the billiard room.

Persys paused in front of one of the many paintings decorating the hall while pondering the matter she had chosen to ignore. It would not be long before she would leave here, most likely never to return. The very thought left her desolate.

"Persys?" the duchess called from her chaise longue in the drawing room. "Come read to me. I would that we finish the book and you read remarkably well. And then we can pray for sunshine!"

Persys suspected it would take at least divine intervention to cause the rain to go away. She willingly picked up the book again to read the last of the adventures of the Dashwood sisters. Her reading was interspersed with acid comments from the duchess and a session of tea during which Persys sipped between sentences. When she finished the book it was time for bed.

She bid the duchess good night and ran up the stairs to her room. Once there she considered what the duke had said during dinner. It was singularly odd that he had suggested a plot in which a heroine believes herself to be in love with a married man. It had to be mere coincidence, surely. Even if he had made a number of remarks that pointed to his guessing her feelings for Katherine's husband, she couldn't believe he would actually say something about it—particularly while at the dinner table!

Once in bed she fell asleep wondering how she'd manage to dye the linen napkins without botching the job. Worry over her future occupied some time. Never once did she think of the Marquess of Torrington nor her love for him.

The following morning she blinked in surprise at the sunshine beaming in her window. To be sure, there were clouds about, but the day promised to be an improvement on the last week or so.

Libby fairly danced as she entered the room. Had it not been for the basin of warm water, Persys thought she would have skipped for joy.

"No ark for us, Miss Persys," Libby said with a wink.

"If I must dye those linen napkins today I may wish it were still raining. Libby," Persys said soberly, "it will not be long before we must leave here. The duchess is healing well, the duke said. Once she is able to fend for herself she may wish me gone. My poor head aches with wondering where we shall go. Perhaps something will turn up for us?"

"Right you are, miss. Look how this job happened just when you had need of it," Libby said with a serious change of expression. "You never know when something will come your way." She helped Persys out of her night rail and into her shift and her oldest muslin dress deemed suitable for dyeing. "I wonder when those cousins are due to arrive? Heard in the kitchen that Miss Charlotte is a one, always demanding this and that. Very hard to please, she is. And if her brother Mr. George is with her, you best mind yourself and never be alone with him. He's a nasty reputation, he has."

"Indeed? I wonder that His Grace allows him to visit, if that is the case," Persys said, sitting down at her dressing table so Libby could attack the long ash-brown hair with a determined brush. "Do not worry, I shan't get near the man . . . if he does indeed come. You take care as well. Too many of these fine gentlemen think they can play fast and loose with a maid if they please."

"Not with me, he won't," Libby promised.

Following a hasty breakfast Persys sought out Mrs. Biddle to inquire about dyeing the napkins. With her she took a pad of paper and a pencil; her memory was excellent but not perfect.

"Bless your heart, it's a messy job. See that you put on a waterproofed apron before you attempt it." Then the kindly woman took Persys across the yard to the laundry where a small stove had been lit and a pail of water was even at that moment coming to a boil.

"First you mordant the fabric." The housekeeper instructed as Persys took notes of every step.

When the housekeeper concluded her directions Persys poked at the pile of napkins and said, "Well, it doesn't sound as though it's impossible, does it? I mean, chamomile tea ought not stain my fingers past redemption. How fortunate the duchess doesn't want them dyed with indigo or cochineal. Even madder root would give me pink hands!"

"Indeed," the housekeeper agreed. "If that is all, I shall leave you to get on with it. One of the laundry maids will be here should you need a bit of help. Not that I think you will."

Persys watched the housekeeper depart, then set about the dyeing.

Sun streamed in through high windows, lighting the room and thus making it most pleasant. The laundry maid scurried about her work. Persys mixed and stirred the dye, then spent the next hour or so poking and prodding the fabric about in the dye bath. It was hot work, and she frequently brushed a wisp of hair away from her face, leaving streaks of pale yellow on her skin. Several hours later she was taking the last of the napkins from the hot chamomile bath, preparing to rinse them, when she heard a noise.

"How does it go, dear Persys?" the countess gaily cried.

Whirling about, Persys was astounded to see the duke and his mother, who was seated regally on a fat cushion in the combination wheelbarrow and Bath chair. She waved gaily at Persys and smiled serenely at the mess in the laundry. Persys doubted if this was a place she frequented.

Dropping the last of the napkins into the hot rinse water, she took wooden spoons to stir, then lifted the fabric from the water, letting it drip and repeating the action until the water ran clear.

"The napkins are very dark yellow," the duchess said with a

little frown. The duke remained behind the odd chair, watching Persys but saying nothing.

"I understand the color lightens as the fabric dries. I think," Persys said with enthusiasm while pushing tendrils of hair off her forehead, "that they are all going to look splendid once dry and pressed."

The duchess appeared to have her doubts and Persys could only hope that what she said proved true.

Moggy trotted into the laundry, inspecting Persys with a wary eye before deciding that this exceedingly warm and bedraggled lady was his.

"Poor Moggy, he scarcely knows you," the duchess said with a chuckle.

"Well, there are streaks of yellow on her cheeks and her hair has tumbled about her head as though she has been in a strong wind," the duke said with a wry smile.

"Do not tease her, Harry. I think she looks charming even if she does resemble a tiger cat. Now, I wish to go into my garden. Join us when you can, Persys."

The pair disappeared from the laundry room just in time, thought Persys. She had come dangerously close to throwing something at His Grace and that would never do!

The laundry maid entered the little building with a cautious step. "Be you done here, miss? Kin I help you with those napkins?"

The girl was cheerful enough and willing to help, although Persys wasn't certain how best to dry the fabric once the napkins had been well rinsed and said so.

"The bushes, miss. They be ever so fragrant and the napkins will dry a treat, they will."

Within minutes the pair had spread the napkins to dry. One look at the disorder in the laundry room made Persys most thankful that she could leave the mess to the maid whose job it was to tend that place.

Persys took off her oiled-cloth apron, tucked her hair under her gardening bonnet, then peered in the cracked bit of looking glass hanging above a stone sink. Horrified at what she saw, she wondered how she could face the duchess and the duke after such an appearance. It took a bit of scrubbing with the fine soap used on the silk washables to clear the yellow stripes from her face and rid her hands of at least some of the dye. What a pity they did not make waterproof gloves for such work. When she was satisfied that she was as presentable as possible under the circumstances, she left the laundry in search of the others.

Voices led her to where the flower garden had been placed along one side of the house. It was quite impressive, with a great variety of flowers.

"Ah, my Persian woman just when I have need of her," the duke exclaimed when he spotted her ambling along the border of colorful blooms.

"Now what?" Persys demanded softly, wondering what scheme the duchess had dreamed up next.

"I say she ought to think of red tulips for next spring and she insists nothing will do but yellow. Do you not think red would be nice?" he coaxed as a little boy might.

Persys laughed at his pleading. Surely if he wanted red tulips, he could have them. It said a great deal for him that he tolerated his mother's whims.

"I prefer lavender, myself," she said, still grinning at him, thus missing the duchess's intent gaze.

"What say you to that, Mother? Lavender would be something a bit different than red or yellow, now wouldn't it?" He spoke lightly but Persys wondered a little at his purpose.

"Lavender it shall be and I will order some white primrose to set them off. Now, what do you think of that?"

"I think I am bested at my own game. I would not be surprised if you planned it that way from the beginning. Will you take over, Persys? I must see my steward." At her nod, he strode away, a tall, handsome figure.

"He is a dear man, is he not, Persys?" the duchess quietly demanded.

"Indeed, he does seem to have his good points," Persys conceded tactfully.

"More than you will ever guess," the duchess concluded lightly.

Moggy had followed them out to the garden and now proceeded to chase a butterfly through the lupine and foxglove. Persys called the cat, to no avail.

"Like most males he knows precisely what he wants and goes about getting it without hindrance," observed the duchess from her ungainly chair. Even with her leg propped up, she maintained a regal air.

"They do seem to have a way about them," Persys agreed. "Although I have known women who were quite capable of achieving their aims. They simply were not as direct about it."

"Subtlety is a trait not often common in men," the duchess replied.

"But one can never underestimate any of them," Persys responded thoughtfully. If Mr. George Russell came with his sister he would likely be a great contrast to the duke. His Grace worked indirectly, seeming to achieve his results without effort when Persys suspected that it took considerable planning on his part to get things just as he wished.

Moggy abandoned his chase, coming to sit on the freshly scythed grass around the flower bed. Proceeding to clean his paws and face, he then stretched out in the sun.

"I sometimes envy a cat," Persys said softly. "How easy life seems for them, doing as they please."

"As long as they have a home and are loved," the duchess gently reminded her.

Her words jolted Persys to recall her own coming predicament. "How long must you remain immobile, Your Grace? Will it not be soon and you will be walking again?" Persys wondered. Given the impatient nature of the duchess, she would not be still a moment longer than necessary.

"Another two weeks, possibly longer—perhaps less. Dr. Fraser comes today. Wheel me to the herb garden, Persys," the duchess suddenly demanded. "I would have you gather some angelica root. As well, I should like some horsetail reed and that will be at the shore of the lake. Harry had them planted particularly for me to use. Is there any feverfew in bloom? I believe a handful of leaves and flowers would be beneficial. A lotion of it is so good to nourish the skin, my dear. When one grows older, looking one's best takes longer and longer."

Persys laughed as was intended and did as requested. A spade leaned against the brick wall of the herb garden, testimony to a gardener's attention. It took but a few minutes to obtain the required root.

Looking at the angelica root, soil clinging to it in a rather unappealing manner, the duchess said, "Would you believe this also makes a wonderful lotion for the complexion? You must try some. I shall have Tessa make us each a bottle."

The feverfew came next and was placed in a small fabric bag the duchess carried in her lap.

When Persys trundled Her Grace along the path to the lake, she found it slow and hard going. Finally, she abandoned the gravel path and parked the duchess on a swath of green.

"Allow me to fetch the reed while you wait here in comfort. It cannot be easy for you to be jounced along this path." Leaving Her Grace in the shade of an elm, Persys ran across the grass until she reached the lake and found the spot she recalled from the day when she had found Moggy on the walk with the duke.

When she returned it was to find the duke seated on a nearby stone bench, chatting with his mother. Persys came to an abrupt halt, then walked forward with hesitant steps.

"This is not the ideal time to gather the horsetail reed; autumn is better. That cannot be helped, I wish some now," the duchess said while investigating the armful of reeds Persys had gathered.

The duke had risen when Persys arrived with her herbs. Now he also inspected the reeds, touching them lightly, inadvertently brushing her arm with his finger.

She felt as though a wisp of fire had blazed across her skin and she gave him a startled look.

"Something the matter, my Persian woman?" the duke said quietly for her ears alone.

"I do not know," she replied, truthful as usual. "It was something, perhaps the reeds . . ." Her voice trailed off as she met his gaze. Somehow she suspected the reeds had nothing to do with that sensation. But if not—what had caused it?

Chapter Five

*I*t was much as Persys feared and hoped. The duchess had improved to the point where she could be on her feet a little several times a day. The doctor cautioned against overdoing, but Persys surmised the duchess would set her own schedule. She always managed to get her way about things one way or the other. The gleam in her eyes when Dr. Fraser pronounced the admonition warned anyone who knew her what would come.

Persys turned from the window in the duchess's sitting room that overlooked the flower garden when Her Grace exploded with annoyance.

"Bother that man," the duchess declared, referring to Dr. Fraser. "Why he thinks I must need these crutches is beyond me."

Crossing to stand beside the irate woman, Persys steadied her hand. "Because you have not walked for a long time and you must be careful," Persys admonished gently. "It will not be for long, you know. Why, I should not be surprised if you send me on my way within days. You shan't need me for long."

"You'll not leave me now!" the duchess cried in alarm. "I'll not have it. Where do you intend to go, may I ask? Have you been illtreated while here? Has anyone been rude to you?" When Persys shook her head, the duchess nodded hers in satisfaction. "You will stay until I say so."

Suppressing a smile at her autocratic manner, Persys meekly nodded. "Whatever you say, Your Grace. But you do realize that sooner or later I must find some occupation or somewhere to go? I cannot continue on here once you are back on your feet."

"Indeed?" Her Grace, Louisa, Duchess of Eddington, grew pensive and a rather crafty look came into her eyes. It was fortunate that Persys couldn't see it, occupied as she was with holding the crutches and assisting Her Grace to balance.

"Now if you will just try again, I feel certain that you will do splendidly."

"What is my mother likely to do, Miss Timothy?" the duke inquired from the doorway. He strolled into the sitting room while studying his determined mother with a barely suppressed smile.

"Walk!" Persys said proudly, as though she was the one responsible for the possibility.

"Harry, persuade Dr. Fraser and Persys that I do not need these ugly things."

"Mother, if the doctor says you need them and Miss Timothy is willing to help you, then you must have patience."

"I should," Her Grace said reluctantly. "It is a good thing you take after your father. He was such a patient man."

The duke nodded, then walked over to examine the wooden crutches. "These are rather heavy. I wonder if the carpenter could think of something that would be lighter in weight and not as awkward for you? I shall look into it at once."

With a fond smile, Her Grace watched her son stride from the room. "He will, you know. He is so thoughtful. He did not even tease you today. You have not angered him, have you?" the duchess asked sharply.

"Not that I know, Your Grace," Persys replied, urging the good foot forward while encouraging the other to follow. It proved to be a tiring occupation and she was thankful when the duchess decided she had had enough.

"Bring me the napkins we colored," the duchess requested in her customary manner. "I would see how they look once ironed." The duchess settled on the chaise longue near her sitting room window, prepared to spend her afternoon there.

However, she looked fatigued and Persys decided that she would take some time in finding the requested napkins.

She slipped from the suite and down to the kitchen, then out to where the laundry maid was at work. There was a never-ending supply of laundry and ironing for the girl. Persys located the stack of buttery-yellow napkins, politely thanked the maid for her help, then walked slowly back toward the house.

"Mother send you off on one of her endless errands?" the duke inquired, joining her in the middle of the service yard. Paths went in every direction: to the stables, the carpenter's shop, laundry and dairy, and the specialty workshops that made the estate almost self-sufficient. "I want you to know that I have the carpenter at work on a pair of lightweight crutches, such as Mother can manage. He had a clever idea of combining some special wood in varied strips that would weigh less." He observed the silence of his companion and bent to inspect her face.

Persys blushed at his probing look. This man could disturb her without half trying.

Harry studied what he found beneath the serviceable headgear she wore. That bonnet scarcely did justice to her delicate face and her gown assuredly did not suit her elegant figure. The duke thought she deserved far better than she had, but he knew better than to suggest *he* be allowed to buy her anything. Her good breeding would forbid any such happening. Now his cousin, dear, aggressive Charlotte, would most likely demand he treat her to a new gown, crying that her present attire was horridly out of date.

How would Miss Timothy look garbed in fragile silks and sumptuous velvets? He suspected she would be elegantly graceful, for even in her humble muslins, she had a quality of refinement about her that caught the eye. Then he noticed her expression. It was not as serene as was her custom.

"You are worried about something. May I help?" He began to draw her off to one side, away from the house. His mother could wait for her companion when said companion had troubles.

Persys shook her head, "Indeed not, Your Grace. There is nothing the matter that time and a bit of thinking cannot solve."

"Perhaps I might assist with the latter. I am reckoned to have a good head." He took her elbow to guide her into the shade of the pergola that was covered with ivy. This led to the edge of the cultivated garden area. Grass grew neatly along the broad grav-

eled path and trees arched over the brisk wall that protected the
kitchen garden on the far side.

"You know"—the duke mused aloud while permitting Miss
Timothy to gather her thoughts—"I am thinking of building a
long conservatory along this wall. I should like to grow camellias and as you might guess they would never survive this cli-
mate. A sensible arrangement of glass walls up against the
brick—giving at least six feet of space or so—would allow the
sun to warm that area quite nicely," he said with a considering
look at the condition of the brick. "There could be a taller central portion in the middle to add to the attractiveness, and aisles
so one could walk back and forth to enjoy the flowers when in
bloom. What do you think?"

Persys was still trying to cope with the sensations he had
stirred within her at the touch of his hand on her arm while he
guided her over the somewhat rough path. She hadn't much to
do with men, being relegated to a position as the elder cousin
and a quasi-chaperone role these past years. But she had to confess that the Marquess of Torrington had *not* affected her so the
few times he had assisted her into or out of a carriage when she
had been with her cousin. What was the matter with her?

There were flutterings within and a feeling she could not quite
catch her breath. It must have been evident she was not herself,
as the duke suddenly glanced down at her to exclaim, "Are you
unwell, Miss Timothy?"

"It is nothing, really." Persys tried to get a grip on herself and
failed when the duke put a protective arm about her shoulders,
looking greatly concerned.

She felt almost weak, and closed her eyes to his nearness.

He guided her to a not-too-distant stone bench from where
one could view the ornamental pond. He had no time for the
pond today. He enfolded one of her hands in his strong, capable
ones as though he didn't quite know what to do with her but felt
he might help by his comforting touch.

If he but knew, Persys thought bewilderedly. The closer he
came to her, the more her heart seemed to panic.

"Were Dr. Fraser here I would have him attend you," the duke declared, giving Persys a concerned frown. "I suggest you tell me what it is that worries you. Maybe that is at the root of your trouble?"

"I must not bother you with my trivial problems, Your Grace," Persys protested. "You have quite enough on your plate without my humble difficulties."

"Now I insist upon hearing them. Difficulties? That sounds serious. Will you not confide in me?" he asked with a meek note in his voice that brought a reluctant smile to her face. He was the most unlikely one to sound meek she could imagine.

"If you insist upon knowing, it is merely that your mother seems so much better that I know I must leave here shortly. And if I had a frown, it was because I cannot think where best to go. You see? Just minor difficulties. I am certain something will occur to me in time. I feel rather foolish, giving way to sensibilities when I scorned such in Marianne Dashwood, that character in the book."

"You must not think of leaving here until Mother is her old self. She leans upon you far more than you realize. Without you she would have no one with whom to converse, or argue with, or involve in little fancies—like dyeing the linens. You have been a godsend, Miss Timothy. Please promise you will not consider leaving here until we discuss the matter thoroughly. I feel as though I stand in place of guardian, you know. I feel, er, responsible for you." Then he appeared to realize it was not the thing for him to sit with his arm tenderly about her shoulder, looking down into her violet eyes. He hastily withdrew the protection he'd offered and sat at her side, saying nothing for a few moments.

Good grief, Harry thought, *I almost gathered her in my arms and went far beyond comforting her. This will never do. She is such a fragile, vulnerable creature, I'd not frighten her out of her wits by a kiss.* The thing to do was to find some reason to keep her here.

Persys glanced up at the duke, wondering what she ought to say, for it seemed an awkward moment, to say the least.

"For now, I suggest you leave everything to me. I'll not have you worrying about a thing. I feel certain the right idea will present itself at the right time." Harry hoped that he didn't look as uneasy as he felt.

Just then Persys spied Moggy trotting along the path, a mouse in his mouth. "Good grief," she said dryly. "I trust he can't get into the house with that offering."

Moggy dropped the mouse before the duke and sat back.

"One would think the beast imagines he is paying for his keep," the duke mused with a grin that altered his face a great deal. "He's a good cat, better than I expected." At this, Moggy, who truly was a perceptive creature, jumped up on the bench and insinuated himself onto the duke's lap.

Persys thought the duke ought to grin more often and just stopped herself in time from saying that very thing. What was the matter with her? In the past she had not been given to such ridiculous urgings. For instance, she felt the most peculiar impulse to lean against his strong shoulder and forget her problems, her uncertain future. If only life were as simple as that! She had depended upon herself most of her life: she had better continue, for there was no rescue to be had from this quarter.

"I see you have Mother's newly dyed napkins with you. Sent you to fetch them, did she?" He stroked Moggy, who issued forth a rough, loud purr in appreciation.

Persys nodded, grateful for more prosaic conversation. "I decided not to hurry for she looked a trifle tired. She *will* walk more than Dr. Fraser suggested, you know."

"Determination to have one's own way is a family trait, I suspect," the duke replied with a wry grimace.

"Why is it that I am not the least surprised at that statement!" Persys replied, laughing now that the strange feelings that had come over her seemed to have disappeared. She rose from the bench and stood for a moment, looking at the pond: such a splendid view. She would miss this all most dreadfully when she left here.

Giving him a brisk smile, she turned to go to the house, only to find him falling in at her side.

"I shall discuss the plans for the new greenhouse with Mother.

You would be surprised at the sensible suggestions she offers at times." He took note of Moggy trotting at their heels and allowed the cat to follow them to the house.

"I believe your mother is a very clever lady, one who may on occasion hide her light beneath a bushel."

"An astute observation," he replied while escorting her through a side door, then walking up the shallow flight of stairs to the main level of the house. "I wonder when Charlotte and George are to descend upon us? I had thought them to be here long before this. Some special party must have arisen that Charlotte decided she simply must attend."

"She decides, not George?" Persys queried before minding her tongue.

"Indeed. Dear George is led around by the nose. Charlotte has an excess of the family trait, you see."

"A very determined young woman, I perceive," Persys replied, thinking it was going to be a revelation to observe the determined Charlotte in action around the duchess.

"She insists she always gets her way. I doubt that, somehow, or she'd not be begging for a visit at this time of year."

Knowing that the Season was not quite over, Persys nodded her agreement of that observation. She was surprised when the duke ambled up the stairs at her side, chatting about nothing in particular as they went. He had been out of sight so much the past week she was puzzled at his sudden change. Perhaps it was as he said, he wanted to consult with his mother regarding the design of the new conservatory.

When they entered Her Grace's suite it was to find her restlessly staring out the window, an open book in her hands—signifying she had been reading.

"Here we are come to amuse you," the duke said lightly.

Persys walked forward with the napkins in hand. "You look rested. I daresay you slipped into a little nap?"

"And you took your time about returning for just that purpose," the duchess returned swiftly, but with a smile so Persys knew she wasn't angry. "Ah, the napkins!" the duchess cried with pleasure. "See how right I was to think of dyeing? I do believe they turned out very well, indeed."

"I suspect the laundry maid wondered if a pot of mustard had fallen into the water," Persys said, smiling with a hint of mischief.

"Well, I have company coming tomorrow so it will be a chance to try them out. Lady Leycester and her daughter are to join us for nuncheon. If I know her, they will linger as long as may be." Turning her gaze from her son to Persys, she added, "That foolish woman still thinks she can promote an alliance between Harry and that insipid daughter of hers, Judith."

"Something to be prevented at all costs," the duke said with a dry manner quite in keeping with the expression on the duchess's face.

"If I can be of any use at all, please do not hesitate to ask," Persys said, thinking she could assist Mrs. Biddle with table arrangements.

"Clever girl. If you do not mind, I shall imply that there is an understanding between you and Harry. Lady Leycester would never repeat the tale—she could never give up on Judith until she actually saw Harry wed."

The duke laughed at this bit, then said, "You would be doing us both a favor, my Persian woman. I believe they were rather fierce, those women. You will need to hold your own with Lady Leycester, but I have little doubt but what you will do a superb job."

"I think this is all very odd—" Persys began, to be cut off by the duchess with an imperious wave of her hand.

"There are a few things I would discuss with you, Mother. First I want you to know that I have invited Burfield for a visit." To Persys he added, "The earl is a friend of long standing and I look forward to seeing him as soon as may be."

"You know I always welcome him—any of your friends, for that matter. And the other?" The duchess gave him a sly smile, darting a glance at Persys, who was edging toward the door.

"I had a splendid notion for a new conservatory along the

kitchen garden wall. I saw an impressive one at Blickling when I was last there. What I envision is a bit different, but long and full of windows. I would grow camellias."

"If you would excuse me," Persys said quietly, then slipped from the room to leave mother and son in comfortable conversation.

Company! And what a lot of nonsense about implying that she had an understanding with the duke! As though anyone would believe such a thing. She scarcely knew what to think. Why, she had not the least interest in the duke. She had vowed never to love another, not when her heart had been given to the marquess. It would take more than a little playacting to simulate an attachment, firm or otherwise, with the duke.

"Libby," she said upon entering her lovely room down the hall, "I need a special gown for tomorrow's nuncheon. Her Grace is having friends to call and, well, she wishes me to attend."

"The lavender stripe, miss. It looks a treat on you, if I do say. I have no doubt you will outshine everyone at the table."

"I shall need every bit of help I can obtain." She made no reference to the outrageous suggestion by the duchess. No doubt by tomorrow she would have forgotten all about it. Perhaps she was taking to teasing Persys as did the duke, calling her his Persian woman.

Thus it was the next morning found Persys arranging flowers sent up from the hothouse, Libby at her side ready to cart away leaves or stems.

"You seem a might nervous for a simple nuncheon," Libby observed.

Persys inserted a tall white lupine into the arrangement of summer flowers and sighed. "Her Grace wishes to discourage the interest Lady Leycester has in uniting her daughter with the duke. I surmise that her ladyship intends to put forth her concerns this noon. If only Lord Burfield will arrive in time. I suspect that would alter the situation some—and for the better."

"At any rate, we had best have you looking as fine as fivepence."

Persys silently agreed. While she might have little personal interest in the duke, she would never let Her Grace down. Whatever she decided to do, Persys would endeavor to follow through.

With Libby's help, Persys carried the flower arrangement up to the dining room on the main floor, then, satisfied all was as it should be, went to her room. Here Libby helped her change her gown for the lavender stripe, fussed over her hair, and found a pretty fan to add the proper touch to one who might aspire to the great heights of Duchess of Eddington.

Walking down to the great drawing room where the guests would assemble, Persys heard a commotion in the entry below. Curious, she peered over the stair rail to see a gentleman entering the hall hand his hat to Portman, then turn to greet the duke. What a blessing! Lord Burfield had arrived just in time.

Thus, it was when Lady Leycester and Judith entered the great drawing room it was to find not merely the duke and duchess but Lord Burfield and Persys as well.

The duchess performed introductions with a charm that Persys could only envy and hope to emulate someday.

Persys glanced about the room, for it was worth many a look. On walls covered in blue-and-silver damask hung a great many portraits of past Russells, while on an easel rested an excellent painting of Eddington Park done by none other than Canaletto. Comfortable sofas covered in blue-and-silver stripe alternated with gilded armchairs upholstered in blue damask. It was on one of these dainty armchairs that Persys perched next to a marble-topped table that had incredibly carved legs of fantastic design. It was an imposing room but not as impressive as the duchess.

Her Grace, the Duchess of Eddington, had dressed in such simplicity as to put every other woman in the shade. Lady Leycester appeared unconscious of her over-adornment for a mere nuncheon and afternoon call.

"How lovely you could come, Hortensia," the duchess intoned in a rich, utterly gracious voice. "It has been an age since we last had a good chat."

Persys had to repress a smile as Lady Leycester's pointed

nose rose a notch when she saw strangers. "Louisa, I trust you are vastly improved? I was greatly distressed to learn you had taken a fall. As soon as we returned from London I made certain to write, hoping you would be able to receive us." Her ladyship motioned a silent Judith to take a seat while she settled on a chair close to the duchess.

"Utter silliness. I tripped on a stone in the garden and stupidly fell. It was a nasty wrench but seems to have taken forever to heal. Thanks to Persys, I am no longer bored to flinders. She keeps me wonderfully entertained."

"Had we been here, Judith could have come over. She is marvelous at entertaining one who is ill." She favored her eldest daughter with a prim smile, then glared at Persys as though she was at fault for simply being at hand.

Old dragon, thought Persys. It was evident now why the duchess could not be enthusiastic regarding an alliance between her adored Harry and Judith Leycester. The girl was as platter-faced as Persys had ever seen and possessed hair the unhappy color of dried corn.

"How thoughtful of you. How are the other girls, Hortensia?" To Persys the duchess added, "Lady Leycester has four other hopefuls at home, all equally charming as Judith."

"I wish there was a school for young ladies I might trust closer than Bath. The nearest one had quite a scandal—the daughter of Lord Chumley ran off with the dancing master and has not been heard from since."

"Never say she was murdered!" the duchess exclaimed in horror.

Persys wondered if the horror was feigned or real. Lady Leycester would not appear to know the difference.

The duke coughed and began a quiet conversation with his good friend, trying to include Judith and failing. The girl would not open her mouth. The duchess and her ladyship continued to discuss the scandal in soft voices.

At last Portman appeared at the doorway to inform the duchess that nuncheon was served. Two delicately carved and yet surprisingly strong crutches appeared from behind the sofa upon which the duchess had half sat, half reclined. With an air of triumph, Her Grace rose with the duke's assistance, then thumped her way to the stairs. Here the two footmen who had served so well these past weeks again carried her down to the dining room where she resumed her halting pace.

"My you are indeed brave, Louisa," Lady Leycester exclaimed. "I would never be so daring."

"You would if you were bored enough," Her Grace said tartly.

At first the meal proceeded rather quietly, with innocuous remarks and the sort of conversation one makes at nuncheon when there are guests.

Then Lady Leycester turned to the duke and, with a fluttering of darkened eyelashes, said, "And when do you marry, Your Grace? Surely it is time for you to settle down and begin your nursery?" she tittered with a fond look and a nod at her Judith. Judith merely blushed and said nothing. She did well at eating, however, Persys noted.

The duchess placed a warm hand over the one Persys had placed on the table. "Well, we have great hopes, do we not, dear?" She bestowed a loving look on Persys and so well did she act that Persys could almost believe she was in line for the position of her successor.

"Your Grace, you will put me to the blush," Persys replied with what she hoped was just the right note.

"Darling Persys has been such help to me—stepping in to do the flower arrangements—which you know I always do myself. And just admire these napkins! My favorite color and I owe it all to Persys. There seems to be nothing she cannot do," the duchess concluded like a proud mother.

Persys thought that was slathering it on a bit thick, but said nothing. What could she utter at this point without looking daft?

"Indeed," Lady Leycester said rather austerely, holding up her butter-yellow napkin as though it might bite her. "I noticed but hesitated to say anything. There are times when the laundry maid manages to put the wrong colors together, you know."

"Clever Persys used chamomile to dye them. And now she

will help the duke design his new greenhouse. Persys has so
many talents."

"But, Your Grace," Persys murmured, distressed at this turn
of the conversation. It was one thing to exaggerate, it was quite
another to fabricate out of whole cloth.

"We have such interesting plans. *I* think that Persys should
sponsor a finishing school for young ladies. She helped her
cousin Katherine, you see. And Katherine is now the new Marchioness of Torrington."

Lady Leycester was seized with a spasm that brought on a
coughing spell of nasty proportions. When at last she could
speak, she said—in a rather strained voice—"I would deem it a
pleasure if the girls could attend. Any school that has your sanc-
tion would bound to be sensible and safe. There would be no
danger of a dancing master who flirted with students in any such
school." She gave Persys a daunting look.

"Indeed, my lady. I do not hold with flirtatious dancing mas-
ters in the least." Then Persys gave the duchess a puzzled look
that dared her to explain what was afoot.

"The duke and I discussed it this afternoon. There is a charming house at the edge of the property that would be perfect for a
school. Persys is always anxious to be occupied and this would
keep her busy . . . for the moment, that is."

Persys blushed at the implication of the remark, particularly
the way the duchess said it and then looked sweetly at Persys.
Good grief, the stage lost a great actress in the duchess.

At this point Lord Burfield said he, for one, could vouch his
little sister would find such a school far better than the one she
now attended in Bath.

The duke sat at the foot of the table and smiled. Persys
thought he reminded her of Moggy when he contemplated a
good meal. Of course nothing would come of the school, but she
actually thought it might be a possibility. She had some funds
and all she needed was a place in which to hold it—plus a
woman of impeccable credentials to help. Smiling wryly, Persys
allowed the chatter that followed to flow over her head. Once

Lady Leycester and her frumpish daughter departed, life would return to normal.

But, Persys decided, she would explore the notion the duchess had unwittingly given her.

Chapter Six

The great drawing room was silent with the departure of Lady Leycester and Judith. The duke strolled over to one of the long windows overlooking the vast park, then turned to face his mother, Burfield, and Persys.

"I believe we survived that well enough," he commented slowly. "That was a clever notion to think of a finishing school for young ladies, Mother."

"I rather thought so myself. As much as I like Hortensia, there are moments when she grates on my nerves."

"You mean there is no such thing as a proposed school?" Lord Burfield asked, with a puzzled look at Persys, then the duke.

"No," Persys inserted, "but I think it might offer the answer to my problems." She turned to the duchess and smiled. "You are truly clever. I had been wondering what I might do and this could be it. Do you not see?" she continued at the speculative expression that settled on the duchess's face. "I was instrumental in assisting Katherine and I feel sure she would offer her patronage for my school."

"And you would have Mother's as well, of course," the duke added with an admonitory look at that lady. "Since it was in reality her idea, she would assuredly wish to support such an effort."

"Oh, indeed," the duchess agreed hastily. "The problem is where to locate it. Lady Leycester said she would like something closer to home for her four girls. Bath is a trifle far in her estimation, although I should think she would not mind that, were it a superior school," the duchess concluded upon reflection.

"My mother would prefer a school closer to home as well. I truly hoped that Miss Timothy was in actuality setting up a school. I believe my sister would like to have Miss Timothy as her schoolmistress," Lord Burfield said. He looked at his friend, then the duchess, finally studying Persys with a curious gaze.

"Schoolmistress?" the duchess echoed with a darted glance at Persys before turning to her son. "Shall we think about it a bit?"

"I have an idea. Perhaps Persys and Burfield would come for a drive with me so I might show them something. I'd rather not tell them in advance so to receive a spontaneous reaction."

"I'm game," Lord Burfield said quickly.

Before the duke or Lord Burfield could offer her a hand, Persys rose from her chair near the duchess. "If you can spare me for a time, I will go with His Grace to see what this surprise might be."

"Go, go," the duchess admonished with a wave of her hand. "I would reflect on a few things. Lady Leycester is ever full of Town gossip. I believe I will write a few letters while you are gone."

With a puzzled glance at the duke, Persys slipped from the drawing room to hurry up the stairs and down the hall to her own chamber. Libby was by the wardrobe putting away some freshly laundered garments and looked up in astonishment when Persys came rushing into the room.

"My pelisse and bonnet, Libby. I am to go on a mysterious drive with the duke and his guest to see a surprise somewhere. Oh, Libby, I may have found the answer to our problems. I shall start a school for young ladies."

"You start a school?" Libby inquired, wide-eyed with bewilderment.

"It was Her Grace's idea, actually, and I believe it just might do." Persys slipped into her lightweight pelisse of violet ribbed-silk. She would have clapped on a simple corded bonnet in a matching silk, but Libby prevented that scandal by arranging the bonnet just so, then tying the ribbons precisely right. Impatient to be gone, Persys picked up the gloves and a reticule Libby offered her and whirled out of the room. Even with her hurry it had taken her some fifteen minutes, considering the flights of stairs and distance involved. It would be twenty by the time she reached the ground floor some three flights below. Getting around the house took time and patience and a good set of legs.

Lord Burfield and the duke were chatting in the entryway when Persys calmly walked to join them, no sign of her dash down the stairs in the least evident beyond pink cheeks and a faintly breathless air.

By the time they went out of the great front doors, the carriage was coming up from the stables.

The open landau was just the sort of carriage in which to view the scenery—if that was what they were intended to do. Persys gratefully sank upon the well-cushioned seat and leaned against the squabs with delight. Treats such as this did not often come her way.

"Well, where are we off to, Harry?" Lord Burfield inquired. He sat opposite Persys and studied her more than he did the scenery. "What is this surprise you have in store for us?"

"It is not what you might think, a small matter, really. Ah, there it is," the duke exclaimed and the landau drew up before a moderate-sized brick house of the Queen Anne period. It was in good condition, as might be expected if it were part of the property belonging to the duke.

"This?" Lord Burfield inquired with obvious astonishment. "It is but a house."

"It would do admirably for a school," the duke replied, watching Persys and not his friend.

At first thought Persys was filled with delight, then she looked at the duke with the knowledge that she had intended to go far away from here. She did not mean to remain close to the duke, although she did not fully understand why.

"Miss Timothy is overwhelmed with her emotions. Let us examine the interior for suitability. It is some years since I've been in the place, for it was rented until recently."

With a puzzling reluctance, Persys allowed herself to be handed down from the carriage, then walked at the duke's side up the straight path to the front door.

"Well kept, I must say," Lord Burfield said upon entering the house.

Persys looked about her. The entry walls were plain white with a simple crown molding at the ceiling. The windows had equally simple treatment with plain draperies of leaf-green damask, while a walnut table stood against the far wall with elegantly unpretentious pewter candleholders at either end.

"Very nice," Persys said, feeling the commendation rung from her. She followed the duke into the first room to find a drawing room free of excessive decoration. The mantel was soft gray marble and the surround of the most elegant design. A few pieces of simple but good furniture remained in the room. Persys could envision a rug of muted blues and greens in the center to harmonize with the leaf-green draperies that were also found in this room.

From here, their steps led to the simplicity of the dining room. Even the chandelier was a graceful but plain item. How nice that leaf-green was such a practical color and so very pleasant, she thought, for the fabric had been used in the draperies and to cover the chair seats as well. Persys murmured soothing sounds that could have meant anything, then followed the other men to the far side of the house where the library met instant approval. Lined with mahogany bookcases, it had simple uncluttered windows and a large desk most suitable for a headmistress of a school for young ladies. Even Persys had to admit that.

From this room they entered another. "This would serve admirably for a schoolroom," Persys exclaimed, warming to the idea of a school here in such proximity to the great house. She had suddenly realized that once established in her school she would see little or nothing of the duke or the duchess, much less their guests. Why it was so important to be independent and out of their sight she didn't pause to examine at the moment.

Turning a glowing face to the duke she said with quiet satisfaction, "I believe it would be perfect, Your Grace. We should have to settle on rent and I must find a respectable teacher to assist me." She slowly turned around in the center of the room, seeing not the bare floor and walls, but a neat arrangement of desks and pleasant girls equally neatly in their places. "But I believe this would do admirably. Do you think your sister would like to come to such a place, Lord Burfield?" she asked as she crossed to the door to the hall, intent upon a discovery of the upper floors.

"Indeed, particularly if the school held the patronage of the Duchess of Eddington."

Persys paused on the stairs, looking behind her to the duke and his guest. "I suppose if I were truly independent I would disdain such, but I can only be thankful for any interest the duchess might decide to take in Miss Timothy's School for Young Ladies."

"Forgive me for saying so, but you seem rather young to head such a project," Lord Burfield said after a glance at his friend.

"Perhaps I had best think of another name." Persys turned and climbed the rest of the steps to the next floor, seeking to inspect all the rooms while mentally making a list of all the things she would need.

Stopping at the door to the second bedroom, she said, "I could dress in very somber garments and wear a proper white cap on my head. Do you not think that might be the thing?"

Lord Burfield took a good look at the eager and very pretty face that gazed at them with such hope and coughed. He turned to his friend and said, "Harry, I believe this one is yours."

"What is the matter?" Persys demanded.

"My dear Persian woman, one look at those violet eyes in that delicate face would raise doubts in most mother's minds. You are a rather fetching piece, you know, and as unlikely a candidate for a spinster schoolmistress as I can imagine."

"I cannot see why a schoolteacher must be ugly and old," Persys said, pushing aside his remark about her being fetching.

"I agree," said another voice from the stairs. "I confess that one of my tutors was so homely he quite turned me off my studies. That is why I am such a nodcock today."

"Hervey, by all that's holy, what are you doing here?" Lord Burfield exclaimed. "The last I saw of you was at a ball surrounded by several excellent young women. Veritable diamonds of the first water, as I recall. You were entertaining them all at once."

"True," Mr. Ninian Hervey admitted without a blush. "It is not because your cousin Charlotte is to arrive here shortly, either, Harry. You know we mutually detest one another."

"Point non plus?" the duke hazarded.

"Cutting a trifle close to the bone, as they say. I thought to rusticate and where else would be better?" Mr. Hervey asked jauntily. Turning to Persys he continued, "I recollect seeing you at your cousin's wedding. Bridal attendant, you were, and smashing in pink, as I recall."

"Ninian has an amazing memory for gowns as well as the women in them," the duke said dryly. "I gather dear Charlotte is to arrive before long?"

"Indeed," said Mr. Hervey with another infectious grin. "Just wait until she sets her eyes on your schoolmistress here. Are you actually turning this into a school, Harry?"

"Miss Timothy seems to think it a viable proposition. Rob, here, would have his sister attend and Lady Leycester wishes a place for her four youngest."

"They look anything like Judith?" Ninian Hervey asked warily.

"So my mother says."

"God help us all. Is the world ready for four more platter-faced women?"

"Mr. Hervey," Persys admonished, "you ought not judge a woman merely by her face."

"No?" He studied her intently until Persys blushed under his gaze.

"Ninian," the duke said with a barely suppressed grin.

Mr. Hervey ignored the warning and said, "I would wager that you are a thoroughly nice person and delightful company. I suspect you are rather clever and I'd fear that. Don't want a clever woman, myself, but I do respect them."

"You would need one to keep the duns from your door—that is, if you'd give her the assets to manage," the duke said with a short laugh.

"Women don't manage estates," Ninian replied swiftly, then with another look at Persys, added, "Although I imagine *she* could. Looks devilishly clever, she does."

"Come, you are putting her to the blush." The duke guided Per-

sys and the men along the hall. They peered into the various bedrooms, all of which Persys saw were in good condition, if very
plain, then paused at the foot of yet another stairs.

"I believe this leads to the servant quarters and attics," the duke
reported to Persys. "I expect they are the usual thing."

Persys resolved to inspect them at a later time when she was by
herself and not in the company of three teasing gentlemen.

"Well, I daresay there will be a great deal involved in the planning of it all, but it might be possible to open a school here this
coming fall, if all things work to my advantage," Persys said
thoughtfully while the four trod the stairs to the main level.

"My steward can handle the clerical details and you can depend
upon him for all and any advice you might need," the duke said as
they left the house. He locked the door, then handed the key to Persys. "I imagine you might as well have this now, seeing as how
you are bent on a school."

"Charlotte will find it most aggravating," Ninian Hervey said
with relish while studying Persys on the drive back to the great
house. He turned to the duke to add, "Sent my groom on to the stables with my curricle and gear. Thought you'd not deny me a roof
for a time."

The duke smiled thoughtfully and replied, "I should think you
would be an excellent buffer, dear Ninian. Rob as well. With Charlotte and George about to descend upon us, it is the more, the mer-
rier."

"Men, of course," Lord Burfield added wryly.

Persys was fascinated at the exchange she guessed would normally not be heard by a woman. Perhaps it made a difference that
she was a relative stranger? Or did a prospective schoolmistress
become invisible? That thought intrigued her so that she fell into a
deep reflection that lasted until the landau stopped before the impressive entrance to the great house.

"Look who we found, Mother," the duke said upon entering the
yellow drawing room, Ninian Hervey, Robert, Lord Burfield, and
Persys in tow behind him. "Hervey has come to visit for a while."

"Well, keep him out of Charlotte's way."

"On the contrary," the duke replied, a decided twinkle in his eyes, "I shan't do anything of the sort. Nothing like a spark of dissent to liven things up a bit, I always say."

"You say nothing of the sort and you know it," the duchess said, but matched his look of suppressed amusement. "However, I shall enjoy a bit of lively conversation. I fancy Persys is vastly tired of playing cards and reading to me. Now she will have diverse pleasures."

"Ah," the duke inserted, "Persys has decided she will leave us as soon as you are on your feet once again, Mother. I took them to see Russell House when we left here. Persys agreed with me that it would be the perfect location for a smallish school for young ladies of the most respectability."

"You play the pianoforte, of course, Persys?" the duchess inquired. "And paint watercolors as well as embroider?"

"Of course, Your Grace."

"I'll wager she had to do her cousin's work while she went out with all her gentlemen," Ninian Hervey said with a grin. "The fair Katherine led Torrington a merry dance before he caught her."

Persys thought it odd that hearing the name of the man she loved didn't cause a twinge, but knew any pondering would have to come later when alone. "Well, let us say that I improved my abilities when I had the opportunity. Katherine had no love for the pianoforte, although she did well at watercolors and embroidery."

"So you would be able to instruct the girls in the finer arts necessary to a lady of quality?" The duchess exchanged a knowing look with Persys, one that held wry amusement at what was considered required education for young women. She and Persys had discussed what also should be included and that was a smattering of history, French, the globe, knowledge of household and money management, plus the previously mentioned arts.

"Indeed, Your Grace. I have given it considerable thought since you first mentioned the possibility of a school. Now all I require is a proper schoolmistress to assist me."

Portman entered the room followed by two footmen with trays of drinks for the gentlemen and one of tea and biscuits for the two women.

"Sustenance," Ninian Hervey exclaimed, reaching for a glass of claret with undisguised relief.

The three men took their wine and sauntered off to the far end of the drawing room, probably, Persys thought, to chat over the Season and gossip a bit. One thing she had discovered was that men were as much gossips as women.

"You liked Russell House, my dear?" the duchess inquired while sipping the steaming bohea.

"It seems quite perfect for my use," Persys exclaimed quietly. "I should not accept so many girls as to risk damage to the interior. Perhaps ten, do you think? Or am I too ambitious? I suspect the knowledge of your patronage will inspire quite a number of enterprising mothers to select my school merely for that reason alone. I have no reputation upon which I might rely."

"I am glad you are realistic in that regard," the duchess said while reaching for another biscuit. "You will be able to plan while you are yet with us. By the time the school is ready I should be up and about without the awful pain I had after I so foolishly fell. I am pleased you are not returning to London. I have grown accustomed to your cheerful presence and you do read astonishingly well, my dear."

Persys blushed and refrained from comment on Her Grace's acting ability.

"Would you play something for me? The men are off in their own world and pay us not the slightest heed." The duchess replaced her cup and saucer on the tray and leaned back on her chaise.

Seeing that the duchess looked tired, Persys agreed with a nod and made herself comfortable at the pianoforte near a set of the tall French doors. The windowed doors offered excellent light at this time of the afternoon. Persys softly performed a Sonata in C-Sharp Minor composed for the harpsichord by Soler.

The duchess kept time with a wave of her hand as Persys played the exquisitely simple piece with great feeling. Even though written in a minor key, the music was lyrical and pleasant to the ears with suitably dramatic parts to delight the duchess, who possessed an ear which liked a contrast.

"Very nice, Persys," the duchess said softly when the music concluded. "I should envy the girls under your tutelage. I once played but not for some time. It seems when one is drawn up in the rigors of a London Season there is little time for such pleasures."

Persys was conscious that the duke had watched her from where he stood at the far end of the room, but he had not joined her and the duchess again, nor had the others appeared interested. Whatever they found to discuss—such as the next horse race or who was lately involved in gaming wins and losses—had captured their complete absorption.

She played until it was time to change for dinner, then walked with the duchess to the stairs where the sturdy footman carried the duchess up the steps and along to her suite.

"Thank you, James," the duchess said politely when he placed her on her feet before the door to her rooms. "Come in with me for a moment, Persys. I would talk with you."

Puzzled, Persys followed the duchess into the suite and waited for whatever it was she had to say.

"Lady Leycester and Judith are bound to come over while Charlotte and George are visiting. Should it prove necessary I would like to continue the little deception we began the last time they were here. Charlotte is so terribly sure of her charms it would do her good to think there is someone else who might capture her cousin's interest."

"Does Charlotte Russell believe the duke could be interested in her?" Persys asked guardedly while the duchess limped over to the closest chair.

"No. But that does not prevent her from flirting with him." The duchess eased herself onto the chair, giving a sigh of relief when she could put her foot up on the small stool before it. "It would be disastrous were she to entrap him into a marriage that could only be calamitous. I cannot imagine any woman I would desire less for a daughter-in-law than Charlotte Russell! She is self-centered and possesses a nasty temper when stirred. That is why I beseech you to play along with the innocent deception I have in mind."

The door had opened silently behind them and now a rich male voice inserted, "And what is this little deception you would have, dear Mother?"

The duchess turned in her chair to study her son. "Charlotte has always had her talons into you whenever she could. I want Persys to continue the pretense of your nurturing an interest in her. If that will drive Charlotte mad, so be it. I think Persys can handle that woman nicely."

"A formidable enemy, Mother," he cautioned.

"Pooh! Persys will be a match for her, as I said. It is long past time that Charlotte look elsewhere for a husband. It irks me no end to see her play up to you in hopes that she might seduce you."

"Dear Mother, you scandalize Persys, I believe," he said with an amused glance at her flaming cheeks. "There has never been the slightest chance that I might think of Charlotte in the role of Duchess of Eddington."

"But she has entertained that thought many a time, I'll vow," the duchess snapped. "And just because you are sensible does not mean that she would not attempt to entrap you into a forced marriage. And you know *that* to be true," she concluded with a narrow gaze. "This is not the first time I have cautioned you about her nor will it be the last—until the day you are safely wed—to another."

"Yes, Mother," the duke replied, taking Persys by the arm to guide her to the door. "Enough of plotting for the moment, I think. You rest for a bit and then I'll come to assist you down for dinner."

Persys willingly went out to the hall at the duke's side. Floundering for something to say, she blurted, "Perhaps it is all a hum. I cannot think I should be required to mislead your cousin as to our relationship."

"But you are staying here and there is the matter of proximity. Charlotte will be inclined to think the worst, imagining another woman to be as she is. When she learns that Mother will sponsor your school she will speculate on why. Knowing Charlotte, she will conclude that Mother is intent upon fostering a relationship between us."

"This is far too much for me to absorb. I cannot think why you simply didn't forbid your cousin from visiting?" Persys stopped before the door to her room to confront the man who not only employed her but also was to assist her in beginning the school that would make her independent. "If she is so clever, she will see in a trice that there is nothing lover-like between us and then what?"

"You have an excellent point there. What a fine mind you have, my Persian woman," the duke purred in a manner Persys instantly mistrusted.

Yet when he reached out a hand to touch her cheek with a gentle finger she made no move to evade him. Like a mesmerized bird, she stood gazing up at him, her breath suspended, waiting. She had not long.

He was careful not to startle her, treating her like the timid bird she felt. With the odd sensation that this had been fated, she felt his lips touch hers, igniting a fire within her such as she had never known before. It was impossible not to respond. Strangely enough she felt no displeasure, no fear of him, no feeling of revulsion whatsoever. Rather, she welcomed his lips, their warm touch on hers, with the feeling that she had longed for his kiss.

Her release came too soon she realized with shame. It could not be that she wanted him to continue? She did not even like him! Impossible! Backing away from him she sought refuge in her room.

"I shall see you later," the duke said, the words sounding like a warning to Persys.

"Not if I see you first," she shot back before thinking. "Oh, this will never do!"

"I agree with Mother. It would be wise to convince Charlotte to look elsewhere for a husband. I would rather not come to words with her. Far better she draw conclusions on her own without a confrontation. Lady Leycester will drop a hint, Judith another, and Charlotte will watch to see if there is anything to what they have said."

Persys stared at him, not saying a word.

"Please?"

Not understanding herself in the least, Persys found her head nodding in agreement and her mouth saying, "Very well." It wasn't what she had intended to say, far from it. Perhaps it was the "please" that had reached her, for he had looked troubled and pleading. "I would be heartless to leave you to be a victim of a scheming woman."

The duke opened her door for her. "I shall see you at dinner. Join my mother when you are dressed and we can all go down together."

Persys gave him a troubled glance before entering her room to thankfully shut the door behind her.

She leaned against the door for a few moments, then crossed the room to gaze down at the garden. That kiss had not happened. She must have imagined it. Surely the duke would not toy with her? There must be some other way to rid him of Charlotte. Strangest of all was her reaction. She still loved the marquess, did she not?

Leaning on the windowsill she considered her feelings. She tried to conjure up the image of Katherine's husband and retrieved only the blurred image of the man. Far too real was the vibrant and virile image of the duke. What could this mean?

"There you be, Miss Persys," Libby said as she entered from the dressing room where she had her little bed. "Time to dress for dinner."

"Indeed," Persys replied absently, her mind elsewhere.

"I pressed your blue-and-silver gown for this evening, miss, seeing as how there are two gentlemen to visit."

"Fine," Persys said from her fog.

She allowed Libby to help her change into the lovely silk gown, then to dress her hair as becomingly as possible, given the lack of fine pearls to interweave or flowers to adorn. There was naught but a simple gold chain for her neck.

Twilight approached as Persys hesitantly knocked on the door to the duchess's suite. Tessa opened the door, admitting Persys with what likely passed as a smile for the dour woman. "Come in, they are waiting for you."

Persys had dawdled as long as she dared, not wishing to be alone with the duchess. Now she faced the pair, so alike in so many ways—not the least appeared to be their love of intrigue. "I am ready."

"I told Mother of our agreement," the duke said with a smile that Persys thought seemed a trifle overwarm.

"Indeed, and a good thing it is. Word just came that Charlotte and George have arrived. Of course dinner has been set back and Cook will be in a fury but it cannot be helped. Their traveling coach encountered a bad stretch of road."

"Charlotte and George are here?" Persys responded to the words that had leaped out at her. "Now?"

Chapter Seven

The trio paused at the top of the staircase, all listening to Miss Russell's dulcet tones as she informed Portman that she simply had to have a bit of sherry and would he be a lamb to see to it for her? Then the lady in question drifted into view.

Persys refrained from a gasp only because she had her mouth firmly shut. Unless she was badly mistaken, Miss Russell was a beauty of the first water.

"I shall carry Mother while you manage her crutches, Persys," the duke said in an undertone.

"And whatever you do, follow our lead," the duchess added, sotto voce.

"Indeed I shall," Persys replied, having taken an instant dislike for the somehow aggressive guest. In her book a young lady did not enter another's house and instantly demand the butler to wait upon her.

"Well, Charlotte, you have not changed an iota," the duchess said sweetly, but with a faint edge to her voice that Persys immediately caught.

"Poor lamb," Charlotte said, oozing sympathy, "I always said your gardening would bring you to grief."

"Gardening had nothing to do with it. I could have tripped on a stone anywhere on the grounds. It merely happened to occur while I was tending my herbs. You must meet our dear Persys Timothy. She has been such a comfort to me these past weeks."

Charlotte shot Persys such a look that made her glad that eyes could do nothing more than see. "I have heard so much about you, Miss Russell. I am pleased to meet you at long last."

At that precise moment a gentleman entered the house, ignoring Portman, intent upon reaching the cluster of people standing at the bottom of the staircase.

"Hullo, dear aunt, Harry." He gave Persys a speculative look, then turned a questioning gaze to his cousin.

"George, Miss Persys Timothy, who has been enormously helpful to me in my time of immurement," the duchess interposed, giving her protégée a warm smile.

Charlotte Russell might have taken an instant dislike to Persys but George was another case altogether. His eyes revealed a warmth and interest Persys found uncomfortable. She would take care to keep her distance; Libby had been advised correctly—the man was a menace.

They all turned to walk to the yellow drawing room where the family usually gathered. The duchess managed to look regal even when stumping along with the new crutches. The duke remained closely by her side.

Persys found herself on the other side of the duke, even though Charlotte had made an effort to insert herself and failed. Darting a look of dislike at George, who strolled along at her other side, Persys sought a means of discouraging those appraising looks he continued to cast her way.

Charlotte smiled thinly at the duchess and declared, "I trust Portman has my sherry waiting for me. You would not believe the horrid trip we have had! Such roads." She walked slowly, darting curious glances at Persys all the while. "We paused at the Leycesters' since the bridge was under repair."

By this point they had achieved the drawing room and the duchess made a fuss about settling onto her chaise longue, draping shawls just so and easing back with great care as though she was too weary to do else. "I saw Hortensia the other day. I trust she remains well?" the duchess inquired with a benign nod.

Persys put the crutches on the floor behind the chaise and wondered if she could ever manage that regal tilt of the head, or the faintly patronizing touch to the voice. She decided it was something that took time to acquire.

"I had a most interesting conversation with Lady Leycester," Charlotte continued, giving Persys a malicious smile.

She refrained from returning that smile. It was not difficult to imagine what had been said or pried during that chat.

George and the duke casually strolled up where the ladies had gathered, George taking a position too close to Persys for her liking. She took an instant exception to his encroachment and sidled away from him, thus closer to the duke.

"How was London when you left, George?" the duke inquired, shifting about so that he somehow came between George and Persys and was standing far closer to her than his cousin.

How clever of him, thought Persys, *to make a subtle point of establishing his supposed interest in me without saying a word.*

George eyed his cousin with disfavor but merely said, "All of a muchness. You know how it can be—the predictable balls and routs, the tedious attendance at Almack's, gracing various Venetian breakfasts and whatnot."

"I wonder that you can bear it, George," the duchess interjected. To Persys she added, "Do not let George fool you. He would be desolate if the invitations ceased and were he to be cut off from Almack's."

"Yes, while Almack's might be dull at times, it has its moments," Persys offered, more composed now that the duke signaled she was under his protection. That she also informed his cousins that she was acquainted with the Society's holy temple she failed to realize. It was not something Charlotte was likely to miss, however.

"You attended the assemblies, Miss Timothy? I do not recall seeing you there." Charlotte's air was of one who intends to unmask an imposter.

Persys smiled. "I suppose my cousin stole most of the limelight. She is now Katherine, Marchioness of Torrington." There was no way Charlotte could pretend ignorance of such a personage, for the romance and subsequent wedding had been the talk of the Season.

"I fear I did not attend the wedding," Charlotte said with a dismissive shrug.

"I was there and you missed a splendid affair," the duke said, adding, "Miss Timothy made a very pretty attendant." He ignored his cousin's ill-mannered sniff of disdain.

"Lady Leycester mentioned something about a school?" Charlotte inquired, not content to leave the call on her ladyship's home fade into oblivion. "I could not credit that my dear aunt would associate herself with anything so common."

"On the contrary," the duchess said with more animation than had been displayed since the arrival of her late husband's niece and nephew. "Our darling Persys will use Russell House to open a school for young women who seek to enter Society. Polishing their graces, you know."

"She is rather young for that sort of thing, is she not?" Charlotte said, sipping her sherry with rather more enthusiasm than Persys suspected was proper.

"Age has nothing to do with wisdom, Charlotte," the duke said with a fond look at Persys. "My Persian woman can do most anything."

Charlotte drew herself up with another sniff, holding out her empty glass in Portman's direction, silently signaling she wanted more sherry.

While the butler obeyed her command, she studied Persys with a less than friendly eye. "Persian woman?"

"My Persian woman," the duke corrected politely. "It is a little family humor, and since you are family . . ."

Charlotte's nose flared with annoyance. "I wish to go to my room and change. I suppose dinner is still at ungodly country hours?"

"We shall dine at six-thirty to please you," the duchess said, a slight edge to her voice. "We are not in the wilds of America, Charlotte. Come winter it is pleasant to dine early in the day and retire early."

"Oh, help," Charlotte muttered as she flounced out of the door, her glass of sherry in hand.

"I gather you will wish to change for dinner as well, George? It will be shortly." The duke gave a pointed look at the tall case clock near the door as he spoke.

Once George left, seeing that he had little choice but to obey his cousin, silence reigned for a time until the duchess said—most quietly, "Well, well. Charlotte never ceases to surprise me. We must be on our guard, all of us. I fear you may expect her wrath, Persys, and for that I trust you will forgive us in advance?"

"Of course," Persys responded instantly.

"You are hasty in agreement," the duke said. "But then, perhaps being forewarned is sufficient."

"You had best not alarm me too much or I will be tempted to flee," Persys said with a laugh.

"That is not the sort of tempting we desire," the duchess declared. "And keep your distance from George. You smile?"

"I have already received a warning from my maid. It would appear your nephew's reputation precedes him." Persys spoke warily, not certain she dare bring the matter up, yet thinking it was time that someone report George's behavior. She thought it unconscionable that he be allowed to pursue his amorous chase without censure.

Ninian Hervey and Lord Burfield entered the room at that point, strolling across to join the two clustered by the duchess.

Ninian spoke first. "I see my nemesis has arrived in all her splendor. Pity she and George met such bad roads."

"They paused at the Leycesters' until they were able to cross that last bridge," the duchess said, then added with a decided snap, "Pity the weather could not cooperate more."

"But you were the one to invite them, Mother," the duke gently reminded.

She glared at him a moment, then shrugged. "Everyone is entitled to a mistake."

"I gather Miss Russell and her brother wish to rusticate awhile?" Lord Burfield said hesitantly.

"Indeed," Ninian Hervey agreed. "Poor Harry will have three of us hanging on his coattails for a time—until he boots us out."

"You know you are always welcome here," the duchess commented. "Amusing people are so entertaining and we need a bit of that. Although I must say that having Persys to read to me has been a great joy. She dramatizes each character so well, you see. What was the name of that book you finished the other evening, Persys?"

"*Sense and Sensibility*, Your Grace," Persys replied.

"That author has other books," Charlotte Russell said from the doorway. "There are several actually—*Pride and Prejudice*, *Mansfield Park*, and *Emma* last December. Buried here in the country you are not au courant with the latest in books, I can see that."

"I had no notion that the novels were so diverting. But then, I had not Persys to read them to me. Harry, order those others from Hatchards, will you?" the duchess begged nicely.

Portman appeared in the doorway to solemnly announce that dinner was served.

Surprisingly enough, dinner proved to be a lively meal with Charlotte chattily telling them the latest news from London, the sort of things that Lady Leycester would never say in front of her virginal daughter and that bothered Charlotte not a whit.

"Scandal? Is that all you can recall, Charlotte?" the duke lazily inquired during a lull in her report, for that was what it seemed to Persys.

"Well, you can scarcely expect me to natter on about gardening!" Charlotte snapped. "My dear aunt knows more about that topic than I could ever hope to accumulate."

"How fortunate I am that Persys shares my interests, in that event. It is always so pleasant to have someone with whom one can talk intelligently about various topics of interest," the duchess said with a sweetness of manner that barely concealed her contempt for so small a mind.

"Her Grace is so very knowledgeable about herbs that I could take notes for a long time before learning all I would know. She has promised me some of her special lotions and as you know, one can never begin to take care of skin at too early an age," Persys said politely.

"I have special potions made for me in London," Charlotte replied as though determined to be at loggerheads with anything Persys did or said.

"Let us hope they are safe," the duchess said before Persys could offer her opinion on lotions that were not homemade and thus possessing known ingredients.

"Well, once I read of the efficacy of Gowland's Lotion I was determined to try it and I think it is marvelous."

"How nice," the duchess said with a grim smile, then turned the subject matter to something else entirely. When she signaled it was time for the ladies to leave for the drawing room and their tea, Persys could almost hear an inward sigh of relief from the quiet Lord Burfield.

After handing the duchess her crutches Persys walked at her side, maintaining a slow, even pace to accommodate the duchess's infirmity. Charlotte flitted ahead, demanding a glass of sherry immediately as they entered the drawing room. She sipped it with the same intent quality as before.

"Relying on sherry a bit much are you not, Charlotte? Take care, excessive drinking can wreak havoc with a girl's complexion."

"I take an occasional glass to settle my nerves, dear aunt," Charlotte replied with what Persys thought to be more than ordinary defensiveness.

"Nerves? I did not know you had any," the duchess replied with a laugh.

Persys drifted from the pair crossing verbal swords to the pianoforte where she settled on the stool. After studying the music for a time, she began to softly play a pretty sonata that the duchess admired.

"Talented at the pianoforte as well, Persys? You do not mind if I so address you? If we are to be here for a time, I scarcely wish to be so formal as though we were in London under the scrutiny of Society. You lived in London, I gather?" Charlotte inquired with a tenacity that Persys found daunting. She wished the girl would go back to the duchess, who could handle her with ease.

Pausing in her playing, Persys replied, "Indeed. I lived with my Aunt and Uncle Talbot for a number of years."

"A charitable gesture on their part, surely. How kind!"

"I have my own income, but yes, it was very kind for them to offer a home to an orphan. My cousin Katherine and I grew up together and rubbed along quite well. I was sorry to see her marry, but . . . it is what is expected, is it not?"

"I fancy you have designs to achieve the same goal?" Charlotte asked with a darted glance at the duchess.

"I imagine that were I to fall in love with a gentleman, I would naturally wish to marry him. That, of course, is not always possible, is it? To marry where one wishes?" Persys gave Charlotte a level stare that had her retreating.

She cast a look of dislike at Persys and sauntered away from the pianoforte, leaving Persys to resume her playing. Charlotte stared off into the fading twilight.

"I like that piece, Persys. Play me another." The duchess waved her hand in the air as though directing an unseen musical group and Persys obeyed.

The evening continued with no further confrontation of any kind with Charlotte. George made one move to join Persys at the pianoforte and was thwarted by his cousin, who had to know the latest in sales at Tattersalls. Since horses were George's second passion, coming very close to women, his interest was immediately captured and Persys temporarily forgotten.

Persys begged to leave them for her room, excusing herself to the duchess with pretty manners.

Charlotte rose at the same time, saying, "I'll join you. That west hall is a trifle dark."

"Persys is next to me, dear," the duchess said. "And if the hall is too dark, see that another candle is lit."

Charlotte gave her aunt a hard look, then followed Persys without another comment.

Wary, Persys took her bed candle and walked up the stairs with the feeling that she would not escape unscathed. She had not long to wait.

"I suppose it is your violet eyes. Men are always such fools for things like violet eyes or a meek, submissive disposition."

Persys thought of the confrontations she'd had with the duke and grinned. "Perhaps. I do not consider myself to be an authority. I had never considered the color of my eyes to be an asset in social situations."

"What? No odes to your violet eyes, sonnets to your delicate face?" Charlotte cried with a laugh. "Surely some gentleman must have found something about you irresistible? Of course you are too thin and look rather exotic with those slanted eyes, but still . . ."

"I fear not. Perhaps I am too practical and thus discourage the poets. Good night, Miss Russell." They had reached the top of the stairs where Persys dipped the slightest of curtsies before turning to head toward her room.

"I do not see how you managed to rate a room near my aunt," Charlotte whispered waspishly as though reluctant to part without a last shot fired.

"I am next door, actually—in the event she might have need of me. Her pain has been a severe trial and I offered to read to her should she have difficulty sleeping."

"Aren't you the little saint."

"I suppose I am, in a way," Persys said with a half-smile. "All Christians are considered saints, are they not?"

Charlotte stormed off in a huff, obviously believing Persys more than she or anyone could bear.

Libby awaited her mistress with soothing words, helping her from her blue-and-silver gown with gentle hands, then offering a pleasant cup of tea.

"I see what your informants meant about Mr. Russell," Persys declared. "There is something about him that makes you feel soiled—just from his stare. A most unpleasant gentleman, all in all. I shall take care to avoid him."

"And Miss Charlotte?" Libby inquired.

"I perceive she is a very unhappy woman, Libby. She consumes sherry as though it was water and is given to making disagreeable remarks. There is not the least reason for her to fear me and yet she attacks as though I were her mortal enemy."

If the maid had her own ideas about why Charlotte Russell might assail Persys, she kept them to herself.

The following morning Persys entered the breakfast room to find the duke at the table, making an excellent meal.

After making suitable greetings, she settled to enjoy her modest repast when he spoke.

"You do not eat enough, Miss Timothy."

She cast a glance at him, then nodded. "I suppose some may think that, certainly Miss Russell does. I have ever been thin despite how much I consume. I shall have to survive without sonnets to my face or eyes, as she appeared to deem desirable."

He digested her comments along with a goodly part of his breakfast before pausing to ask, "Do you have any letters to go out this morning? I must order all those books for Mother." When Persys shook her head, he persisted, "What, no letter to your cousin, the new Marchioness of Torrington? I should have thought you would write to her, surely." He watched Persys while he spoke, something of which she was supremely aware.

The pain Persys expected didn't come. Instead she felt a nothingness inside, a complete lack of emotion that she had not anticipated. Not given time to ponder this, she merely shook her head. "I have had not a moment in which to write. Your mother keeps me quite busy." When he would have spoken, she continued with a wave of her hand, "Please, I do not mind, she is the dearest woman imaginable and I am coming to quite adore her."

"You do not find her daunting?" he asked with a curious expression.

"Not in the least. You should have known my Aunt Talbot. Now, there is a woman who daunts with the best of them!"

Any further conversation between them was prevented by the entrance of Ninian Hervey and Lord Burfield, followed shortly by George Russell.

"A flower in a garden of thorns," Ninian said with glee. "Miss Timothy, we are your slaves. To brighten our day by joining us for this morning meal is surely beyond the call of duty."

"Miss Timothy has a busy day ahead of her, she needs a hearty breakfast," the duke said while eyeing the disappearance of the modest bit of egg and toast Persys had accepted.

Before the others could ask, Persys inquired, "And what am I to do today?"

"Why, go over to Russell House to decide what you need. There are desks to order, other supplies. How do I know what is required for a school?"

"Why cannot the carpenter here make the desks?" Ninian asked. "I have seen the work he does and it is excellent. I trust costs are just as important here as in any business."

"I am surprised at you understanding business costs, Ninian. You usually are contriving means of avoiding your share of them," George Russell said with a trace of malice.

"That is why I understand them so well. Why do I not accompany Miss Timothy on her task? I am a useful person, skilled in holding measuring tapes, estimating required furniture, all matter of helpful things."

"Really, I had no idea you were so talented," the duke said dryly. "Very well, if Persys will accept your escort, go with her and make lists. I feel sure her maid will be happy to join you," he concluded, reminding Ninian and the others that he would brook not the least bit of incivility toward Persys.

"I shall leave here within the hour, Mr. Hervey," Persys said after a last sip of tea. She had never been able to enjoy the coffee the men appeared to relish. Give her a cup of bohea any day. The footman assisted her from her chair and she paused at the door to add, "My maid will be able to carry the tape measure, the pad of paper for note taking, and perhaps a few other things I consider of help."

Following her departure George leaned back in his chair to study his cousin. "Pretty little thing, your Persian woman. Why do you call her that?"

"Her name," Harry replied patiently. "Persys means Persian woman."

"But yours?" George persisted, nothing if not determined to dig for as much information as possible. It had always been his wont to assist Charlotte—as everyone well knew.

The duke merely smiled mysteriously, giving George an enigmatic look that said a great deal, none of which George could define or repeat to his sister.

"Anyone wish to ride? The gamekeeper informs me that there are birds to be had should someone wish to do a bit of shooting, not to mention we have had fine fishing in the stream." The duke addressed his friends in general, offering a good day.

"Always the perfect host," George said, but this time without any malice in his voice. "I am off for a bit of shooting. Burfield?"

"I believe I would go as well, if that is agreeable with you, Harry?"

"Yes, by all means. I have some correspondence to catch up on first, then I may join you myself."

The men left the table, each to their rooms before taking off in various directions.

Persys was thankful that the others seemed to be housed in a different wing. She had no fear of encountering the odious George coming from or going to her room. The tacit understanding that she was in some way an interest of the duke's was certainly a benefit. Perhaps the aggressive Charlotte would tire of her game and go away sooner rather than later? So far nothing had been seen of her this morning and that suited Persys to a tee.

Pausing to consult with the duchess, Persys found an eager participant in her plans for the new school. "I would like to go with you if it is not terribly inconvenient to you, my dear."

"Mr. Hervey has offered to assist me, ma'am. Do you still wish to come?" Persys grinned at the instant reaction to her words.

"That scamp? He is most entertaining and I wish to come more than ever now." The duchess gave Persys a twinkling look most reminiscent of her son. "Allow me a few minutes and Tessa shall have me ready to go."

Thankful that another woman would be along besides Libby, Persys agreed. It was also a sensible idea to include the duchess in the planning since it was their property and as such nothing could be done without her blessing, as it were.

The crutches were easily stowed in the carriage, with Mr. Hervey making certain they did not bump her leg while the carriage traversed the short distance to Russell House.

"It has been years since I was last here," the duchess exclaimed softly as they walked to the entrance of the house. She looked about her with curious eyes, making note of the improvements and changes that had been made.

"It is much the same, save for the lack of paintings on the walls and much of the furniture. I see your maid has a note-taking pad. Let us begin."

If Persys had ever held the notion that the duchess was indolent or given to idleness the very thought was banished forever in the ensuing hour.

"Egad, Your Grace, you leave me quite breathless," Ninian Hervey said when they had whirled through the ground floor rooms. "Not but what I do not agree with your assessments. And I am pleased you agree that the estate carpenter will do a splendid job on the desks. It ought to save not only time but money."

"Time is money, Ninian. I read that somewhere and it is true. One can waste so much time trying to find a bargain that a good deal of life can be missed altogether, if you see what I mean."

Mr. Hervey gave her a puzzled look but did not disagree. Persys had noted few did, other than Miss Russell. She seemed to have her own ideas about everything.

The duchess turned to Persys. "Make a note to go through the attics for beds and dressers. There must be any number of them, for my mother-in-law completely redid the house some years ago. I doubt there is a thing wrong with anything other than she did not approve of *her* mother-in-law's taste. How fortunate I liked all that was here. It saved much aggravation; my husband did not care for change."

"Indeed, ma'am, I shall do just that. I always enjoy prowling through attics. One can find such interesting things."

"You have vastly different tastes from Charlotte. You couldn't drag her to an attic unless she was after a fortune—one way or another."

"You are very hard on Charlotte, Ninian," the duchess said pensively. "Why?"

He strolled to stare out the window for a few moments, then turned. "A good friend of mine had the misfortune to fall in love with Charlotte. She not only rejected his suit but was unnecessarily cruel in doing so. Since then, I have had no time for her, nor patience with her dramatics. I trust you will not allow her to cut up your peace, Miss Timothy?"

"No, indeed. I have had to deal with selfish, unpleasant people a good deal in my life. There is little Miss Russell could say that could touch me," Persys answered with a hint of irony. Aunt Talbot could take prizes in any contest.

"Well, if Ninian can help me with the stairs we can decide what else in addition to the beds and dressers may be needed." the duchess made a slow way to the first floor, examining the stair rail and the walls as she went. Little seemed to escape her notice.

"There is a patch of damp on the north wall in this first bedroom. Make a note of it, Persys."

"Make a note of what, Mother?" the duke said from the doorway.

Persys was surprised at the flood of pleasure that surged through her at the sight of him. As pleasant as Mr. Hervey might be, he was nothing compared to the duke.

"The patch of damp up there." The duchess pointed to the obvious gray blotch.

"I gather Persys is taking notes to be given me or my steward?" he quizzed, reaching out to take the pad from her unresisting fingers. In so doing he brushed her hand and again Persys had that wave of peculiar sensation sweep through her. Fastening a confused gaze on him, she wondered if he had also experienced the shock. Apparently not, for he certainly gave no indication he had noticed anything unusual, but his touch had left Persys quite disturbed.

Chapter Eight

"You are certain you have no letters for me to frank, Miss Timothy?" the duke inquired politely. Since their return from Russell House he had been distant and exceedingly civil. His behavior reminded her of when she'd first met him at the wedding.

"I do have a short letter to my cousin," Persys said, wondering if he could sense her change of heart. It was odd, but she no longer felt that pang of sadness when she thought of her cousin married to the man she loved—or thought she loved. Now she wondered if she truly loved the marquess or merely imagined it. Yet she must love him. Had she not suffered a great deal at that wedding?

"I am glad to see you have written her. At least one of your relatives should know where you are. I fancy you left an address with your aunt's butler?"

"Yes. It is possible my cousin might write me, but I imagine she is very busy, adjusting to her new role in life." Again Persys wondered a trifle why she did not experience that gnawing pain when she considered Katherine and the marquess. It simply was not there. Perhaps time was a healer as so many said.

"She will be pleased to hear from you, I am certain," the duke said, seeming to thaw a little. "Perhaps she will invite you to visit her later? If so, you must go, for their home is indeed splendid. You were very close to your cousin, I believe. It would be a shame to break that attachment."

He inclined his head, ever courteous, giving her a searching look before checking the letters in his hand, then gathering the ones on the hall table so he could frank them before sending with the groom to the nearest post town.

Persys stood rooted to the spot, wondering how on earth she could visit her cousin. Surely the pain would return when she saw the marquess again? Much as she enjoyed Katherine's company, there was a limit to what Persys could endure. To watch her cousin and her new husband exchange lovers' looks went beyond all bounds of forbearance. Well, she doubted an invitation would ever reach her and if it did arrive, Persys could always claim pressures from running the school as an excuse not to go.

She watched the duke walk down the hall, then she turned to hurry up the stairs. Mrs. Biddle had promised to take Persys to the attics this afternoon. A feeling of excitement crept over her as she considered selecting items for her school. Her school and the demands it would make upon her time was the answer to all her problems. And although she no longer disliked the duke, she thought a distance from him would be prudent.

The housekeeper was waiting for Persys in the central hall, an apron draped over one arm. "Best put this on, Miss Timothy. The attics are not often dusted. You are bound to acquire a film of dust on your clothes otherwise."

Gratefully donning the enveloping apron of Holland cloth, Persys followed the woman through the door at the end of the hall and up a narrow flight of stairs until they reached another landing. From here there were two doors to the opposite ends of the house.

"This one first, I reckon. When you finish with this end of the house, you can do the other. It will likely take you days to go through everything." The housekeeper shook her head in amusement. "Everything not wanted is sent up here—big and small. Do not be surprised at what you find."

Persys thanked her, then began to wander through the collection of things from the past. The click of the door closing behind Mrs. Biddle brought total peace. It didn't take long before Persys spyed the furniture the duchess mentioned. There didn't seem to be a thing wrong with it. Of course it was old, but very well constructed and simple in style, which made it most suitable for young girls.

Tugging her mobcap more firmly over her hair, Persys set to

work with a will. She counted enough beds and dressers, just as the duchess predicted. Persys tagged them all, then continued on, finding nice looking-glass that would be a pretty addition to various rooms, plus old rugs rolled up in piles. She investigated and tagged a few that proved suitable. That moths had ventured to the attics was obvious, for holes appeared here and there in many rugs.

"Chairs—I need a few chairs, one for each bedroom, and assuredly desks as well." As she explored, she encountered a few cobwebs, a great deal of dust, and many fascinating items.

There were chests of old clothing, some going back to the reign of Queen Anne. Neat boxes of extremely plain candleholders she tagged, for they were always needed.

Back in a dim corner she discovered a group of chairs, none matching but graceful and just the thing for the bedchambers.

"If only I could find a few writing desks for the girls. It would be difficult to ask them to do their lessons without a writing desk of their own," she complained, then renewed her exploration.

She was deep in the shadows of the far end of the attics when she heard a noise. Although not given to hysterics, nevertheless her heart pounded with sudden fright. She had no love for mice or rats or any other creature that might find a way into the upper reaches of the house.

Clutching a copper warming pan that was missing a lid she advanced to stand in the narrow pathway that had been left between stacks of stored items.

"Oh!" she cried with relief as a familiar figure loomed in the dim light. "It is just you. I mean, not just you, but at least not some creature about to frighten me half to death." She set the battered bed warmer back on the pile of odds and ends she had just left, not wanting to meet his gaze.

The duke chuckled at her rambling, jumbled explanation.

At this unexpected sound, she looked up at last. "What are you doing up here and wearing good clothes?" she demanded, although attempting to be polite about it. "There is dust everywhere and your valet will have a fit of the vapors if you return covered with it."

"My valet knows better than to blink an eye at any condition I might acquire." There was a trace of haughtiness in his reply that Persys found amusing, for it was so precisely what she had anticipated.

"Indeed, I expect that to be the case. I'd not considered that, Your Grace. I keep forgetting who you are, you know." Persys gave him a dry look, tilting her head to examine his perfection. Unfortunately, her action dislodged the large mobcap that then slid over one eye, obscuring her vision to some degree. Before she could right the matter, the duke was at her side, pushing the mobcap into place, smiling at her chagrin.

She ignored his proximity, for it was enough her heart was behaving in a foolish manner. Instead, she gestured wildly to the chairs and rugs and other things she had tagged. "I have made a splendid start. You will have to approve each item as suitable and permissible, of course. I'd not want to take family heirlooms or something of the sort."

"My great-grandmother was a practical woman and selected durable, if plain, furniture. My grandmother disliked it the moment she set foot in the house. She banished it to this attic and now you have found it again. I think it sensible to put it to use. I should hope the girls will not abuse it excessively." He remained close to Persys. Oddly enough she found it difficult to think clearly with him standing so close to her. She took a step away from him, only to find he followed.

"You are not afraid of me, are you, my Persian woman?" he asked, his voice having that deep, husky quality that had intrigued her on more than one occasion.

"No, of course not," she whispered, backing away another step. She cleared her throat of a sudden obstruction. "And I do wish you would cease calling me that silly name. People might receive the wrong impression."

He leaned against a tall chest, studying her as one might a strange, unknown creature. "And what would that be?"

"Why . . . that I am your woman. And you must know that would never do." She gave him a wary look, feeling uneasy. He presented no threat; she was convinced of that, but he did daunt her. He was a duke, termed "Most High, Potent and Noble Prince" by the court and the king addressed him as "Our right trusty and right entirely beloved cousin." Persys had read that when she had searched for the proper form of address for Katherine's husband, and Katherine, as well, when directing her letter. The marquess was merely The Most Honorable Marquess of Torrington and she his marchioness, which was not nearly as impressive.

A prince? Indeed, he gave that perception when he issued an order he expected to be obeyed instantly without question. Potent? Powerful, that's what the word meant, and at times he exuded a sort of commanding presence, as when he spoke to George Russell, even Charlotte. It was clear who was head of the family without a word being spoken. His word was to be obeyed without question. Only to his mother did he unbend. And, Persys admitted, at times to her as well, although why, she couldn't imagine.

What all this had to do with her was puzzling. She was nothing more than a temporary companion to his mother and the hopeful mistress of the school to be held in Russell House.

"I suppose it might give a wrong impression," he said with what seemed like regret. "You are a delight to tease, you know. You become all flustered and tilt that charming chin in the air, give a little sniff, and slant those violet eyes at me with a challenge flashing in them." He chuckled, then added pensively, "Do you know I believe you are the only person I have encountered who has not behaved in a meek, servile manner? You even manage to forget who I am from time to time. You are an intriguing woman, Persys Timothy."

"Indeed?" Persys scarce knew what to say. She certainly had never thought of herself as anything out of the common way.

"Now, what remains to be found?" he said briskly, destroying the strange mood that had settled in the attic.

Trying to match this new attitude, Persys consulted the list she carried. "I have found chairs for the bedchambers, and beds and chests, of course. There are not near enough rugs and you *know* how cold a floor can be on a winter's morn. As well, I believe it would be good to have some manner of credenza in the entryway, or at least a cabinet where callers can place parcels or whatever."

"You *have* given this thought," he said, guiding her to where another collection of furniture stood. He pointed out a simple, though elegant bit of furniture.

"Ah, the perfect hall table," Persys said with satisfaction, nudging aside the sensations that had coursed through her at his touch. It was nothing more than her overactive imagination.

"I believe there is a small spinet at the other end of the attic. My mother requested a pianoforte when they became popular and the old spinet was relegated here. The harpsichord was placed in the great drawing room. Mother thought it went well with the furniture."

"I should appreciate a spinet, for then I could teach the girls how to dance."

"The waltz?" he queried softly.

"That would be required of a girl about to have her come-out in London. Even before she is given the nod at Almack's she is expected to know how to waltz."

"So you know how?"

"Of course. I learned when my aunt hired a dancing master to instruct Katherine." Persys made the error of turning to look behind her and up into his eyes. His expression, although quickly gone, made her tremble. "You would not object, Your Grace?" she whispered. That fleeting glance disturbed her.

"What is it, Persys?" he asked, instantly seeming to sense her unease.

"I cannot say," she said slowly. Then, ever honest, she continued, "I sensed something strange for a moment." Then she moved away from him and returned to examining the furniture. "Pay me no heed, I am becoming fanciful."

They worked in harmony for a time, tagging a few desks, several more suitable rugs that Persys claimed would do. "There are a few moth holes, but put under the bed they will never be noticed. If I have time, I can attempt to mend them."

"Is there nothing you will not try?"

"Of course. Do not think I am a total fool merely because I attempt a school when I have not taught before. Perhaps inviting trouble?"

"I suspect teaching would come easily to you." Again he studied her with that odd expression on his face.

"I cannot think why you might say such a thing, but I hope you are right as usual."

"You believe I am always right?"

"As far as I have observed, yes," she admitted.

"That places a great burden on my shoulders, my Persian woman."

"Your Grace, you said . . ." she admonished, albeit with a smile.

"So I did." He turned to lead her to the other end of the attics where he located the spinet and a goodly number of other items save for the writing desks she wanted.

"We shall buy a few. There cannot be that many," he decreed.

"I did not wish to cause any expense. I shall have a hard time meeting costs as it is."

"Since my mother is sponsoring your school, I think it only proper she invest a sum to further it along."

"That is most welcome, Your Grace," Persys said, invoking his title once again, for it helped to keep him at a distance. "Thank you, for it comes from you ultimately, does it not?"

He glanced at her but said nothing more.

At last he dusted off his hands and pulled her mobcap from her head. "Your hair is a total devastation, I fear." He shook his head as he attempted to smooth unruly curls.

Then he paused, his hand atop her head, to stare down at her. With a muffled groan, he drew her against him and quite thoroughly kissed her.

It was unlike anything Persys had experienced in her life. She felt as though she was truly alive for the first time, knowing the touch of his mouth, the feel of him against her. She didn't know what to make of that storm of emotions racing through her, just that she felt at home in his arms, close to him with his lips pressed against hers.

He withdrew and Persys knew a great feeling of loss. She turned partly away from him, so he could not detect the play of emotions she felt certain lingered on her face.

"Sorry, my Persian woman," he said, not sounding terribly sorry to her way of thinking. But perhaps a duke had a different set of attitudes, contrary to mere mortals?

"Please . . . forget it. It is the atmosphere, our proximity. I did not intend to tempt you, nor would I ever place you in a position of compromise. You must know that!" she said fiercely in a low undertone. "Perhaps it would be best were you to leave the attics. I shall look for a few things I have remaining to locate. It is drawing late and will be time for dinner before long."

"You accept all the blame for our kiss? That is doing it too brown, Miss Timothy." He stood quietly studying her from frosty blue eyes before turning on his heel, leaving her as directed, and snapping the door shut behind him.

"Well, of all the . . ." Persys declared, plumping herself down on a trunk. "I do not understand him in the least!"

Unable to concentrate on the job at hand, she shortly followed him, closing the attic doors with regret. If he had not been a duke she might have—what? Deep in reflection, she slowly walked down the steps to the upper floor, intent upon reaching her room.

"Well, well, if it isn't the Persian woman," Charlotte said with a sly smile. "*His Grace's* Persian woman. Just how well do you perform in that capacity, Miss Timothy? Well, I trust? Although perhaps not recently."

Persys clutched the mobcap in hand and stared at Charlotte, dismay filling her within. "I do not know what you mean, Miss Russell."

"Now, now, Miss Timothy! I saw my dear cousin come down from that attic not minutes ago looking thwarted, unsatisfied. And you are here, hair mussed, looking as though you were not beyond a bit of dalliance, but definitely not as though you'd had a love tryst. I can add very well—particularly when it comes to the human sort of addition."

"You have everything wrong, Miss Russell," Persys said coldly. "I have been in the attics searching out furniture and other items for the school. His Grace came up to see how I did and to agree as far as what I had tagged. My cap mussed my hair."

"You expect me to believe that nonsense? My dear, I was not born yesterday." Charlotte's beautiful face contorted with scorn.

"Again I must say I have no idea what you mean," Persys said, fear clutching her heart. She cared little for her own reputation, for that was paltry at best. But the duke was another matter. His name and reputation must remain untarnished, at least as far as she was concerned. If he erred, it was not going to be placed at her feet!

"He is a very handsome man, not to mention wealthy and of high rank." She took a threatening step toward Persys. "Can you deny you have fallen in love with him? I can see it quite plainly!" Charlotte's mouth twisted into a grimace of a triumphant smile. She stood in the middle of the hall, thus making it hard for Persys to brush past her without difficulty.

Persys wanted to tell the beautiful Charlotte to crawl back under her rock, but of course she dare not say such a thing to the duke's cousin. Instead, Persys gathered all her courage together and gave Charlotte a smile she hoped was serene. "I think you are mad." Rather than risk saying something foolish, Persys pushed past the taunting woman, marching down the hall to her room. At her door she paused, looking back to meet Charlotte's icy stare, then entered.

"Are you well, miss?" Libby asked, turning from the wardrobe to give Persys a curious perusal.

"It is nothing, Libby." Persys took a turn about the room then paused before the window to gaze down at the flowers. "Oh, it would have been better had I not come here."

"But the school, miss," Libby queried, clearly at a loss from her mistress's words.

Persys wrapped her arms about herself, pacing back and forth before the small fire burning in the grate. In spite of summer, it seemed chilly to her now and she was grateful for the warmth. "I shall be fine. Pray that I may collect the furnishings for the school as quick as may be. Then we can leave here and take up residence at Russell House."

What Libby thought of these brave words was not said.

"Best set out one of my better gowns, Libby. Miss Russell is quite the critic and I would arm myself as well as I can," Persys declared in a bitter manner.

Obviously puzzled even more, Libby still held her tongue and did as bade. After assisting her mistress to cleanse herself of dust, she helped her into clean underpinnings, then a pretty gown of lavender sarcenet accented with silver bows and violet roses.

Watching as Libby twirled her hair into a soft mass of curls, Persys wondered if she could survive this evening unscathed. She would have to enter the yellow drawing room as though nothing had occurred—that the duke had not kissed her, nor Charlotte uttered nasty, implicating words. It would not be easy, but then it couldn't be for long. Soon she would be away from here and the duke as well. He would scarcely come to check on her often.

Then she considered Charlotte's words, spoken in such heat and with such venom. What *were* her true feelings? Persys wondered. Did she, indeed, love the duke? Nothing was simple, nothing clear-cut, and she assuredly did not know what was in her heart any longer.

"The dinner gong, miss," Libby cautioned. "Best be on your way."

"Indeed. I must cease my woolgathering; 'tis a bad habit I have acquired." Persys gave her maid a forced smile, then left her room.

The yellow drawing room was well occupied when she at last reached it. Ninian Hervey and Lord Burfield stood chatting with the duke while George Russell was in conference with his sister. The duchess was ensconced on her chaise. She surveyed Persys, then quietly asked, "Are you well? You seem a trifle pale."

"Perhaps I overdid while in the attics, Your Grace. It is easy to get carried away when intent upon a goal." Persys looked up to meet the duke's eyes, knowing he had likely heard what she said, for she did not attempt to lower her voice.

The duchess also noted the exchange and pursed her lips.

"I should think that depends upon what the goal might be," Charlotte said in a throaty voice, sending the duke a knowing little smirk.

"And what would you know about goals, Charlotte?" the duke inquired. "I was unaware you spared any thoughts for *goals* other than a new gown, a ball, that sort of thing. Never say you have taken a notion to be intellectual?"

"An intellectual? Never," Charlotte scoffed. "I shall leave that sort of thing to Miss Timothy. Although in her lavender gown she scarcely *looks* the intellectual."

"Did you find what you wished, Persys?" the duchess inquired, breaking into the banter with a ruthless cut.

"There were chairs, beds, and chests, just as you said, and rugs and other pieces as well. The school is fair on the way to being furnished."

"What is lacking?" Her Grace asked pointedly.

"A number of writing desks for the rooms, a few bits and pieces for the main rooms. I shall require dishes, I suppose, and it would be best to order those from a supplier to schools, I fancy."

"My, you sound so, ah, authentic," Charlotte said with spite ringing in her voice.

"I should hope so," Persys returned calmly, although her pulse was beating faster than normal. "If I do not appear to be capable I shan't have much hope of obtaining pupils, shall I?"

"When do you move out of here?" Charlotte demanded.

Persys was saved from answering by Portman announcing dinner was served. She walked by the duchess, unobtrusively helping her to the table.

Once seated, the duchess surveyed those at the table, particularly her son. "I believe I shall give a party so Persys will have an opportunity to meet those who might have daughters eligible for the school. It is about time I did something to entertain my friends and why not those who have girls of an age?"

"Your Grace—" Persys began, only to be cut off by the duke.

"Why, I believe that to be positively brilliant, Mother. If you are to sponsor this school it had best do well, I think." He stared at Persys as though daring her to say something.

"But—" Persys began only to be thwarted by Charlotte.

"A party? With music, of course. What fun!"

The duke smiled, a trifle grimly, Persys thought.

"I suspect that would be agreeable, Charlotte," he said. "Then Miss Timothy can demonstrate that she is acquainted with all the required dances."

"Never say you can waltz, Miss Timothy?" George Russell inquired.

"I can," Persys replied quietly. Since the duchess seemed determined to have a party, Persys would do what she could to assist her. "I would be pleased to help with the invitations, Your Grace."

"By all means, let Persys write them all. She can demonstrate her fine handwriting," the duke said, sarcasm clear to Persys's finely tuned hearing. "We would not have all those parents think that Miss Timothy is unlettered."

Persys opened her mouth to rebut his caustic words when the duchess placed a cautioning hand over hers.

"You are kind to offer your help and I shall accept at once," the duchess declared, just as though there had been any question about Persys doing all the work involved.

The duchess indicated to Persys that she wished to leave the table. Persys at once assisted her, and walked at her side to the stairs. Here James helped her up to the yellow drawing room.

Once again on her chaise and duchess resumed her plans for the party. "A week? Two weeks?" They debated until the duchess found a satisfactory date, followed by the number of guests, then the musicians.

When all been settled to Charlotte's satisfaction—for she appeared to know a great deal about such things—the duchess relaxed, obviously pondering about arrangements.

"Which room will you open for use, dear aunt?" Charlotte inquired.

"The Great Drawing Room I believe. The ballroom is so huge and rather overwhelming for a modest gathering such as I plan." She rose from her chaise, motioning the girls to go with her to the larger and more formal drawing room. They paused at the doorway to the very impressive sight. It was indeed vast, and with a bit of rearranging it could hold a goodly number of guests.

"Well, it will be interesting to see Miss Timothy cadge for students," Charlotte said lightly.

"There are times when you overstep, my girl. Be careful that you do not anger me," the duchess said with serene calm, quite as though she was not issuing a warning. To Persys she added, "I expect that by the time of our little party I shall be no longer requiring these crutches. In fact, I think I shall try a walking stick to-morrow. My knee feels much better."

"I am very glad for that, ma'am. The school will take me away just when you no longer have need of me."

"I may request you call at times. The winter days are dreary."

"Surely you intend to go to London for the next Season?" Charlotte inquired sharply.

"Perhaps. We shall see how things go," the duchess concluded with a thoughtful look at Persys, which Charlotte did not miss.

Chapter Nine

The following days kept Persys in a whirl of activity, what with writing invitations, assisting with the menu and decorations, not to mention her consultation with Libby regarding a proper gown.

"I shall need to look eminently respectable, Libby; a lady to whom these people can entrust their daughters without qualms. Perhaps my gray or the blue sarcenet would be suitable?"

The maid gave a reluctant nod. "Either one is nice, miss, but hardly the thing to go against Miss Russell."

"I do not wish to compete with her, Libby. I am not in the same class with the cousin of the duke, you see." Persys gave her maid a vexed look. As if Persys could compare with the dashing and elegant cousin to the duke!

"I see she hopes to snare His Grace, miss. 'Tis the talk below-stairs." Libby assumed a mulish expression for a moment, before returning to her more normal bland appearance.

"That will do, Libby," Persys said. His Grace had indicated he was not pleased with Miss Russell, that he found her conduct improper, or something of that nature. Had he altered his opinion? "Perhaps I had best go with the blue. What is it they say—true blue? As well, it is quite simple in line."

Libby nodded with what appeared to be relief. The blue was indeed simple, but it had an exquisite cut that bespoke a mantua-maker of the highest skill.

Several days later when Persys went down to breakfast she discovered Charlotte Russell at the table, looking all sweetness and light.

Persys gave her a wary glance before selecting a light meal, then joining the other woman at the table. "It is a lovely day, is it not?" Persys said politely while wondering what went on in Charlotte's mind.

"Indeed." She fidgeted in her chair, toying with a piece of toast, crumbling it onto her plate.

"Is something troubling you, Miss Russell?" Persys asked at long last, after enduring a good number of speculative looks.

"I feel so badly, you see," Charlotte said softly. "I have been utterly beastly to you merely because you seem to have captured my aunt's interest so completely. There was absolutely no reason for me to treat you so and I wish to apologize. Aunt has made it clear she is giving the party mainly to assist you in the school. It was unkind of me to believe there was more to her attentions than that."

Persys placed her fork on the plate with care, studying the delicate design that bordered it; garlands of ivy and oak leaves. Had Charlotte thought the duchess intended to bestow wealth on Persys or something equally silly? Moments later she studied Charlotte's gaze: her blue eyes seemed to be honest and direct. Could she believe the woman's sincerity? Persys would have sworn Charlotte utterly detested her and wished her to the ends of the earth. Why the conversion?

"I certainly accept your apology. Let us pretend the unpleasant words exchanged never happened," Persys said graciously. But inwardly she resolved to be cautious. She had never been one to believe in tigers changing their stripes for spots.

"Perhaps I might help you with the coming party?" Charlotte offered meekly.

Persys put her napkin down, then rose from the table, offering a hesitant smile. She had no clue to this sudden gesture from Charlotte Russell, but considering she was the duke's cousin and had far more right to be here than did Persys, the overture from Charlotte must be accepted.

"Come with me, then. There are the decorations to settle. The duchess wishes something simple but I have yet to figure out precisely what her notion of simple might be."

Charlotte left the table to join Persys. Once in the hall they observed the butler with a large parcel in hand, heading toward the library.

"From Hatchards, Portman?" Charlotte guessed.

"Indeed, miss," the dignified butler replied. "It would appear the books have arrived."

"Good. You may read to us this evening, Persys. Aunt will enjoy the new books," Charlotte said more pleasantly than Persys had imagined she could speak. "Read them in order, beginning with *Pride and Prejudice.* I prefer *Mansfield Park*, myself. Miss Austen, for that is her name, is an excellent delineator of character."

Thankful to be on a more agreeable footing with Charlotte Russell, Persys drew her into the planning for the party while still resolving to exert caution. There was nothing about Charlotte to give an indication of falseness—yet Persys knew a wariness within.

"Ah, my dear sister and our Miss Timothy. Pity I cannot call you my Persian woman as my cousin does," George Russell said with a joviality that sounded a trifle forced to Persys. Perhaps she was being overly sensitive?

"I am no one's Persian woman, you may as well know, sir," Persys said with a hint of reserve. She turned to attend to the acceptances that had arrived and was startled when Mr. Russell touched her on the shoulder.

"I may not be as clever as my cousin, but I do have eyes in my head. I sense something between you two and I refuse to believe that Eddington would finance a school for just anyone. No, my pretty Persys, you are here supposedly to keep my aunt company, but can you deny that my dear cousin has made advances to you? Improper ones?"

George watched her with an intent gaze that pierced uncomfortably close to the truth. The duke had whisked her away from London before she could look elsewhere for a position. He teased her with far too much familiarity. And he had kissed her while in the attic. Persys hoped she did not blush, for that would give away her secret at once.

"The duke is most proper," Persys said shortly. "I doubt he would ever do anything to jeopardize his position, particularly with the woman he wishes to be no more than schoolmistress at

Russell House." With rising anger she watched George stride from the room. How dare he accuse her of a liaison with the duke! Yet she had wondered about the school and its proximity. While she would be away from the house and see the duke rarely, would it make her vulnerable to him in the long run? What would he expect of her?

"Do not pay the least attention to my brother," Charlotte advised kindly. "He is out of sorts because you pointedly ignore him. He likes to flirt, you see. Until Eddington marries and has a son, my brother is the heir to the dukedom. George is accustomed to a girl knowing this and he enjoys a certain amount of flattery because of it. It will do him good to realize that he cannot count on so tenuous a future to assure him a respectable marriage—or for that matter, an agreeable flirtation. Eddington is bound to marry one of these days."

Persys knew a peculiar lurch in her chest and gave Charlotte a confused half-smile, returning her unseeing gaze to the table whereon the notes for the party were spread. She pretended to search for a paper. "Excuse me, I must check a minor detail with His Grace. He promised to arrange for music and I would have that information."

Charlotte nodded agreement, then sauntered to the door where her brother had disappeared minutes before. "I shall check with Mrs. Biddle regarding the pastries," she said obligingly.

It took but moments for Persys to hurry down the hall to the library. A gentle rap on the door brought an invitation from the duke to enter.

"What is it, Persys?" he inquired, looking up from where he was seated behind a vast mahogany desk. The window behind him revealed a wooded knoll with the lake in the distance. To either side of the large window were books that Persys longed to read. To be able to dip into any and all of them was most tempting. The duke cleared his throat, thus drawing her wandering attention. "I have seen so little of you I might be forgiven for thinking you were avoiding me. That is not the case, I trust?" He placed his chin on steepled fingers, studying her with the same sort of intensity that George had.

It was the reason he'd not seen her, but Persys was not about to reveal her motive for making certain she was never alone with him, nor ever close to him. "I came to inquire about the music, Your Grace."

"I suppose it is hopeless to beg you call me Harry?"

"Not even Charlotte or George call you Harry," Persys protested. "It would not be seemly. I am, after all, a companion, soon to be a schoolmistress," she said, her recent conversation with George fresh in her mind.

"Never say someone has had the temerity to offend you regarding your position in this house?" the duke asked with narrowed eyes.

"No, indeed not," Persys answered. George had merely hinted that she was here because the duke had designs on her, one way or another. After that kiss in the attic, Persys wasn't certain where she stood and she was too much the coward to confront the duke on it. She needed to leave this house so as to be away from any more such challenges.

The duke slowly rose from his desk, pausing to stare out the window a moment before turning to face Persys. "I had wondered if you avoided me because you found my, er, attentions in the attic repulsive." There was no hint of his inner feelings; his face seemed almost mask-like.

"Repulsive" was scarcely the word that came to mind when thinking of the duke's kiss. Persys shook her head, turning her eyes away from him. She could not meet his gaze and fabricate some tale.

"Hmm," he murmured, then walked around the desk, watching her as he drew closer. "I have ordered the spinet brought down. You must tell me where you want it. The other furniture will be sent to Russell House as well. Tomorrow take time from this party that Mother has thrust upon you and see to the placement, will you?"

"I shall be pleased to do as you wish. Charlotte is being wondrously helpful, Your Grace. I shan't have near the work now that she has taken over so many little tasks for me." Persys turned to leave and was detained by his light touch on her arm.

"Charlotte is helping you with the party?" When Persys reaffirmed this unusual fact, he frowned, adding, "I wonder why?"

Persys had wondered as well, but was far too cagey to agree with him at this point.

"What about George? Does he help as well?"

"George goes his own way, Your Grace. Perhaps he will attend?" Persys asked with a strained smile.

"Indeed. You are not finding this party too overwhelming?" When Persys shook her head he continued, "You have a suitable gown, I suppose. You always seem to be attractively garbed." His eyes searched hers, probing, pinning her in place with whatever his intent might be.

"I shall wear a blue sarcenet I believe will seem proper for a schoolmistress," Persys offered with the hope he might release her from this hold he maintained—without even touching!

"Which means I probably will not like the thing," the duke grumbled. "And I believe I know you well enough to expect a refusal were I to offer an appropriate gown for the party? Mother says it is important you make the right sort of impression."

Persys flashed him an angry look. "My blue gown is simple but adequate for the *schoolmistress*. Remember, I am to be no more than that."

"Did George or Charlotte say something?" When Persys refused to answer, he continued, "I shall ask George first, then Charlotte, if you prefer. I'll not have you plagued with insinuations, Persys."

"Charlotte said not to worry about George. He was merely annoyed that I would not succumb to his charms nor offer flattery. I doubt he would impose upon me, truly." Persys backed toward the door, intent upon escape before the duke might probe more deeply.

The duke gave Persys an amused look. "Tell me if he attempts anything you do not wish."

"I cannot think why you might have the slightest notion I'd entertain attentions from Mr. Russell," Persys said, her voice frosty. "Excuse me, Charlotte is waiting. Oh"—Persys paused at the doorway—"the musicians?"

"A group has accepted the engagement at the date my aunt wished. It seems playing at a ducal party sweeps anything else aside." One of his eyebrows rose and that firm mouth which had felt so warm and remarkable on her own tilted into an attractive grin. Persys fled from the room.

He was the most impossible man she'd ever met and she scarce knew what to make of her jumbled emotions. She tried to remind herself that she was still in love with another man and thought it odd that she could not recall his face. Disturbed a little by this defection but with no time to examine it, she set to the remaining tasks involved with the party. By concentrating on which flowers to use and what china pattern would be best, she was able to set aside her inner confusion.

That evening began the first devoted to the reading of *Pride and Prejudice*. Persys fell into the charm of the book with the first words and reluctantly put it down when she had read until threatened with the loss of her voice. "Tomorrow," she promised the duchess, who was sorry the reading ended.

"I said you would like Elizabeth Bennet excessively," Charlotte pronounced with a grin.

"Just tell me this," the duchess demanded, "does she marry Mr. Darcy in the end?"

"I shan't," Charlotte said rising from her chair with a flounce. "It would spoil it for everyone else. I must say you read with excellent expression, Persys."

She accepted the encomium with good grace, resolving to look ahead to the end so she would have an idea of dear Miss Elizabeth's future. Of course she would wed the scornful Mr. Darcy, it would be unthinkable that she not. But one never knew. Look at the previous book. Persys thought Elinor ought to have married the colonel and Marianne, Edward Ferrars. It proved that Persys would never make an author; she had no notion of proper pairing.

A fine mist gave way to mere overcast the following morning. Persys consumed a hasty breakfast, then dropped the key to Russell House into her reticule before setting off in that direction. She intended to see precisely how long it would take to walk.

She had not gone far when she heard the sound of a carriage behind her. She paused to look and was dismayed to see the duke approaching at a fast clip.

"You did not tell me that you intended to walk, Miss Timothy."

"I was unaware I must tell you of my every movement, Your Grace," Persys declared, giving him a cool look. How, she wondered, did one manage to maintain a pleasant relationship with the owner of the house wherein you intended to have a school while at the same time discouraging any other sort of relationship? It was like crossing a fallen log over a stream; you worried every moment that you might take a tumble.

"Get in," the duke commanded, offering her a helping hand.

Knowing better than to counter his will, Persys stepped up into the curricle, settling back and keeping her distance from him as much as possible given the narrow confines of the carriage seat.

"I do not bite," the duke said sharply.

"I did not think so," Persys replied sweetly, deciding she had better not argue with him. She was saved from further conversation by their arrival at Russell House.

A large dray stood before the house and several men could be seen carrying furniture inside.

"Just in time to tell them where everything is to go," the duke said dryly.

"I intended to do precisely that," Persys snapped, her resolution to be agreeable flown as a cloud on a windy day. "I wanted to walk here to see just how far it was from your home. Driving is deceptive."

"It is but a mile, Miss Timothy, although why you should be so concerned about that point, I cannot imagine."

He assisted her from the carriage and, to her discomfiture, strolled along at her side into the house.

"The spinet, miss?" the older of the moving men inquired.

Persys put aside the turmoil seething inside her and motioned to the drawing room.

"Excellent location," the duke said with approval, his undertone spoken close to her ear.

Persys flashed him a questioning look, wondering if that was sarcasm she heard or if she was being touchy.

He possessed a bland expression, wandering along at her side as she informed the men where each piece of furniture went—for she had given considerable thought to suitable position.

When the contents of the dray had been removed and placed in the house, the men left. The house was extraordinarily quiet, every footfall sounding like an explosion in spite of the few rugs now in place.

Persys spun around, liking what she saw, even if there was still a great deal to be done. "They repaired the damp patch in that bedroom," she said to break the stillness.

"I should like to inspect it, if you do not mind."

"But it is your property," Persys pointed out. "I could have no objection."

"You have the key now. You will pay rent and as such will be a tenant. I do not intrude on my tenants, Miss Timothy."

"Well, dear me," Persys muttered, following him up the stairs to pause in the doorway of the room that had the repair done to the ceiling and roof as well.

"Appears to be complete," the duke said quietly, walking about the room with hands clasped behind him, examining not only the ceiling but the furniture placement there as well.

"I shall rearrange things once the remainder of the furniture and rugs come," Persys said, unexpectedly acquiring a touch of nervousness. Just why she should suddenly feel skittish, she wasn't certain. Perhaps it was because the duke was alone with her and he had once kissed her.

As though he guessed her thoughts, he crossed the room to stand before her, touching her lightly on the cheek.

"You do not flinch. That is a step in the right direction, I suppose." He stepped away to the hall, then turned to look back at her.

"You would not harm me, I think?" Persys said, not meaning to ask a question but make a statement, only it hadn't come out that way.

"Never." He smiled and Persys felt as though the sun had emerged from behind a cloud.

"I did not think so. After all, I am merely a schoolmistress and as such—"

"As such you feel safe from further kisses or attentions?"

Persys frowned. She didn't know why his words sounded wrong, but it wasn't the way she'd have phrased it.

He seemed pleased that she could not answer his query, for he grinned and ran lightly down the stairs to the main floor. Persys followed, deeply in thought. This man continually surprised her, confounded her, and in general confused her to bits.

That evening he joined the little group in the drawing room to listen to Persys read from the novel by Miss Austen. He stood by the fireplace, one arm draped along the mantel while he watched her with intent blue eyes.

"I think it a pity that Elizabeth and Jane must endure the rest of their family," the duchess said when Persys paused following her reading about the Netherfield entertainment. "One can suffer greatly from relations."

"Would you agree, Miss Timothy?" the duke inquired, his gaze sharply upon her.

"Indeed, I can. Relatives can be the bane of one's life or the completion of it. It all depends on the relatives, Your Grace." She marked her place with a finger, resolving to read until the end of this chapter, no more.

"Oh, neatly put, Miss Timothy," George drawled. There was no mistaking the sarcasm in *his* voice, she decided.

Persys ignored George and returned to the book.

"And does Mr. Collins declare himself?" the duchess asked once Persys put in the bookmarker and had shut the volume with a snap.

"That will come tomorrow and I shan't reveal a thing in advance. It would ruin everything," Persys said with a laugh as she rose. "And I shall take the book with me. I'll not have anyone looking ahead!"

"Miss Timothy does not like to know what is in store for her, I perceive," the duke said so softly that Persys doubted anyone else in the room heard his words. He had strolled over to look at the book in her hand and had his back turned to the others in the room.

"I enjoy the book, and you are wrong, Your Grace. I would like to know the future as much as anyone else." She gave him a steady look, then added, "However, I can guess at mine: I shall teach school to a cluster of charming young girls and grow old with Moggy at my side for company."

The duke smiled, giving her an odd look. "That shows how little you know, Miss Timothy. Given decent odds I would wager your years ahead will be vastly different."

He left before she could quiz him on the preposterous statement. To her knowledge there was no one who was remotely interested in asking for her hand, nor could she think of a single man she would wed.

Once in her room she continued to ponder the matter, trying to recall the image of the man she had wished to marry. She was disturbed when instead of his dear face, the mocking visage of the duke intruded in its place.

Sunshine greeted her the following morning, a distinctly pleasant change from misty rain or mere overcast. Libby assisted Persys into a simple pale-blue muslin with a fluted white trim at the neck. "I shall be at Russell House again, should anyone seek me. I am determined to have the place in order so that we may remove there as soon as possible. I fear I impose here once the duchess is back on her feet."

"But Her Grace ought tell you when you are no longer needed. Or perhaps His Grace, since he retained you," Libby pointed out with a servant's wisdom.

"True, but yet, I would be ready to move," Persys insisted with her own logic.

Libby knew better than to argue with her mistress. With troubled eyes she watched Persys flit from the room.

Charlotte was nowhere to be seen, fortunately. Persys quickly took a few rolls and cheese, wrapped them in a napkin, then hurried from the house. She wanted no confrontations of any sort this morning.

The sun was pleasantly warm as she marched along the avenue leading to where Russell House was sheltered among a grove of trees. After a time she began to sing, more loudly as she continued until she was caroling at full volume. There was not a soul to hear her.

The mile proved to appear much longer than expected, she reflected once she reached her goal. She sat on the front steps, absorbing the sun for a time while she rested her tired feet. Unfolding the napkin she put a bit of cheese on top of a piece of roll, to savor the delight of enjoying simple fare in the fresh air.

Thirsty, she explored the house and found a workable pump in the kitchen. Her hand proved an acceptable cup for the spring water that gushed forth once the pump was put into action.

"This will do nicely," she said with delight, spinning about in the center of the entryway.

"I'm pleased," the duke said from the doorway. "I'd not wish you haring off in some senseless manner for an even more stupid reason."

"Are you determined to annoy me? You cannot! This is far too wonderful a day to make me angry over anything." Persys grinned at him, looking, had she but known it, like a gamine flirt.

"I suppose I seem a trifle dour to you," he suggested.

"After reading Miss Austen's estimable novel I could wonder if you intend to take a page from the one I read now. Are you a Mr. Darcy?" Persys taunted gaily.

"Never!" the duke declared, his expression softening as he watched Persys float about the room in her happy mood.

"Oh, I think perhaps you are. You are determined to think the worst of me, I suspect. And my aunt is nearly as bad as Mrs. Bennet, is she not? My uncle bears a resemblance to Mr. Bennet, withdrawing from any guidance girls so need. I could have used a bit of help at times," Persys said wistfully, forgetting there was someone to hear her, wrapped up in the past for a moment.

"I do not think the worst of you, Persys," the duke said with deliberation, taking her arm to bring her pirouette to a halt.

Persys stood quite still at his touch, her eyes meeting his with confusion and a trace of alarm. That quickly vanished when she saw the smile deep within his eyes.

"I feel happy today and no one can spoil my joy," she said, grinning at him. "Your mother is almost healed, certainly she has quite enough to keep her occupied for a time. This house is near ready. Soon I will be doing something toward my future."

"Poor deluded girl." His eyes mocked her and his mouth twisted into an amused sort of expression.

She took instant umbrage. "You *are* like Mr. Darcy. You do disapprove of me." She pretended to punch him in the arm, then froze as she remembered.

"What happened just now?" he wanted to know.

"I'd forgotten who you are again," she whispered ruefully.

"Then I shall as well," he countered. With that, he reached out to envelop her in his warm clasp and kissed her.

It was not the devastating kiss of the attic, but it still stirred her, made her want more. She leaned against him, tilting her face so better to receive that kiss, to encourage him to do she knew not what. She only knew that this was what she had wanted since that moment in the attic when he had touched her lips with his.

The sound of the dray coming to a halt outside the front door brought both the duke and Persys to their senses. While the men began to unload the rugs, she stepped back to stare at him, wondering if what she suspected could be true. Had Charlotte been right when she accused Persys of being in love with the duke? Could such a thing be possible?

What a blessing he would never know—if indeed she loved him and she much feared she did. Such irony! He had sought to help her and she'd accepted to flee memories of a love lost forever. Now she had found a love she could not possibly lose, for she could never have it in the first place!

"What is it?" the duke questioned softly. "Have I become a dragon or Mr. Darcy?"

"No, n-not in the least," Persys said, her confusion making her sound quite as befuddled as she was.

"It is not your doing, you know," he said quietly. "This time I demand full responsibility."

Persys was at a total loss for words. She could not even imagine what he intended next.

Chapter Ten

Considering all the invitations she had written, Persys knew she ought not be surprised at the flood of guests into the Great Drawing Room. It was a good thing that much of the furniture had been moved elsewhere or the guests would have been hard pressed to gather.

The musicians sat cozily on a raised dais at the far end of the room surrounded by palms from the greenhouse. She listened as they played soft music designed for conversation, not for the dancing that was to follow.

Persys was enormously conscious of the duke wherever he happened to be. It was as though she had developed a special sense that was attuned just to him. Confusion reigned in her heart. How could she think she had loved the marquess? It must have been admiration, nothing more. It most assuredly had been nothing like what she felt now.

The duchess interrupted her mental wanderings, bringing Persys down to earth with a thump.

"My dear, I want you to meet Lady Thorpe. She and the baron believe they would very much like to try our little school. Dear Drusilla became so homesick at the Bath school that Lady Thorpe did not have heart to return her there. Russell House is vastly more convenient."

Persys curtsied, then stood chatting quietly as Lady Thorpe looked her over from head to toe. Apparently she decided what she found acceptable for she said she would enroll Drusilla once the school opened.

After that, Persys endured a succession of introductions to women who had daughters of an age to be schooled in the ways of Society. Watercolors, needlework, and dancing were considered obligatory, but polite conversation, French, how to arrange for entertainments, not to mention understanding of polite manners won approval from all parents.

"You cannot know what a hoyden my dearest Araminta is; how I fear she will never take," Lady Caswel declared. "Her father spoiled her dreadfully and now we pay the price." She glanced across the room and sighed at a chestnut-haired girl of perhaps seventeen who was slouched against her chair, twisting her reticule cords in her fingers.

Persys began to perceive that her life was to be no bed of rose petals if she had to mold girls such as Araminta into acceptable fodder for the marriage mart in London. Time later to discover if the girl had an acceptable dowry: money usually went a long way to assisting a hoydenish girl into a suitable marriage.

She had curtsied politely to Lady Caswel when she found the duke at her elbow.

"Mother would like the dancing to begin now." He offered his hand to Persys, who frowned at him.

"What about the Marchioness of Tavistock? Precedence, you know."

"This is special. The marquess will lead out Mother, and George will take care of the marchioness. We have let it be known that this is an informal affair. It is your night to be known and to shine." The duke smiled at her, his eyes twinkling in amusement at her hesitation.

Persys suffered him to take her hand—thank heaven it was neatly gloved—and lead her out to the center of the room while the musicians played an introduction to a rather pretty country dance. It was customary to begin a more formal dance with the minuet, but that was waning in popularity and far be it for the duchess to be out of date.

Persys faced the duke with a pounding heart, most thankful that she was skilled enough in the ways of Society to mask her true feelings. The duchess and her partner joined them and the music began—a lively tune that was far from the more stately melodies for the minuet. Conscious of all the parents watching, debating her merits as a teacher, and most likely speculating on her connection to the ducal household, Persys wondered that she could remember to put the proper foot forward or offer the correct hand in the complicated movements of the dance. She should not have been the least surprised at how excellent a dancer the duke proved to be. He would most likely put every man in the room in the shade no matter what he did.

"Splendid, my dear Persian woman," the duke said in a low, teasing voice as the shortened dance came to an end and a number of other couples drifted out to join the original four in the center of the room. "How well you flash those violet eyes and whirl about in the figures of the dance. I believe you are becoming a bit of a flirt after all."

"I should hope not, Your Grace," Persys denied with a quick shake of her head. "I must appear proper to these parents—particularly the mothers. Else the school will be a failure before it begins." And if the school failed Persys would leave here to retreat to a village deep in the countryside where no one would know her or the ways of Society and she could live in peace with a truly broken heart.

"If nothing else, they shall see how accomplished you are at dancing, my dear," the duke whispered. "You did well."

Persys imagined her supposed connection to the ducal family had far more influence than any dancing skills she possessed, no matter how graceful.

She accepted Lord Burfield as her next partner and was glad to see he was quite as deft on his feet as the duke.

"It goes well, I believe," his lordship said while capably spinning Persys about in a figure of the dance.

"I hope so. Her Grace insists she owes all these people engagements, but I am very aware that she makes a point of mentioning the school to one and all. I daresay the mainstay of my little school will be the daughters of the people at this party. Many of the girls are here and I fancy I have my work cut out for me."

Persys did not add that the prospect of teaching the girls had assumed daunting proportions. How could she, but a few years older than many of them, hope to instill the proper training to enter Society unless they really cooperated? How had she allowed the duchess—and the duke—to sweep her into this mad scheme? Because, another voice in her head reminded, at that time you were being a stupid girl over a fancied love with your cousin's husband.

Ninian Hervey led Persys out for the quadrille and she ably acquitted herself, but upon his praise informed the gentleman that she had him to thank for his expert partnership.

"You are a gifted dancer, sir, and make no mistake on it." She laughed at his returning sally, then observed Charlotte partnering the duke, laughing up at him with coy glances and flirtatious smiles. To make matters worse he was returning her smiles, flirting lightly with her in what Persys supposed to be an acceptable manner. While Charlotte was his cousin and not to be considered in the light of an acceptable wife, it reminded Persys that it would not be long before he would require a spouse, a gracious lady who was trained to be his duchess.

It was far worse than when she had observed her cousin with her fiancé, then husband. Even though the duke was unmarried, Persys knew full well he must make an advantageous marriage to a woman of wealth and rank. She was naught but a mere Honorable. Soon she was to be a mere schoolmistress in a house he owned on the edge of his property. Her lone consolation was that she was unlikely to see him at all once her classes began. Excuses not to present herself at the Great House when he was in residence would be a simple matter.

It was after she had danced with George Russell and endured his awkward footwork that she decided she needed to get away from the throng of people for a few minutes. Although it wasn't excessively warm, it was crowded and the scents of many perfumes combined to oppress her. Actually, she had barely refrained from sneezing on several occasions, so strong were several fragrances.

Slipping from the room, she wandered to the library, concealing herself in one of the great chairs at the far end of the room. Should anyone enter she would not be seen and could have a quiet time to herself until sufficiently composed to return to the gathering. There was a wealth of contentment to be found in the library, what with all the books and the comfortable chairs, not to mention excellent Argand lamps for reading.

She had been enjoying the sputtering of the low fire for several minutes when voices intruded on her peace. She at once recognized Charlotte's dulcet tones.

"Thank you, cousin, for assisting me to a breath of air and a bit of quiet. Your mother certainly is a clever hostess, but difficult to match in spirits. I envy her the energy she has—at her age, too."

"My mother does well at this sort of thing, but then she has had a great deal of practice. I doubt, however, if you truly have a hard time matching her in energy. What is on your mind, Charlotte?" the duke inquired.

"You have gone to a great deal of trouble over this stranger, your Persian woman—as you call her," Charlotte said, seeming curious, no more.

"I suppose some might think so," the duke acknowledged.

Persys felt her heart flutter madly at the sound of his voice. The memory of his kiss was still too vivid for her to be calm in his presence.

"Why?" Charlotte demanded.

"That is not for you to know," he countered, his voice firm and chilly.

"Some might think you had a particular motive for singling her out to settle here with your mother." There was a silence during which the duke said nothing and Persys wished she might peek around the corner of her chair so as to see his face.

Charlotte was nothing if not persistent. "Did you have a reason for bringing her from London?"

"Yes," the duke replied and Persys shrank back into her chair as she heard his footsteps pacing about the other end of the room.

"I would wager it was not to be a schoolmistress," Charlotte said with a bright laugh.

"No," he admitted. "That was Mother's idea."

Persys held her breath, wondering what Charlotte would ask next.

"If not to be a schoolmistress, what? Russell House is most convenient."

"What you say is true, Charlotte. But know I would not do anything improper." It was impossible to guess what his expression might be, for his voice held no inflection whatsoever.

"What might be considered improper for an ordinary being would not apply to you, I think," she said slyly.

"Are you quite finished, cousin? What my designs are in regard to Miss Timothy are none of your affair. I shall leave you to complete your rest; I shall return to my guests."

Persys heard his footsteps grow distant, then Charlotte's exasperated sigh. "Oh, drat the man!" And with that, the flurry of soft slippers left the room and Persys to her thoughts.

So . . . he had designs for her? And what sort of designs might they be, pray tell? Persys wondered, her ire rising to the fore. Did he plan to keep her close at Russell House so should he desire a kiss or more she would be convenient? She knew to her mortification that she had little resistance to his charm. All he needed to do was touch her and she caught fire, all opposition melted.

She leaned back in the chair, contemplating the words she had just heard. For one thing, she surmised that Charlotte had no motive for her questions other than to tease her cousin. No one had observed Persys slip away from the party, nor had either the duke or Charlotte caught sight of her in this great chair. Had they, one or the other would have said something.

What could she do in regard to the duke's designs, whatever they might be? Naturally, he had kept them from Charlotte. He was far too much the gentleman to reveal intentions however questionable they were.

Bitter thoughts and feelings assailed Persys. She felt so cheap! Why had she not queried the duke more regarding his intentions for whisking her from London? Stupid girl . . . she had been so infatuated with the marquess she scarcely knew what she was about! Small wonder that the handsome and persuasive duke could persuade her to leave London so easily. Of course, she had needed a place to go and he had taken advantage of that need. But why?

There had been no plans afoot to begin a school until his mother popped out with the notion. And that silly business with pretending to be the duke's particular interest was truly nonsense. Persys felt as though her head was whirling while attempting to figure out the riddle.

"Miss Timothy? Are you in here?" Ninian Hervey inquired.

Knowing she had better not continue to hide, Persys reluctantly rose from the chair to face him, hoping she did not look as pale and shocked as she felt.

"Mr. Hervey, you caught me out in my refuge from the mad squeeze," Persys said in a strained voice.

"I thought you might welcome a bit of supper. Her Grace is known for her splendid repasts, although I suspect you were responsible for this one." He walked to her, taking her hand in his to lead her from the room to where the supper was in progress.

Across the room Charlotte was sitting with her brother and Lord Burfield as well as the young Araminta. They were laughing and consuming the delicacies with obvious pleasure. It was evident that Araminta would be a handful at the school, she looked to be far too forward.

The duke was circulating about the room, not eating but making polite conversation with one and all. When he caught sight of Persys at Mr. Hervey's side he paused in his steps, looking at her in a rather odd manner that no one else appeared to notice.

"Come, I have found you a chair. Save the one at your side while I find us some of the excellent food." Mr. Hervey wended his way through the clusters of people to heap a couple of plates with the delectable viands.

Persys did as bid, sinking onto the small gilt chair with gratitude that she did not have to speak to the duke at the moment. Lord Thorpe had collared him and launched into a discussion of a topic evidently dear to his heart. His Grace was far too well mannered to cut the man short; thus Persys could take time to gird herself for their inevitable meeting.

Charlotte paused by Persys on her way from the room. "You are undoubtedly the belle of the evening, right from your first dance with the duke. You are pleased your school will likely be a smashing success upon its opening?"

Resolved to be polite at all costs, Persys dredged up a smile, thankful Ninian Hervey joined them at that moment. "Indeed. I would be a fool not to appreciate all Her Grace has done for me. She is a most wonderful person."

"And my cousin?" Charlotte demanded softly.

Persys forced her eyes to meet Charlotte's compelling gaze without flinching. "His Grace is an excellent manager of his estates and investments. Undoubtedly he sees a school as a profitable venture."

Charlotte appeared disappointed with the reply Persys gave her and flounced away from the little table with visible ire.

"What was all that about?" Mr. Hervey queried. "Did Miss Russell have her claws into you? Everything she says or does is not without purpose, I'd wager."

"You are very hard on her," Persys protested, forking a dab of salad to her mouth, not tasting any of it.

"She has earned it, if you recall. I have little mercy for the woman."

"I venture to say she has her uses. She was enormously helpful in preparing for this party," Persys said, determined to be fair. And unspoken was the thought that without Charlotte's probing Persys would not have learned that the duke had ulterior motives for bringing her to his estate.

The duke at last appeared at their sides, smiling cordially at both. He chatted social nothings, then turned to Persys and asked, "There is to be a waltz following supper. Would you partner me? Mother vows to show all the parents you are quite up to snuff on the latest dances."

Persys fought the panic that assailed her, successfully pushing it aside. "Thank you, Your Grace, I should like that very much."

He bowed slightly, then wove his way through the tables to talk with his mother.

Persys allowed her gaze to trace his path.

"May I ask what that was all about, or is it too arcane?"

She had to smile at Mr. Hervey's expression of fascinated eagerness, as though intent upon discovering secrets of the most scandalous sort.

"Nothing at all. His mother most graciously seeks to advance my cause." Did the duchess know she inadvertently advanced the cause—whatever it might be—of her son as well? Persys doubted that very much.

There were only so many ways she could push the food around her plate; only so long she might stall for time. Eventually she must face the duke. Perhaps it would be better to put the ordeal behind her as soon as possible. She rose from the little table, looking across the room to where the duke stood. He lounged against the wall, apparently watching her. Why, she couldn't imagine, unless he wanted to know when she would be ready to perform that waltz.

"Excuse me," she murmured to Mr. Hervey, who had been watching both parties with interested and very alert eyes.

Terribly aware of the duke—the way his black satin evening breeches fit him so superbly, the dark wine velvet coat hugged his athletic figure perfectly, the exquisite fall of his neckcloth emphasized his masculinity—she began her journey across the room. There wasn't a man in the room who could touch him for elegance or pride of bearing.

"It would seem time for our waltz," Persys said with more civility than she thought she possessed. He nodded and took her arm to guide her from the supper room.

When she and the duke entered the Great Drawing Room, the musicians had been playing a spirited tune. Because Persys had been dawdling at her meal, most guests had already returned to the lovely blue-and-silver room and mingled in conversation, with a number off to one side deep into playing cards.

At a signal from the duke the musicians paused a few moments, which served to draw attention to them. Then they struck up the introduction to the waltz. Persys faced her partner, wondering how best to immure herself to his touch. She would think of the school, concentrate on what she must accomplish there, and a future life without the duke remotely involved.

No matter how she had steeled herself against his touch, it had not been enough. The heat of his gloved hand burned through the thin fabric of the blue sarcenet gown and into her skin as he drew her close. As she turned to face him, her skirt brushed against his body and she was obliged to place one hand on his shoulder, with the other entrusted to his care.

While the music might captivate and charm, Persys could well understand the resistance to the dance. It brought two people closer than arm's length and facing, almost as lovers. The next logical step would be a caress, a kiss. Persys made an effort to keep her mind away from that and failed. It was an intimate dance, far from those country dances and quadrilles that kept the partners a good distance apart.

The dance made it difficult to be distant with him. He guided her around and around in the ever-circling path, taking care to keep her from others also venturing the relatively new dance. Persys raised her gaze to meet his. What *was* his motive for bringing her here? Could she ask? She thought not. She wasn't like Charlotte, who dared anything. It could well be something Persys would rather not hear and anyway, why force the issue? If there was a plan in his mind, she would learn it eventually—if he held to it.

"You dance very well," he said, giving her a probing look.

"As you do, Your Grace," she responded stiffly.

"It ought to reassure these good parents that you are quite capable of anything, even teaching the waltz."

"I can only hope that the woman I need to assist me can be found."

"You have sent an advertisement to a paper as yet?"

"No," Persys said. "But I shall quite soon." Perhaps Charlotte had grasped the wrong end of the stick? Maybe he merely intended to be kind to Persys, felt sorry for her, and had wanted to help her out of the dilemma she faced with her aunt. She foolishly had told him she needed a place to go immediately. Of course one as generous and kind as the duke would have thought of a situation with his mother. Persys relaxed at the very idea.

He pulled her a trifle closer and apologized, "Sorry, there was a couple about to collide with us. That is one thing you seldom have to worry about when performing a country dance." But he did not release her again, continuing to hold her closely against him in defiance of all proper dictates.

"Your Grace?" she queried from the folds of his neckcloth.

"Of course," he replied with a sigh.

Before Persys could say another word, the waltz ended and he stepped away from her side, his face a mask of polite civility.

"Charming, utterly charming," the duchess proclaimed as she joined them.

"Thank you," Persys murmured, then excused herself to hurry to the side of the room.

"You did that well," George Russell said. "I must say I am all admiration."

"Thank you, Mr. Russell." Try as she might, Persys could not like George Russell. There was something about him that repelled her. What a pity it was that he was heir to the duke. It was to be hoped that nothing happened to His Grace before he wed and produced at least one heir of his own.

"I cannot hope to match the duke in ability to dance. I wonder if you would join me in a quiet stroll? We could look at the conservatory—I understand there are lanterns lit there this evening. There will probably be a good many to inspect the place—you know how impressive the plants are."

Persys suspected it would be a romantic spot she ought to avoid, but she did want to keep a distance from the duke. What it would be like to venture there with him!

"It has become rather warm in here. I should like a bit of fresh air, if you please," she replied, wishing someone else had thought to invite her for a stroll.

Oddly enough Mr. Russell was quite as he ought to be, polite and for him, rather entertaining. Persys wondered if she had misjudged the man.

"I must say, you look very well in blue, Miss Timothy," Mr. Russell said. They passed a footman guarding one of the private rooms off limits to guests. If he saw them it was not perceptible by so much as a flicker of his eyes.

Surprised by the kind words, Persys thawed a trifle toward Mr. Russell.

They entered the conservatory where the rare orchids and other unusual plants His Grace indulged his mother with all thrived. It took the efforts of two gardeners to care for this collection, Persys recalled. And of course Her Grace oversaw the plantings. Undoubtedly it was the duchess who had the various plants in bloom arranged to be most attractive.

"We could sit on this bench if you like, enjoy the light fragrance of the flowers."

Persys tossed him a grateful glance. "There seem to be a goodly number of people who poured the contents of a perfume bottle over their persons this evening."

"I had noticed," he admitted, then fell silent.

Persys didn't mind his lack of words. As matter of fact, she preferred it that way.

After a time he grew restless and rose to his feet. "Why not walk along this side to better view those orchids? The white show off rather well even at night."

Agreeable to what seemed to be an innocent suggestion, for he had not attempted the slightest liberty with her—Persys rose to her feet as well.

They had gone about ten feet when Persys found herself nudged against a thorny plant by Mr. Russell's clumsy loss of footing.

"Sorry," he muttered. "I hope you haven't torn your gown. Allow me to help untangle it." He bent over, taking the delicate cloth in hand to carefully remove it from the clutch of the thorns. It involved lifting her skirt so he could see better and Persys was most thankful that no one was present at that moment to see him, *or* her immodest show of petticoat and stocking-sheathed leg.

"Persys, are you quite all right? Charlotte said you were feeling faint," the duke inquired as he rapidly covered the path to where she stood, embarrassed and devoutly wishing she were elsewhere.

The duke halted, absorbing the scene and Persys wondered what he saw. Did he see a flustered young woman with a gentleman attempting to free her from brambles or did he think he caught a man in the act of seduction? Persys was not so sheltered that she had not learned the things to avoid and this scene was one of them. Of all the idiotic things to do was to come to the conservatory with George Russell!

"Excuse me," the duke said in a voice guaranteed to freeze one solid. He turned and marched away so fast that even had Persys called to him she doubted he would have heard her.

"Sorry about that, my dear," said the unctuous voice of one Persys now realized must be an enemy.

Pulling the fabric of her gown from his hands, heedless of any damage that might occur as a result, Persys gave him a withering glare. "I expect you have achieved what you wanted with that nonsense. But *please*, do not ever speak to me again. I would deem it a very great favor." She whirled about and retreated to the shelter of the withdrawing room where the maid assigned to perform just such tasks helped her pin together the tear to her gown.

Fortunately the guests had begun to depart. Charlotte stood by her aunt, who beckoned to Persys with an imperious hand to join them in the entry hall.

"Are you feeling more the thing, dear? Charlotte said you were a trifle faint. The party was such a crush," the duchess said with justifiable complacency. Every hostess desired packed rooms overflowing with happy, if crowded, guests.

"Indeed, Your Grace, I am myself again. I fear my gown suffered a bit of damage while strolling in the conservatory. That plant with the thorns, you recall?" Persys turned to look at Charlotte, giving her much the withering look that had been bestowed on the hapless George. "How fortunate I am able to replace the gown, but the maid in the withdrawing room kept me from being indecent."

"Dear girl, you shall have ten gowns, for you were such a success this evening. I believe there are at least ten of the girls whose parents expressed interest in the school."

"All I need now is an assistant," Persys murmured, wondering where she would be once the duke informed his mother of what he had observed in the conservatory. Well, at least she had spoken first, for the duchess had not been told that Persys had been found in a most compromising position.

"You had best find a capable woman as soon as you can, Miss Timothy, one who could take over should it prove necessary." The duke gave Persys a cold look, then devoted his attention to his mother.

Charlotte gave Persys a serene smile and drifted up the stairs to her room.

Chapter Eleven

"*I* would that you tell me precisely what happened in the conservatory last evening, Persys. And do not fob me off with that tale about thorns," the duchess demanded in a soft voice that brooked no denial. She was being her usual high-handed self again and there was no denying her when she sought information while in that mood. She tapped an impatient finger on the table, waiting. "I want details. Why did Harry look like a thundercloud and speak in *such* a manner to you?"

Persys looked about the cheerful breakfast room, buttery yellow splashing sunshine on walls and chairs offering no comfort. Her poor heart was battered and near defeated this morning. The duke had believed what he thought he saw and condemned her out of hand, without an explanation. Persys cast a frowning glance out of the window. It seemed she was destined to love not only imprudently but rashly as well.

"Mr. Russell suggested we stroll in the conservatory. He said there were some white orchids that looked rather nice even at night because of the lamps."

"And?" the duchess prodded impatiently. "Continue." She tapped her foot silently on the blue-and-yellow rug. Even though silent, her testiness could be felt in the room.

"Mr. Russell appeared to lose his footing on the slate floor and stumbled, pushing me against one branch of that thorny plant—I do not know the name of it," Persys added in an aside. "He insisted upon helping me free my gown from the thorns. When His Grace came charging down the path, I fear my dress was lifted to an inappropriate height, revealing far too much ankle and petticoat to be proper. What he thought, I cannot say. But I suppose that is why he suggested in that manner he has when he is angry that I hire a woman who would be capable of taking over the school. I fear he means to supplant me."

The duchess stopped tapping her foot and her fingers curved around the teacup before her while a pleased expression crept into her eyes—for a few moments only. "He shan't dismiss you while I am here to prevent it." Her chin rose a notch and that odd smile returned to her eyes again. "I quite believe you. George was out of line and so I shall tell him. As to that lovely gown, I insist you permit me to replace it. You can ill afford to lose so charming a garment and I am well able to provide you with a replacement. I shall instruct my abigail to see to it immediately." She made a notation on a pad of paper she normally used to write memoranda regarding her herbs and other plants. "As to my son . . . he mistakenly believed George was attempting to seduce you."

Persys took a seat at the table, stunned at the notion that George or anyone else would seek to seduce her while in the conservatory or anywhere else. "Absurd, Your Grace! I cannot believe he would do such a thing while he's a guest in your home to one you employ . . . who isn't a maid."

The duchess gave Persys a sharp look, then murmured, "Something will have to be done about George."

Feeling immensely better now that the duchess accepted her story without question, Persys poured a cup of tea and proceeded to sip it. At least *one* of the family believed her.

"I would advertise for my assistant. What papers would you suggest, Your Grace?" Persys inquired hesitantly. You never knew quite what the duchess would do or say when asked a question. She had strong opinions and made no bones about voicing them.

"There is an agency in London that has always sent me excellent help: I have never had to dismiss any of their people. Why do we not see what they have to offer? I believe that to be a better path than advertising in the newspapers. Heaven only knows what or who might apply!"

Seeing the wisdom of this, Persys agreed at once and obeyed the suggestion that paper and pen be put to use immediately. Persys wrote the agency's direction on a separate slip, thinking she might have use for such a firm herself if the duke decided she had to go.

The letter written and tea consumed, Persys begged leave to go to Russell House to oversee the furniture placement and make a list of kitchen and stillroom needs.

"Go, go. I will consult with Mrs. Biddle regarding the meals and such while you are gone. I shan't inform George of your whereabouts, I promise," the duchess added with a significant look at Persys. "However, it would be wise to arm yourself in the event he decides he cannot bear *no* for an answer."

"I had no opportunity to say anything other than to beg him to release my gown," Persys replied indignantly. "Since he did not, I tore it and—"

"Ran off." The duchess looked vexed, then shrugged. "There is a sturdy umbrella in the entry hall. Take that."

Shaking her head at the suggestion, Persys did as bade, however. In spite of gentle clouds that held no hint of stormy gray, she grasped the large red umbrella in her hand, and having tucked a paper and pencil in her reticule, set off on the one-mile walk.

The parklike setting held little appeal this morning. Ordinarily she would have reveled in the neatly scythed grass and perfectly trimmed shrubbery. Even the trees were placed at the precise location where they enhanced the view from the house. Mr. Capability Brown had been indeed a master of the landscaping art. Today her mind was otherwise occupied.

There was no sound of a carriage this morning. If the duke was out and about on the estate he was not here, nor had he chosen to see her this morning, and Persys supposed she ought to be grateful for small mercies. If he didn't talk to her he couldn't fire her.

Russell House looked charming in the early morning sun. The grass beyond the low box hedge that bordered the path was now properly scythed and urns overflowed with bright red geraniums to either side of the front door. Windows sparkled and the brass knocker on the front door gleamed with polish.

Inside Persys found much improvement as well. It was amazing what could be accomplished in such a short time. The lengths of fabric in a pleasing shade of green made attractive swags that did not spoil the view beyond. Furniture fairly glowed with polish.

The woman overseeing the transformation of the house appeared in the hall, a short cloak over her shoulders. "Be you pleased, miss?"

"You have done wonders, Eliza." Persys had been surprised that not only had the butler been permitted to marry but that his daughter, Eliza, held a position of trust in the household. It was not often the case, most people seeming to prefer unmarried servants.

"Thank ye. I'm going to the house for a few supplies. I shan't be long." The woman whisked herself from the house and was marching up the path before Persys could think of anything to bring back with her.

Putting the red umbrella on the entry hall table, Persys walked slowly through the rooms of the house, inspecting each in turn for needed supplies, or missing, but necessary items.

"A lamp for the hallway," she murmured as she added the item to her growing list. Eliza Portman had used good sense in placing the furniture; there was little that Persys would alter. She had returned to the hall with a chair she thought might serve for someone waiting to be greeted when the door suddenly opened and George Russell entered.

Persys placed the chair on the marble floor with a decided click. Then she prudently edged toward the table where the red umbrella so innocently reposed.

"Good morning, Mr. Russell," she said with frigid politeness. Whether or not George had intended to cause trouble last evening she could not know, but he had, and therefore was not to be trusted an inch.

"Morning, Miss Timothy. Place looks amazingly good—real welcoming, if you know what I mean. Have you seen the duke yet this morning?" George strolled about the entry, looking at a landscape painting on the wall, then peering at the rooms opening off from there with a curiosity she found puzzling.

Wary of this effusive friendliness, Persys shook her head, curling her fingers around the handle of the umbrella now so conveniently at her back. "No. I had a conversation with Her Grace earlier. I have been occupied here since then. Was there something you wanted?"

"Indeed. You are alone here. I just passed Portman's daughter on the way to the house." He paused in his admiration of the drapery above the entry window, then turned to look at Persys, a speculative gleam in his eyes.

"And what has that to do with anything, sir?" Persys asked quietly, moving away from the table so better to be free to swing her most unsuitable weapon if necessary.

"I endured an unpleasant scold from my aunt this morning. That is not the way to treat the heir to the dukedom!" His hands balled into fists and he looked extremely angry. George Russell appeared to be the sort who wanted a certain amount of toadying from lesser mortals.

"No?" Persys could well imagine the scathing tongue-lashing meted out by the duchess. When her anger boiled over, the lady was truly impressive.

"I believe I merit compensation for what I was denied last evening." At the look of outrage from Persys he went on, "Do not claim you were unknowing of what I desired, have desired for some time."

"I am not a servant girl who dare not repulse your advances, Mr. Russell. I have independent means and do not need *this* particular position to keep me fed and clothed," Persys stated firmly, while surreptitiously bringing the umbrella down to her side.

"You will not refuse me, however," George declared, taking a threatening step in her direction. When he drew close enough Persys took a chance and struck him over the head as hard as she could.

George didn't reel, as she expected; he slumped to the floor in an ignominious heap.

"Well done, my Persian woman," said a rich, deep voice from behind her. "I thought I'd have to come to your defense. Mother's umbrella?" the duke asked as he looked at the sturdy wand of bright red that remained in Persys's hand.

"How did you know? That is, where did you come from?" Persys stuttered. She had just clobbered the duke's heir and probably ruined his mother's umbrella. Most likely the ribs were in a sad state after connecting with George's hard head.

"I happened to see George set out in his curricle. Then I spotted Portman's daughter, Eliza, who informed me that you were here alone in the house. It didn't take much intelligence to add two and two." The wry note in his voice brought a flush to Persys's cheeks.

"I thank you for your concern," Persys said, shaken with the implications of what she had done. "I truly am not certain what I would do now by myself."

"George does not look so threatening when collapsed in a heap, does he?" the duke asked lightly, staring down at his cousin. "I suppose I ought to dump a pot of water over his dishonorable head so he will come to, but I hate to disturb our peace like that."

"Well, I imagine he will be very angry with me for hitting him . . . but I had no wish for him to kiss me, nor anything else, for that matter. I do not like your cousin, Your Grace. He may be your heir but he is a ramshackle fellow, for all that."

"He is, isn't he?" the duke agreed. He hesitated a moment, then walked around her, hands behind his back while he seemed to mull over what he intended to say next. At last he paused, looking directly at her. "Persys . . . I must apologize for last night. I jumped to conclusions and I ought to have given you the opportunity to defend yourself. I didn't, and that was wrong. I'm sorry."

"That is a handsome admission, Your Grace," Persys said, thinking how odd it was that she felt no fear of the duke, but had trembled at the presence of George Russell. Yet both men had found her alone and defenseless—or supposedly so. "I had never appreciated what excellent weapons umbrellas make," she murmured while carefully placing the battered protection against rain on the hall table. It had served her well as protection against another type of adversity.

"Mother always did say they were handy articles," the duke replied in kind. He stepped nearer and touched Persys on her shoulder, bringing her around so she was not only close but also directly before him.

Persys stared into his eyes, wondering what *he* wanted. Why was it that men always seemed to want something?

"I believe I deserve a reward, even if I didn't bash him on the head."

"Because you were here as an alternative?" Persys queried with a softened expression. "Had I not knocked him out, I expect I would have had quite a struggle. I caught him by surprise," she concluded simply.

"He was not the only one you caught by surprise," the duke said, but did not explain those cryptic words. "Well? I would claim my reward, but not if you intend to hit me with the umbrella."

"And the reward?" Persys asked, beginning to enjoy herself while placing a tentative hand atop the umbrella.

"This," the duke replied softly. His kiss was gentle, and while it sent tremors of delight through her, today it did not overwhelm, nor did his kiss threaten as she had feared.

When he withdrew she blinked her eyes and sighed with pleasure. Gathering her common sense about her, she scolded him. "This will never do. Think what an effect that would have upon impressionable girls!"

"I'd not worry about that were I you," he answered, again with an enigmatic remark she failed to grasp. "I had best remove my cousin from here and be on my way. Open the door and I'll simply dump him in his curricle. He can wake up on the way back to the house."

Persys chuckled at the irony in the duke's voice and did as bade. She stood watching in the doorway as George was not too carefully placed on the curricle seat. She was about to close the door and resume her work when the duke turned to her.

"By the way, you will be pleased to know your cousin is to arrive tomorrow, along with her new husband. I thought you might enjoy a visit with them, and Torrington has long been a friend as well as a relative." With that remark he leaped into the curricle, picked up the reins, and took off up the avenue, his horse trotting along behind like nothing more than an obedient dog.

Persys was not thinking of the remarkable horse, however. Her mind focused on seeing her cousin and her handsome husband again. What if she had been wrong? What if she still was in love with him? Could she be in love with two men at once?

"Oh, help," she moaned, and gave up the notion of any more work that day.

The following morning she was up bright and early, restlessly pacing her room when Libby brought her the tray of chocolate and toast Persys favored.

"Out of bed, are you?" Libby asked pertly. "Lady Torrington that was Katherine comes today. Afternoon, most likely."

"Indeed. What a happy day for us all! Lord Torrington is a distant cousin to His Grace and a most welcome visitor. I am somewhat surprised that they would take a trip so soon after their wedding," Persys said with a glance at her maid. Servants always knew things that their betters didn't.

"As to that, I heard His Grace invited them to come. Perkins, his valet, mentioned it to me before dinner last eve. 'Tis odd, but that's the Quality for you, begging your pardon, miss," Libby added as matter of form. She bustled about the room, bringing out a pretty day dress of violet sprig muslin along with the necessary underpinnings and slippers.

Persys sipped the chocolate while surveying the distant rolling grounds and the corner of the lake visible from her room. "It will seem strange to see Katherine again, a happily married woman with a large home to run and a husband who adores her."

The maid paused by the dressing room door to study her mistress. "Happen it will."

The hours dragged by and Persys occupied her time by taking on every job she could find.

"Goodness," the duchess exclaimed after nuncheon, "I shan't know what to do without you once you are settled in the school. I have become quite attached to you, Persys."

"Thank you, Your Grace." Persys picked up the cane the duchess had begun to use that day. The knee was truly healed and there was not the least reason for Persys to remain. Yet nothing had been said about her removal to Russell House. Perhaps they waited for her assistant to arrive?

When the sound of an approaching carriage was heard the duchess and duke, Ninian Hervey, Lord Burfield, and Charlotte

Russell, along with an anxious Persys, gathered in the entry to greet the guests. George had remained in his room and not a word had been said about his absence.

The footmen rushed forth to open doors, remove luggage, and in general make themselves useful. The marquess exited first to be followed by a laughing Katherine. Persys watched as he helped her from the carriage, his hand lingering on hers and his eyes caressing her most lovingly.

"Oh, my dearest cousin!" Katherine cried when she saw Persys. "How pleased I am to find you here. What a nice surprise! I had no notion you knew the duchess until I received your letter," Katherine bubbled as she walked beside Persys into the house.

Persys didn't know how to answer this so remained silent. This was just as well, because Katherine hadn't required an answer. She paused in the entry to look about and become acquainted with her husband's friends and relatives.

The duke greeted his cousin, made sure everyone met, then turned to Katherine and said, "A kiss for the bride, I believe. I did not have that treat at the wedding."

Persys watched as he kissed Katherine lightly on her lips then stood back, his gaze fixed on Persys of all people.

She, in turn, found herself lightly kissed by Katherine's husband and felt . . . utterly nothing. Confused, yet relieved, she was sure she smiled. She took Katherine's hand to walk at her side, not hearing much of what was said while they strolled into the yellow drawing room. She took surreptitious peeks at the marquess, puzzled by her complete disinterest in him. How could she have such a change of heart?

"You do not much resemble one another," Charlotte said to Katherine, quite the picture of demure amiability. "I vow, Miss Timothy has such unusual eyes."

Katherine blinked at this comment, then studied her cousin before replying, "Persys has always been an original, particularly with those violet eyes. Thank goodness she is also my best friend as well as cousin. I cannot tell you how delighted I was when you wrote to say you had found a position with Her Grace, who happens to be one of Christopher's favorite relatives, the duke being the other. When he sent the invitation to visit I was pleased, for then I could see you again and thank you."

"Whatever for?" Persys wondered.

"Not merely all you did at the wedding, but the comfort and help when Christopher was courting me." The look exchanged between the two cousins was filled with memories of a wooing that had brought tears and laughter, not to mention more than a little heartache before the resolution.

Persys sighed, thinking of how foolish her infatuation with the marquess had been. But he had been the most handsome, elegant figure to enter her life—however remotely—to that point. Now that she had met the duke, Lord Torrington paled in comparison.

Across the room her gaze sought and found the duke, laughing at a story being told by Lord Torrington. What a pity there would not be a happy ending to her little love affair—if you could call such a one-sided thing an affair. He turned his head and his eyes met hers. He appeared as reluctant as she was to break that thread of contact when his cousin spoke to him and Katherine demanded Persys to accompany her to her room.

"How does Lady Jocelyn fare? Is she still living with you?" Persys inquired, thinking of the haunted face belonging to Lord Torrington's sister.

"No, indeed. When we returned from our wedding trip it was to discover she had gone off to the west of England to visit an old school friend. Perhaps she will remain there. She has written nothing about returning to live with us. Which is as well, for I suspect I am in the family way."

All thoughts of the interesting Lady Jocelyn were abandoned with this marvelous news. Persys plumped herself on a chair while Katherine settled on a chaise near the window of the elegant room that was hers, part of a guest suite that Persys deemed fine enough for royalty.

"When? And you must be pleased," Persys said with her beguiling smile.

They shared the delightful details of coming motherhood— Katherine not bothered the least by nausea or spasms or any of common ailments often plaguing expectant mothers.

When they had exhausted this topic Katherine asked, "And what about you? Do I understand rightly you are to run a school for girls—to prepare them for their come-outs?"

"It was Her Grace's idea. I had no notion of where I ought to settle. Society is opposed to a young woman establishing her own household, even if she can afford it."

"Mother?" Katherine hazarded.

"Told me to leave immediately following the wedding." Persys had decided she would not protect Lady Talbot from her daughter's ire. Katherine knew full well what her mother was like. "Fortunately His Grace happened to be there and suggested I keep his mother company while her badly injured knee healed. It was a godsend and I have come to adore her. She has so many interests in life and normally is quite active—in spite of her white hair and that deceptive look of age."

"You are happy here," Katherine said, her brow furrowed in thought. "And the duke?"

There was no way Persys could prevent the blush that tinted her cheeks, not after that kiss yesterday. "He is a fine man, a good steward of his property, and a good son. I have a tendency to forget who he is, however, and that creates a problem now and again."

"But I think there is more," Katherine said slowly. "I see that blush. I also know what is expected of a duke by his family and Society. Oh, Persys," she said, compassion clear in her voice, "how perfectly dreadful for you, to fall in love with someone so far removed from you."

"Do not be silly," Persys said with a grimace. "And I very much doubt if hearts truly break. The crack in mine shall mend and I'll be as good as new."

"If you say so. When do you leave here? I should think the sooner, the better."

"As soon as I can find an assistant, I shall move from here to Russell House and most likely shan't see the duke from one end of the month to the next. He has been kind to me, but I expect it is the sort of kindness he would extend to anyone in need."

"I wonder?" Katherine murmured. "I suspect that had you not

possessed gorgeous violet eyes and a charming figure, to say nothing of a delightful personality he would not have given you a second look."

Persys rose from her chair and paced about the room, turning at last to face her cousin. "He calls me 'his Persian woman' at times, I suppose to vex me."

"How decidedly odd," Katherine replied, repressing a smile and utterly failing. "His Persian woman? Oh, Persys, how droll."

At that fortuitous moment the marquess entered the room and Persys escaped before she forgot her cousin was a lofty marchioness and threw a pillow at her.

Once the door closed Katherine smiled adoringly at her husband. "Persys is in love with the duke. At first I pitied her, for he has a high place in Society and would be expected to marry equally high. But Chris, he calls her 'his Persian woman.' And she admits that she tends to forget who he is. Now, what do you think of that?"

"Hmm. Intriguing bit of news. I managed to keep watch on him as well and he found it dashed difficult to keep his eyes off Persys. I could feel his glare when I dared to kiss her—no matter it was light and brief."

"Well, well, who would have thought it. Do you suppose we might stay on for a bit? I should like to help Persys if I might. She was a great comfort to me when those rumors of Felicia Rochmont reached my ears."

"I imagine I owe Persys a debt of thanks for that bit of support."

"Indeed, she fiercely refused to believe ill of you. Since she has always been quite astute about people, I took heart and here we are."

"You feel well? The coach ride did not upset you?"

"Oh, pooh, not the least. You must know that nothing bothers me as long as you are at my side." At her inviting smile, the marquess found it necessary to postpone changing for dinner and tend to more important matters for a bit.

Persys hastily changed her gown for a delicate violet faille with a simple lace ruff at the neck. It was not dashing, but had a look of quiet elegance about it. She left her chamber to make her way to the yellow drawing room where she imagined all would gather as usual.

At the top of the stairs Charlotte joined her. "My, don't you look fine as fivepence," Charlotte trilled, clasping Persys by her arm. They discussed the new arrivals, the pleasure of company, then at the bottom of the stairs Charlotte paused to say, "My vain brother insists upon remaining in his room until that lump on his head subsides. He refused to tell me what happened? Do you know?"

Unwilling to reveal her part in the matter, Persys took refuge in a noncommittal murmur. "Accidents happen, I imagine."

"I suppose they do," Charlotte replied doubtfully, then left Persys to join Ninian Hervey and Lord Burfield.

"You had a pleasant chat with Katherine?"

Persys stiffened at the warm touch of the duke's hand on her bare arm, just above her glove. Why did she have this outrageous urge to throw herself into his arms and demand he kiss her again? She had always been the most proper one in the family, used as an example to the others.

"Yes, I did. I was thrilled to learn she is in the family way. That is good news, indeed," Persys didn't know whether to take comfort in his touch or edge away. She remained close to his side. She would be gone from here soon enough.

"You like children?" His Grace inquired as he ushered Persys from the bottom of the stairs to the double doors leading to the yellow drawing room.

"Yes, I do. I should wish for several."

As he left her side Persys would have sworn he murmured, "We make progress." But that made no sense at all.

Chapter Twelve

The duchess surveyed the letter newly arrived from the London agency she had used for years, smiling as she concluded her reading. "This woman sounds most agreeable, Persys. I think you ought to send for her. Should she prove acceptable your worries are over . . . on that regard."

"Laura Woodhall. It is a pretty name. Perhaps she will prove quite as nice," Persys said in total agreement. She had been impressed with the credentials offered in the letter and was bent upon securing the teacher as quickly as she might.

It had not escaped her attention that the duchess had increased her interest in the school. Now that her knee was nearly back to normal she was into everything. Persys wondered that she didn't want a house of her own, or perhaps she considered Eddington Park hers to do with as she pleased? She had lived here a long time, after all.

It took but a few minutes to write a letter requesting Mrs. Woodhall to present herself at Eddington Park as soon as possible. Travel funds were to be given her by the agency, which would be reimbursed by the Russell man of business. Persys handed the neatly folded and sealed paper to Portman with the request that it be franked when the duke had time.

"Persys?" Katherine called out as she sedately descended the stairs. "See how proper I am become? No more running like some hoyden. Mama would be amazed!"

"Indeed," Persys said with an affectionate grin. While she had no love for her cold-hearted aunt, she bore no resentment against her pretty cousin. Now that Persys had come to realize her supposed love for Lord Torrington was no more than a mild infatuation, she was even happier with Katherine and her excellent marriage.

"I wished to go riding this morning but Christopher insists I must not. He has such concern for me, Persys. Am I not the most favored of women in the world?" Katherine dimpled an impish smile, then continued. "So, I thought perhaps we might take a carriage drive. Unless you prefer riding?"

"Of course Persys would like to ride," the duchess pronounced in her autocratic manner. "I, however, would adore a drive in the carriage with you; Persys can ride that docile mare eating its head off in the stables. We shall make a party of it. I am certain that Katherine has not seen anything of our lovely countryside and Persys has been so involved with her school that she needs a breath of air as well."

There was no arguing with the duchess if, indeed, anyone had wanted to. Within minutes it was decided that all in the house—even the repellent George, would make up a party to ride to a nearby ruin said to be very picturesque.

Thinking it might be pleasant to escape from her duties at the school for a few hours, Persys hurried to her room to find Libby removing her simple blue habit from the wardrobe.

"I never cease to be surprised how word travels so quickly around here."

"Well, miss, I happened to be in the hall, taking your cleaned dress to your room, when I heard Her Grace. She has a voice that carries, she does."

"Help me change. I would not keep anyone waiting." Persys wanted to be first down so she could remain in the background. The duke had retreated to his usual aloof self and while Persys didn't know what to make of him, she did desire to stay out of his notice.

Thus it was that Persys arrived in the entry to be shortly followed by Ninian Hervey and Lord Burfield, then George Russell, looking like a thundercloud. Persys was engaging Ninian Hervey in polite conversation regarding the proposed jaunt when Lord

Torrington and Katherine, with Charlotte drifting along beside them, joined the waiting group.

"Where's Harry?" Lord Torrington inquired. "He is usually the first ready."

"I expect he wanted to make certain the correct horses are brought up from the stables," the duchess replied as she descended the stairs in what could only be described as a cloud of butter-yellow froth. She waved a parasol at Persys with a twinkle in her smile.

"I shall take great care of my parasol today, although I doubt you shall have need of it." She darted a narrow look at her nephew as she crossed the entry to stand beside Katherine and her solicitous husband.

"Don't be a nodcock, Christopher," the duchess said quietly. "Katherine is a healthy girl and will come to no harm on a simple outing. Women have been having babies for hundreds of years—it is nothing new."

"Ah, but this is my first, dear aunt. Therein lies the difference." He smiled bewitchingly at Katherine as he led her from the house and out to where an elegant landau awaited the ladies.

Charlotte and Persys were assisted to their mounts, to be followed by the gentlemen. At last the duke came around the corner of the house astride his favorite horse, Empire.

"We are all assembled like so many sheep, dear cousin," Charlotte called out gaily. "I suspect you are come to herd us to greener pastures."

"And what would you know about that, sister?" George asked, his tone cynical.

"I know a great deal about seeking greener pastures, George, and so should you," she retorted. She dashed ahead of the others to be followed by Ninian Hervey and Lord Burfield. George Russell gave Persys a look of dislike, then followed, leaving her to ride with the duke at midpoint between the carriage and the others. Lord Torrington remained close to the carriage to keep an eye on his precious wife.

"Do you know," the duchess said to Katherine once they were settled in the carriage and making their way down the avenue, "I read that Hippocrates insisted on boiled water and clean hands when he was attending patients. He also approved rest, quiet, and barley water. I trust you will see that your midwife does the same," she instructed, looking fondly at her newly acquired niece.

Aware of the affection and caring in that demand, Katherine wisely smiled and agreed. The two women, quite in charity with one another, proceeded to delve deeply into the requirements for the heir to the marquessate, for there was no doubt in Her Grace's mind that it would be a boy.

"How good it is that Katherine and your mother agree so nicely," Persys said, attempting a neutral subject.

"Mother is pleased with Christopher's choice in a wife." He urged his mount forward and encouraged Persys to canter as well. When they were separated from the others by space but not sight, he said, "And how was it, to see him again?"

Persys shrugged, not about to allow him to know of the foolish regard she'd held for Lord Torrington. "It was nice to see Katherine and her good husband. I have missed her."

"You deem him good?" He watched her face closely and Persys chose her words with caution.

"He seems a nice person and obviously cares for her deeply. I am very glad she married him—he is just right for her." Persys stole a glance at the duke to note he wore an exceedingly thoughtful expression. Although what in her prudently chosen words might provoke that, she didn't know.

"And she for him," he slowly replied. "Oddly enough, I had the idea that you were, shall we say, enamored of him at one time."

Persys gasped and bit her lip, suddenly realizing that the duke had seen far more than she believed or intended. Again choosing her words with prudence, she replied, "I believe there was a brief time when you might have said I was slightly infatuated with him—he is handsome and has many admirable qualities. That girlish fancy is fortunately behind me. I have far too much to occupy my days to give him much thought."

"And your nights? Do you dream of him?"

"That is far too intrusive a question, Your Grace, but to satisfy your unwelcome curiosity, my answer is no. Even my dreams are otherwise inhabited." She tilted her chin, giving him a frosty look from beneath the brim of a plain, but stylish hat.

He laughed and replied with careless grace, "Forgive me. I was being too prying and without the slightest right."

But Persys noted that he did not give a reason for his intrusion into her private life. She cantered on ahead of him, joining Charlotte and the others.

"Where are these ruins, Miss Russell?" Lord Burfield inquired, edging his horse close to the blond beauty.

Flashing her green eyes at him with great effectiveness, Charlotte gave an impudent grin and spurred her mare forward. "Follow me. They are most romantic and I would show you the tower, for it is the best of all."

Ninian Hervey was not to be left behind and he dashed after Charlotte immediately after Burfield.

George watched them for a moment, then turned to Persys. "So how do you go on now?"

Amazed that he could act as though she hadn't conked him over the head, thus rendering him unconscious and leaving him with a knot and a thundering headache, Persys said, "Quite well, thank you."

"Persys keeps busy at the school most days, George, as you might know," the duke said, silently joining the pair. "When Mrs. Woodhall comes there will be a cook and maid added to the staff. Applications are already being received. The house will be a hive of activity."

Persys gave the duke a startled look. It was the first she had heard of actual applications arriving at the house. Why had the duke kept that knowledge from her? She longed to tax him with the matter but would not give George the satisfaction of a confrontation. That odious creature already had too knowing an expression to please Persys.

"Come on, you laggards," Charlotte cried. "We are nearly there!"

Needing no other excuse, Persys dashed forward to again join the others, leaving the duke and a disgruntled George together.

The ruins were rather lovely, Persys decided when they turned a bend in the road to find them standing at drunken angles—leaning every which way, lichen-covered, the tumbled stones weathered to mottled hues. With Ninian Hervey's aid she dismounted, then strolled about the ruins with admittedly romantic eyes.

"You look pleased, Miss Timothy," Mr. Hervey said at last.

"Oh, I am. Would that I could write as does Miss Austen. What a marvelous setting for a novel—romantic ruins, lovely old grounds. I wonder who lived here so long ago?" She paused in a yet-standing archway, her hand caressing the sun-warmed stone.

"Some ancestors of mine, Miss Timothy," said the duke, his voice more friendly than it had been in days. "They were set upon by robbers; most all were left to die."

"They didn't, of course," Persys said, fascinated at this bit of history. "What happened?"

"Apparently a goodly number feigned death. Once the robbers left the burning buildings behind, my forebears decided to relocate the house rather than cope with the ruins. Thus you have the present house—much added to and altered through the years." He gave Persys a bemused look, and she wondered what was behind his expression.

"Now that is a romantic tale, you must confess, Mr. Hervey," Persys declared, taking her gaze away from the too compelling figure that leaned so casually against a stone wall. He had removed his hat and his black hair stood out against the warm grays of the stone. The blue of his eyes was no longer that cold hue she had first seen. Now they were a warm shade and most beguiling.

"Well," Charlotte cried, "I am off for that next rise. Does anyone want to go with me?"

"Take care, cousin," the duke said sharply.

"Pooh, nothing shall touch me," she snapped and dashed off with Lord Burfield in hot pursuit.

"Perhaps this was not the best idea," the duchess said quietly to her son. She and Katherine had been strolling through the ruins, trying to imagine what sorts of gardens might have existed then.

"Charlotte will do as she pleases," the duke said, not taking his gaze from the fast disappearing figure.

"Always has, always will," George added.

Persys picked up on some nuances but couldn't identify them, things being what they were. She left the group to walk away on her own, her thoughts returning to the applications to the school that had come. Why did he keep them a secret?

She came to a halt by an ancient rose, its vines climbing everywhere like a brambleberry. "You are angry with me," the duke said from behind her.

"Should I not be angry?" she quietly demanded.

"I have my reasons."

"Which you do not share," she pointed out reasonably.

"You enjoyed the book you read to us? *Pride and Prejudice?*"

She turned to face him at that, surprised at the sudden change of topic. What one had to do with the other, she couldn't imagine and said so.

"There is a gulf between the central characters—imagined of course. Do you feel as Miss Austen that lovers can overcome such a social chasm? Or must we be hidebound to conventions?"

"I suppose if true love exists most anything is possible," Persys said, looking away from the duke to the gently rolling hills dotted so untidily with trees and bushes. What would it be like to have a love like that? "There have been many instances of such."

"Your father was a baron. Your mother?" he casually inquired.

"Mama was the daughter of an earl, married beneath her for love I was told by Aunt Talbot. My aunt thought it foolish. I thought it romantic, but then I am ever the absurd one." Persys did not look at the duke, unwilling for him to see the film of tears she must blink from her eyes. To lose one's parents at such a young age, then have them belittled by the one to whom you were entrusted, was above all things detestable.

"I scarcely think it is absurd to admire your parents." He took her elbow to guide her along a rough path. "Come, see the view from the top of the hill. Quite splendid, I should say."

She walked at his side making comments on the plants, wild herbs his mother would appreciate, but avoiding anything more of a personal nature. In the distance Charlotte could be heard teasing and laughing, her voice high and fluting. The gentlemen provided a nice bass rumble as counterpoint.

At the crest of the gentle slope they could see across a broad valley. Below were spread out fields and hedges, winding roads and magnificent old trees as far as the eye could see. A farmer plowed his field, cattle meandered along a stream, and a lone carriage jogged along a dusty road.

"This blessed plot, this earth, this realm, this England," Persys whispered at last.

"This happy breed of men, this little world, this precious stone set in the silver sea," the duke inserted somewhat out of sequence. "Shakespeare was not only an excellent composer of plays, he loved his country."

"I can see why your ancestors found this a superb hill upon which to build. Pity they felt compelled to move—not that your present location isn't wonderful. It is. But this? I think you must come here often to enjoy such a view."

"I am pleased you find it so agreeable. Charlotte finds it a dead bore."

"Charlotte is to be pitied," Persys said, turning to glance up at him.

"My Persian woman, promise you will stay here no matter what happens?" His earnest plea caught her by surprise.

"At Eddington Park?" She ought to have said Russell House and couldn't think why she hadn't.

"Promise?"

"I do not lightly give my promise on anything, Your Grace." She considered what he had kept hidden from her, those applications for the school about which she was to know nothing.

"I would expect nothing less from you. But promise?"

"You are vague, but yes, I will promise," she finally replied, suspecting she might regret her words before long. "Although I cannot think why you insist upon a promise."

"I have my reasons."

"You have not told me of the applications that have come. Am I to be surprised with them or do you wait for Mrs. Woodhall?" Persys froze, waiting to hear what excuse he offered, if indeed he offered one. Dukes often felt that sort of thing unnecessary.

"I thought perhaps you would wish to go over them with her,

reap the benefit of her experience, if she proves to be worthy of the position." He draped a casual arm across her shoulder, quite as though he forgot who she was for the moment.

"If her qualifications are true, she is far more fit to run that school than I, truth be known."

"Indeed," he replied and Persys knew an awful, cold feeling in the pit of her stomach. What plans lurked in the back of his mind? What was his intent that he made her promise not to run away, for that is what he meant.

Charlotte called to them, urging them to return, as the rest wanted to go back to the house for nuncheon.

"Gladly," Persys said to herself, spinning around. She would have fallen when her foot caught in a hummock of grass had the duke not caught her at her waist, preventing a tumble in the long grasses.

"Thank you," she said politely, barely aloud.

His gaze caressed her face as if seeking to memorize every line, every change of expression. "Violet eyes. They have a blue cast today from your habit. You ought to wear violet always. I like it."

"Alas, I cannot please you in that. My wardrobe is adequate but not vast." She glanced to where his hand held her against him, then raised a questioning brow.

"Persys?"

"You know full well who I am, what I am. What do you want?" she softly demanded, wishing with all her heart that she might probe his mind as he did hers.

He kissed her then, a light claim of her lips, quickly—before the others might notice. But Persys was aware of his touch and she wondered at it. That made several now and all of them precious, if different one from another. Did he think so little of her that he could dally with her as a maid? Or was it customary in his group, his sort of people? She wished she knew.

She broke free of his encircling arm and ran down the grassy path until she reached the duchess and Katherine beneath the shade of a massive oak.

"You admired the view from the crest of the hill?" the duchess said, ignoring the pink bloom on Persys's cheeks.

"It is lovely, Your Grace."

If anyone wondered why it was that Persys was so quiet on the ride home no one said anything—at least no one but George.

He sidled up to Persys where she rode slightly ahead of the carriage and said, "Think you to marry the duke, you are daft, woman. He might give you a kiss on the sly, but nothing more. I saw you. Have you never wondered why he brought you here? Why he's allowing that school? Think on it."

Persys tilted her chin, longing to refute his words, wishing she could toss his words back in his face as Charlotte would. She was not Charlotte. Persys merely gave George a withering look and dropped back to the carriage for far more amenable company. She worried a trifle, however. She'd best avoid George unless in the company of others.

Following the ample nuncheon it commenced to rain. The men wandered off to the billiard room, while the women gathered in the cheer of the yellow drawing room, close to the fire and its warmth.

"Read to us, Persys," the duchess commanded. "What is next? *Mansfield Park*?"

"Oh, do," Katherine begged. "You read with such feeling."

And so Persys read until the men joined them later. Naturally they had to be told of the story and the plot was discussed over wine and biscuits. "This evening I think we shall join you. Persys reads with such drama it would be better than cards, I think," the duke suggested to his friends.

George grunted and looked as though he'd eaten a green apple.

Much later when she was abed, Persys thought back over the day, fastening her memory on the time spent at the crest of that splendid hill with the view to forever. What had he meant by that daring kiss when his own mother was almost within view? Anyone could have ambled up that hill to join them. True that kiss was swift and light, yet she felt there had been a possessive touch about it, a claiming. What it all meant she couldn't guess. Her sleep was troubled and she woke the next morning determined to get away from the house for a time if she could.

Nothing could have been easier. Katherine decided to laze in her room, not liking the misty, foggy rain. Charlotte wanted to read.

The duchess studied garden catalogs, planning spring blooms. Persys was able to slip from the house without anyone being the wiser.

The red umbrella offered not only protection against the inclement weather, but its bright color made the day seem not quite so bad. Indeed, she felt almost cheerful by the time she reached Russell House.

Upon inserting the key into the shiny brass lock, she entered the house to find someone had been there before her. Fires burned gently in the drawing and dining rooms as well as the entry hall. Upstairs, several bedrooms also had small fires, taking the chill away and giving her a feeling of welcome. Attired in apron and protective cap, it was not long before she was dusting and sorting the things that needed tending.

She was in one of the bedrooms warbling only slightly off-key when a noise at the doorway brought her about. George. Persys stiffened, recalling the red umbrella was in the entry drying off from its soaking. Nervously she looked about her, seeking something for protection. There was no fire in the hearth, nor any poker to use.

"We have a score to even, Persys." He took a step into the room, looking smugly complacent.

Deciding she had nothing to lose by trying to return to the lower floor, Persys bravely marched to the doorway, intent upon reaching the stairs. To her surprise he failed to grab her as she pushed by him.

"I do not know what you mean." She walked sedately, taking care with each step and clinging to the railing so he couldn't knock her down if that was his intent.

"Nice day out, in spite of the mist," George said, looking well-pleased. "Pity the other women all kept to their rooms. The chaps are involved in a rousing game of billiards and I know I won't be missed. Will you?"

Persys knew she wouldn't be missed by anyone, for she had said nothing as to where she intended to go. She had wanted to be alone, to think unhindered by the need for conversation.

"I cannot imagine why you think we have a score to settle, Mr.

Russell. You made an unwelcome advance and I protected myself. And I will do it again if it proves necessary."

"Think you so? Miss Timothy, you are alone and the duke will not spring to your aid this time." George paced about the entry hall much as he had the previous call, glancing at her from time to time like a cat circling its prey. "He is enjoying his game of billiards, not thinking of the soon-to-be schoolmistress. What shall you do when you must leave the comfort of the Great House for this?"

"Mrs. Woodhall will be here soon, not to mention a dozen young women we will teach. Sir, be gone with you. I have no patience with an idler who can think of nothing better to do than taunt a respectable young woman."

"Respectable? That's rich. A respectable woman does not permit kisses on the sly, not unless she has an engagement ring on her finger." George grinned at Persys, an evil look that frightened her likely as much as he intended.

Persys scanned the entry hall for the umbrella and discovered it missing. She frowned in dismay for she was certain it had been here before she went upstairs.

"Looking for something?" George taunted. "If it is the red umbrella, it now sits outside the door. I'll not have it creasing my skull again."

"You deserved every bit of it, you cowardly fool. Preying upon a woman so!" she snapped. Persys decided if she was beyond hope, she would wound with as many words as she could. As George said, there was little chance of someone coming to her rescue today and her only hope for a weapon was the umbrella now outside the door!

Then recalling the fire burning gently in the drawing room, she wondered if there might also be a poker close by. She edged her way to the door, then entered the drawing room to seek the warmth of the fire . . . and a poker, if possible.

She was most careful not to search for one, nor when she saw it, pick it up . . . just yet.

"Here, what are you doing? I am speaking to you," George complained. He followed her, looking more like a toad than a threat.

Yet Persys knew he was all of that and possibly more. Had she not been so nervous she would have laughed at him and his paltry complaint.

Suddenly he strode across the room, halting before her, touching her. "My patience is at an end, Miss Timothy. I will have you now."

"I am not a food you can have dished up to eat, Mr. Russell," Persys objected. Nausea gripped her and she fought not to panic and scream. She suspected George might well enjoy a good scream.

"No? I shall prove otherwise."

He grabbed Persys and she knew a distinct feeling of déjà vu, only this time she was not lucky. She couldn't reach the poker and George held her so tightly she could scarce move in any direction. His mouth descended upon hers with all the appeal of a slimy leech.

Then she recalled what Libby had taught her to do when confronted with a situation such as this, and she swiftly raised her knee.

George, let her go and shouted words Persys had never heard before and hoped not to hear again. He reeled and hopped and yelled at Persys, who was momentarily frozen at this display of manly outrage. The slam of the entrance door brought her head up sharply, her fears flooding back at once.

"I saw the red umbrella and thought to bring it in for you, lest it be blown away. I gather George is being George again," the duke said dryly while striding to her side. "Did he harm you in the slightest way? You are all right?"

"I shall be fine once away from him," Persys murmured, longing to throw herself against the duke and cry her eyes out. She was gathered close in his arms and contented herself with that comfort.

"Can you not stay out of trouble for a day?" the duke grumbled.

Mortified that he could possibly think she had invited such a scene, Persys tore herself from his comforting presence and ran from the house, pausing only to catch up the red umbrella.

Within Russell House, the duke strolled to where his distant cousin cringed in the best chair, one he thought would save him from further harm.

"Now hear me, George. You will be packed and out of my house come morning, not to return. I trust that is sufficiently clear—even for you!"

Chapter Thirteen

"*I* suppose you know that George left this morning?" Charlotte inquired, hostility ringing clear in her voice while she stared at Persys, quite as though it was all her fault. She put a plate of beef and salad on the table, then signaled the footman to pour her tea.

"He most likely has other interests? Other places to visit?" Persys suggested, feeling upset merely at the recollection of George's mouth against hers, however brief the contact might have been. What she might have done had the duke not appeared at that moment, she could not think. She hadn't asked him how he happened to ride by at that particular moment. He had mentioned seeing the red umbrella on the front steps and perhaps he had come to investigate. She was most thankful that he had. Her walk home had been one of serious reflection.

The duchess looked up from a perusal of her nuncheon plate to interrupt whatever Charlotte intended to say next. "My dear niece, I trust you are not going to blame anyone for George's behavior—other than George. He exceeded the bounds of propriety and let that be an end to the matter."

Charlotte gave her aunt a pouting glance, then subsided in her place. She kept studying Persys as though contemplating some evil she might like to do her. Persys shivered with the feeling of ill will.

"Are you cold, dear child?" the duchess asked, causing Persys to realize that she was more observant than she thought.

"Geese walking over my grave, as they say," Persys said lightly. "I rarely take a cold. Even a stroll in the rain yesterday did me not the least harm."

It had, in fact, been a salutary experience. She had calmed her nerves, reminded herself that the duke had a reason for her being here and that it remained a mystery. She hoped to learn what it was, but expected she'd find out one way or the other eventually.

She had managed to feel washed clean of George's touch by the time she reached the end of the walk. The duke had passed her on his horse, though she doubted he saw her, as far off the path as she'd been. Somehow, a tramp through the grass and shrubbery, dripping wet and splattering what dry spots of clothing she had left with water, suited her mood to a tee. Of course, she was soaked by the time she reached the house and Libby scolded her roundly. But Persys had felt more at peace with herself, and that was what counted.

"I think it is rather nice that Persys could come here when she needed a refuge. But then, the duke was always one to take in strays and lame creatures." Charlotte took a sip of tea, then cast Persys a sly glance. "I imagine Persys fits the stray category quite well."

"I rather thought it was a mutual thing, Charlotte," Persys said calmly, determined not to let the other rile her. "He wished for a young woman to be companion to his mother and I wanted a place to stay until I could make arrangements for the future."

The stare from Charlotte was so skeptical Persys nearly laughed aloud. But then, Charlotte would find it hard to believe that others didn't have her sly nature. Persys had tried to like her and simply could not. That early scene at the top of the stairs with Charlotte stuck in the back of her mind, refusing to be put aside. As well, she had not forgotten the duke's words to Charlotte the night of the party. He had brought Persys here for a reason that had nothing to do with her being a schoolmistress. He had refused to tell her what his designs regarding Persys might be—and rightly so, in her estimation. Charlotte had no business asking in the first place.

Then Persys added, "But doubtless you are right and he extended pity to one who badly needed a helping hand. I greatly admire a man so considerate and generous."

"Admire?" Charlotte whispered cunningly. "I suppose that does cover a wide range of passions."

"Charlotte, you will kindly mind your tongue unless you wish to join George," the duchess said, looking up from the seed catalog that had appeared to occupy her attention throughout nuncheon.

"Well, what I meant was—her *admiration* must be more like *gratitude*." Charlotte gave Persys a guileful look, thought a moment, then added, "I pity Persys having to turn to an occupation. How sad it is that she had to come down in the world. 'Tis a far cry from being a baron's daughter."

"I shall be a baron's daughter until the day I die. Perhaps I may even be something else. It is better than hanger-on, let me tell you," Persys said, her patience evaporated and anger at being twitted by someone like Charlotte overcoming all good sense and manners.

"Bravo, Miss Timothy!" Ninian Hervey said from the doorway. "Pity you are not able to remind Charlotte of that from time to time."

"*You* dare speak?" Charlotte stormed, ignoring the duchess completely. "I would wager you are the champion hanger-on of all time!"

"But *I* am always welcome," he replied with deadly quiet. He gave Charlotte a narrow look, then offered an arm to Persys, who had intended to slip from the room while the battle raged. "I should like to join you if I may," he said with a glance back at Charlotte, as though daring her to utter another acid-dripped word.

"Thank you," Persys said with a sigh. She walked silently at Ninian's side until they reached the door to the yellow drawing room. "Why do you imagine she dislikes me so much?" Persys asked thoughtfully. "I cannot see that I present her the slightest obstacle to anything she wishes."

"Difficult to say. I know that she dislikes me—I see through her," Ninian replied with equal consideration. "You are quite lovely—those violet eyes are unusual and compellingly attractive. Beyond those damning qualities you seem to have caught the eye of the man Charlotte would like to claim for herself."

"He only asked me here out of pity. His mother could have coped without me," Persys protested, ignoring the remark about her violet eyes. She had lived with those too long to be the least impressed with them.

If Ninian had his own views as to the reason for her presence at Eddington Park, he didn't voice them. "You enjoyed your time with the duchess?" They entered the drawing room, winding their way among the furniture that populated the room to reach the tall double doors on the far side.

Persys looked about her, at the basket holding the ever-present collection of nursery catalogs, the notebook the duchess used for her herbal remedies, the stack of the latest novels the duke had ordered from Hatchards. "Yes, indeed. She is a fascinating woman. A very kind one, as well."

Ninian guided her through the room and out to the terrace that overlooked the narrow garden to either side with the long pool immediately before them and down several steps. Three fountains shot thin sprays of water arching many feet into the air and birds darted in and out of the droplets. Neatly trimmed topiary stood sentinel at each corner of the pool, while boxwood marched around the perimeter of the protected enclosure.

Persys left Ninian's side, not wishing him to think she wanted to invite his interest. Walking down the shallow steps to the level of the pool, she knelt to dip her fingers in the water. "It is cool. How inviting it must be on a steamy day."

"When is this teacher to arrive?" Ninian inquired, targeting the matter that had been lurking in Persys's mind all morning.

"Since she appeared quite eager to have a job, I fancy she should come at all speed," Persys said. She rose, shaking drops of water from her fingers, then gazed across the lovely pond with pleasure tinged with regret that she must soon move away from this house, not to mention distance herself from the owner. "The instructions I sent suggested she avail herself of a post chaise, which means speedy transport, does it not?" Persys turned to find the duke had joined them. She dipped a polite curtsy, then gave the duke a hesitant look. "Your Grace?"

"Indeed, she could come anytime." Turning to his good friend, he said, "Ninian, there is something I want to show you. Come with me now, will you?" The two men bowed politely to Persys, then commenced upon whatever topic interested the duke without delay.

Persys watched as the two men strolled off on the graveled walk around the large pond. The fountain's spray made it impossible to hear what was said, but it must have been amusing for Ninian Hervey laughed. It was a charming laugh and she decided had she not given her heart to the duke that Ninian Hervey would be a very nice partner.

"So come down in the world, Miss Timothy. You had best become accustomed to men ignoring you as though you did not exist," Charlotte said, a hint of waspishness in her voice. She leaned against a pillar, her gaze spiteful.

"Oddly enough I do have a dowry, although a modest one," Persys was stung to say in reply, then scolded herself for being stupid and permitting Charlotte to needle her.

"Well, it certainly would not catch you a duke, my dear," Charlotte said, allowing a chuckle. "Perhaps you might find an agreeable tutor, or even dare hope for the local squire. I hear he is hanging out for a third wife to look after his brood of children. Indeed, Miss Timothy, the squire would suit you quite well, I think."

"When I left London for Eddington Park the last thing on my mind was attracting the duke or anyone else—be it tutor or squire," Persys declared with perfect truth. "And I doubt if a ready-made family is to my liking, squire or not. My father would never have permitted it."

"And now?" Charlotte sniped, sauntering down the steps to confront Persys. "Your father is no longer here to help you, my dear. *You* had best look to your future. Or do you wish to teach school forever? Know that when I reside here you will not remain!" Charlotte stood, smiling at Persys in so abominable a way that she longed to push her into the pool. That would never do, Persys decided with real regret. But oh, she was tempted.

"Persys, dearest cousin," Katherine caroled, sounding as though she had been separated from Persys for a year instead of a day. "I am so pleased the sun has decided to shine. You promised to take a gentle stroll with me when it did. I would see the topiary garden as well as the herb garden. Her Grace said she would meet us there later." Katherine walked onto the terrace twirling a pretty blue pagoda parasol of the very latest design. The fringe swayed with each step and Katherine looked to be an expert at manipulating it. She peered out from beneath its shade with a most innocent visage, offering a white parasol to Persys while totally ignoring Charlotte, quite as though she didn't stand there looking like an ogress in all her anger.

Thankful to once again escape from Charlotte's nasty tongue, Persys accepted the parasol and offered her cousin a helping hand down the short flight of steps.

"Silly me, I must take such care, Christopher says. As though a stroll through the gardens would tax me beyond belief." She giggled quite as she had when a child.

It was surprising how much ground could be covered in spite of appearing to stroll when one wanted to hurry.

"Thank you, Katherine," Persys murmured, then glanced behind to make sure Charlotte hadn't taken a notion to follow them. "I cannot like that woman, no matter how hard I try. For a time it appeared she wanted to be friends. Then Mr. Russell was compelled to leave and that ended any attempt at friendship, warm or otherwise."

"Darling, she is jealous of you. You are younger, and have lovely skin and perfect posture. Your hair is like spun silk and as for your eyes, well—ordinary green eyes cannot compare. Actually green is so appropriate for her, for she is stuffed full of envy," Katherine concluded in a whisper and a giggle.

"My hair is mouse-colored and violet eyes are freakish," Persys said with eyes agleam. "My back is rigid, as are my morals, and I have a sharp tongue," she declared. "And even though I have a dowry, however modest, I am assured by Charlotte that it is *not* enough to tempt the duke or any other gentleman above the rank of baron, and perhaps not a baron. I might"—and Persys held up a hand—"be so fortunate as to attract a tutor or possibly the squire who is looking for a third wife to care for his large brood of children. Do you think I could perhaps manage a baronet?"

"Silly goose," Katherine said, tucking her arms close to Persys, and pausing to examine several of the splendid topiary while they made their planned turn around the gardens. "You are worthy of a prince at the very least. Since our only prince is not worth having, we shall have to find you someone who is."

Persys chuckled as intended and settled into a comfortable coze with the cousin she had missed more than she realized.

By the time the two had reached the herb garden they were as silly as a pair of schoolgirls, giggling and laughing.

The duchess, looking up from her bed of bee balm to see what the noise was about, smiled at the closeness of the pair. How easy it would have been for Persys to be jealous of her lovely cousin and her advantageous marriage.

"It sounds as though you two enjoy each other very much," the duchess observed.

"I hope that when there is a school break Persys will come to stay with me for a time," Katherine said. "By then the baby ought to be here and I would deem it a great favor if she would be godmother to him."

"You are so certain it is a boy?" the duchess asked, her eyes crinkling with amusement.

"I am now. Christopher has decreed it. That child dare not be a girl," Katherine soberly pronounced.

"Unless it might be twins," Persys added with a touch of mischief.

"Mercy!" Katherine cried, pretending to reel from the shock of the very thought.

"Do twins run in the family?" the duchess asked Persys, a considering look in her eyes.

"Indeed. There are ever so many pairs scattered about the family tree. I suspect it is time for twins to appear in our generation. Think about it, Katherine," she said with an infectious giggle.

Any nonsense Katherine might have replied was prevented by the arrival of a footman who requested Persys to follow him. "Mrs. Woodhall has come, miss."

Persys tossed an apprehensive look at her cousin, then followed the stout footman inside the house. Katherine could enjoy an enlightening discussion on the various herbs and their properties. It was time for Persys to assume her duties.

Standing in the magnificent entry hall and looking not the least intimidated by the splendor, stood a lady of medium height, garbed neatly and appropriately in sensible dark blue. She turned when she heard Persys crossing the marble and curtsied politely. A face that looked to place its owner in her late thirties peered from beneath a very proper straw bonnet and her plump form gave Persys an instant impression of compassion and comfort.

"Welcome," Persys said, extending her hands in a warm greeting. "Come with me, I would discuss a few matters with you before taking you to see Russell House, where the school is to be held. I hope you shall like it."

Mrs. Woodhall possessed a pleasing voice and Persys thought she detected a country sound to it. Certainly, while she revealed excellent knowledge of all required she was not pretentious or arrogant in the least.

The subsequent interview proved to be most agreeable. Persys couldn't imagine a more capable person, or a more likable one.

"You say you are a baronet's daughter, Mrs. Woodhall? And I am a baron's daughter. How good that we can put our society training to use this way."

"Miss Timothy, perhaps you will do the honors?" the duke said as he entered the library where Persys had been instructed to handle the interview. His eyes had a question in them and Persys rightly guessed he wanted some manner of signal from her as to the outcome of the meeting. She gave him a barely perceptible nod. Mrs. Woodhall seemed all they had hoped she would prove.

"With great pleasure, Your Grace." Persys watched as the duke charmed Mrs. Woodhall right out of her sensible bonnet. Within moments she was smiling shyly and accepted the offer of tea with just the right amount of hesitancy.

"I have instructed someone to remove your trunk and valise to Russell House. Miss Timothy will go down with you to show you about the place and help you settle in." He turned to Persys, adding, "I imagine you will want to join Mrs. Woodhall on the morrow?"

Just like that. She would be gone tomorrow. There would be no more cheerful dinners, or evenings during which she would read from Miss Austen. "Indeed, Your Grace. If I could have the applications from you, I can go over them with Mrs. Woodhall." If there was a hint of questioning in her voice it was because she had yet to see those dratted items. She might love the man but he could be infuriating at times.

He strode around his desk and searched through a drawer while Persys poured the tea brought in by Portman. Mrs. Woodhall had accepted a teacup and a biscuit when he came up with a clutch of papers in hand.

"Here they are." He came back to where the two women were seated and placed the untidy stack on the table by Persys.

"I had not realized there were so many," she said, awestruck at the thickness of that stack.

"It is just as well I reserved them, is it not?" he said with a smile. "I feared you would take one look and run."

Persys frowned, not replying to his attempt at a touch of humor. Protecting her sensibilities had not entered her mind when she debated as to why he kept the applications from her.

"The local squire has applied to have his two eldest girls in your tutorage. I understand he is on the lookout for a third wife. Take care there, both of you," he said, eyes twinkling.

At this, Persys did chuckle. "Indeed, so Charlotte informed me. I believe he has a sizable brood of children who would be the better for a mother?"

"Do not even think of it," the duke said quietly.

Persys set her teacup down with a clink and rose from her chair, a signal to Mrs. Woodhall that it was time to depart.

Portman must have sent for Libby, for she was in the hall with a shawl for Persys. "Shall I pack, miss?"

"Indeed, Libby. Pack everything. I shan't be returning here."

It would have been difficult enough to leave without the realization that it was forever. Now, Persys felt as though she possessed leaden feet. Had Charlotte really insisted that she intended to reign in this house? Somehow, Persys doubted it, but stranger things had happened. In that event, nothing could persuade her back, not even for an afternoon call.

There was a small gig at the door, suitable for the use of a schoolmistress. The chestnut that served to draw it was most appropriate. Someone had the entire arrangement most carefully calculated.

"This carriage is to be kept for your use—both of you," the duke added with a look at Persys. "I imagine you will want to venture forth to the village upon occasion for little things. Mother insists that foodstuffs will be sent down from the House. Your cook has settled in, and with Libby and another maid you ought to do well enough for the time being."

"We appreciate the arrangements, Your Grace," Persys said, wishing she might have thought of something else to say. She offered her hand in farewell to be brought up short by the look of amusement in his eyes. He thought it was humorous that she was departing? She longed to crown him with the red umbrella.

"You will return here this evening, remember? We shan't be so very far apart that we need to say farewell."

He didn't know the half of it, Persys thought grimly. She whirled about to enter the gig with a decided snap to her movements. It took firm resolution not to look back at him or the house.

"What a lovely area, beautiful grounds, and such a house," Mrs. Woodhall said while they jogged along down the avenue, all admiration for the scenery.

"The gardens are incredible. I feel sure the duchess will not mind if I show them to you when we have a free moment."

Persys guided the sedate chestnut—just the sort of animal deemed proper for two elderly ladies—up before Russell House. Neatly pulling to a halt, she sat in the gig while awaiting a reaction from her new partner.

"I am impressed. I cannot help but think any parent would be as well. You are fortunate to be given such an agreeable building for the school."

Persys smiled. It would go well, she felt it in her bones. They entered the house and Mrs. Woodhall proved ecstatic over the furnishings and in particular the spinet.

Persys explained and it was while she talked with her new schoolmistress that the other paused to urge, "Call me Laura, please. May I call you Persys? Somehow I feel as though our working together is going to be a good thing."

"I feel the same," Persys agreed, then took Laura up to see her room, expressing hope that all was agreeable.

"More than agreeable. Wonderful! I have been caring for an elderly aunt who had driven me nearly mad with her demands. A dozen girls will be nothing, especially with a haven like this for my own."

They went through each room, discussing the few items that would add to the pleasure of the residents.

"You have done remarkably well, you know," Laura remarked as they returned to the ground floor from the bedrooms. "How did you know what to acquire?"

"Recalling what was in my room when at school and what I had wished to have," Persys replied with a grin.

They met Cook and the maid, inappropriately named Rose. With a sallow skin and sad brown eyes, the girl looked like anything but a rose.

"Your dinner will be served up when you wish, ma'am," the cook informed Laura.

They agreed on a time, then the two schoolteachers-to-be walked back to the entry.

"I shall join you sometime tomorrow," Persys said, stifling a pang that she would be so removed from the one she loved. "If you like, you could go through that folder of applications to see what we have in store for us. I fancy we must accept them all, for they are children the duchess had directed to us."

"I want to learn the names and as much as I can about their backgrounds," Laura replied sensibly. "And I shall remember to avoid the squire when he brings his daughters around." Her eyes gleamed with impishness and Persys knew then that she and Laura would rub along well together.

The gig had been taken away to the rear where a small stable stood. Apparently there was a groom or man of all work around the place and Persys thought that a very good thing, what with three women alone in the house.

Rather than summon the gig once more, she elected to walk

back to the house. The exercise would do her good, clear her mind, and allow her to come to terms with her future.

Her reflections didn't last long, however.

"Miss Timothy," Ninian Hervey called as he approached in his curricle. "Allow me to take you back to the house."

There was such a hopeful look on his face that Persys was only too glad to agree. "How nice. I had not wanted to bother the Russell House groom for the gig, so I intended to walk."

"And are you a great walker?" Mr. Hervey inquired with an admiring look.

"I suppose I am, for I have done quite a bit of it since I came here. One of my school friends lived in the Lake District and I envied her the scenery she must often see from her home and her walks."

"Then you must go there someday. I understand a good many couples travel there for wedding trips. They stay at The Swan and enjoy lengthy walks in the hills."

"It sounds delightful," Persys said with a smile. What a nice man he was, and he didn't like Charlotte, either.

When they reached the house they met the duke striding up to greet them. "Well, Persys, and how did Mrs. Woodhall like Russell House and what you had done so far?"

"She was most pleased and had but a few suggestions."

"Come with me now, for I would hear them," the duke insisted with that lord-of-the-manner attitude Persys thought a shade pompous.

She turned to give Mr. Hervey a rueful look and a faint shrug of her shoulders. "Thank you. I appreciated the little drive with you, sir." She curtsied and turned to enter the house with the duke.

"Not nearly as much as he did," the duke murmured in a quiet aside that Persys only dimly heard.

"*That* is a lot of nonsense," Persys said almost as quietly.

Anything else that might have been said—or learned—was cut short by the duchess who came into the hall at that moment. When she caught sight of Persys she demanded to know all the details of the meeting with Mrs. Woodhall and what Persys thought of the woman. This took a great deal of time as the duchess had any number of questions. In the back of her mind Persys mulled over the odd remark the duke had made as they entered the house. Surely he didn't think that Ninian Hervey had an interest in her? Never!

Dinner seemed a festive affair. Charlotte insisted that it was scarcely necessary to fete Persys, since she wasn't going far away. "She will be teaching school and I daresay we will see her from time to time with her students."

Persys thought it was highly unlikely that Charlotte would so much as glance her way, but made no comment.

"Come into the drawing room at once," the duchess commanded at the conclusion of dinner. "You men can have a glass of port while Persys finishes reading *Mansfield Park* to us. We will not be favored with her excellent interpretations once she leaves the house. She will be far too busy."

Thus it was that her last evening at the Great House was spent in dramatizing *Mansfield Park* to the best of her ability to a delightfully appreciative audience—with the exception of Charlotte, who muttered from time to time until called to account by the duchess.

"We shall miss you very much, Miss Timothy," Ninian Hervey said to Persys as she was about to go to her room after the reading was done.

She thanked him, but noted that the duke said not a word.

Chapter Fourteen

Within a few days it seemed to Persys that her time at the great house had been no more than a dream. Her removal from there had been accomplished with remarkable speed. Of Charlotte she had seen nothing prior to departure. Katherine had offered a scented cheek for a kiss and promised to visit one day before they left. The duchess had quietly informed Persys that she would see her often, possessing an enormous interest in the school, not to mention a curiosity as to how the two women would manage their venture.

Persys quickly fell into a new rhythm in her new abode. Her small chamber at Russell House was now home to her and Laura was the best of companions.

"You have no idea how pleasant it is to join you for breakfast and not have to listen to my aunt's carping," Laura said, unconsciously echoing Persys's sentiments.

"Indeed, I admit I do not miss Charlotte's everlasting quibbling. I felt the target of a thousand tiny darts—all poison tipped."

"I have met people like that," Laura mused over her teacup. She set her cup down with a clink, then pushed her chair from the table. "I suggest we go over the applications and make our replies."

It did not take long to realize they must accept every application that had been sent to the duke, then given to them. Laura offered to write the letters and Persys decided she would go over her list of things they still required.

The house was very still. The cook was occupied in the kitchen, a small wing jutting from the back of the house. The maid might be the plainest woman Persys had ever seen, but she was frightfully efficient, whisking through the bedrooms and dusting with astounding speed.

Persys thought to consult her regarding the needed items when the knocker on the door was given a resounding thwack.

Rose scurried to open the fine oak door to reveal the group from the main house. Charlotte, Ninian Hervey, Lord Burfield, Katherine and her husband, the duke and his mother all clustered before the house, with the duchess pointing out the finer details of the exterior to Katherine.

Laura left the desk in the little room they had decided would make a good office to join Persys in greeting their first guests.

"How lovely to see you all," Persys exclaimed with delight. Yet she felt very apart from them all now, almost a stranger. After all, she was in another world—the world of those who had a living to earn, the employed.

"I trust we have not come at a bad time. Everyone" and the duke looked at his mother with that word—"wanted to see what you have done with the house, how you get along."

Laura curtsied, then spoke quietly to Rose, who promptly bustled off toward the kitchen.

Although Laura joined the group, she remained quiet, allowing Persys to serve as guide to the others through the house, pointing out what had been altered and added, the attic finds as well as the pieces made by the estate carpenters. They concluded the modest tour in the little office. The gentlemen peeked inside, then retreated to the entry hall to discuss the merits of a local horse Ninian Hervey had seen offered for sale.

The women investigated the various aspects of the office, a floor-to-ceiling bookcase the carpenter had made for Persys, the elegant little desk from the main house attics, and the lovely old carpet—a few moth holes mended and well concealed beneath the desk. A new Argand lamp sat next to a very old and somewhat battered inkstand of ornate design that Persys had found in the attic and instantly loved.

While Katherine and Persys recalled happy days at their school, the duchess inspected the few books on the shelves, and Charlotte poked around at one thing or another. Suddenly she gave a great gasp of horror.

"Oh, dear Persys, I am so sorry! I was merely admiring the unusual inkstand on the desk and somehow it tipped over. I fear it has stained all those letters! How clumsy of me." Charlotte appeared remorseful but Persys doubted if she was sincere. For one thing, it had been evident that her animosity toward Persys had not changed one whit—so why regret damage? Persys had noted the hostile glances and barbed comments while they toured the house, now school. Charlotte had not one kind thing to say while inspecting the rooms.

Laura rushed to the desk at once, mopping up the spilled ink with the dust cloth Rose had left behind before sent off on her errand.

"What was on the desk?" the duchess asked quietly.

Persys held up several letters splotched with dark brown ink, nearly all writing obliterated. "The applications! I cannot think how we can read one of these now!" She turned to Charlotte and said, "Had you wished to cause trouble for us, I cannot imagine a better way."

"Charlotte, how could you be so awkward?" the duchess demanded, her ire with her husband's niece very clear. "You had no business poking about that desk in the first place."

"What happened in here? It sounds like bedlam," the duke inquired as he stood in the entryway. Had Charlotte wished to escape, he effectively blocked her way.

"Your cousin Charlotte spilled ink over the application letters. I do not know what Persys and Mrs. Woodhall will do now," the duchess said with an exceedingly dark look at Charlotte.

"How fortunate for us that the first thing I did was to enter each girl's name, the parents as well, plus their direction into our book," Laura said clearly into the beginning conflict. With a glance at Charlotte she removed a ledger bound in dark brown leather from a side drawer to show the duke, rightly assuming he would be in charge of any confrontation.

"Ah, yes, I had that sent down, thinking it might prove useful," the duke interjected into the chatter around him. He exchanged a glance with Mrs. Woodhall, then turned to a subdued Charlotte.

"I believe tea is prepared for us in the drawing room, Persys?" He gave her a significant look, then escorted Charlotte from the room, leaving the others to straggle behind.

"How clever of you, Mrs. Woodhall," Katherine said when she had a chance to speak quietly with her.

"I had no notion there would be a disaster, merely that the ledger was in the desk and it seemed a sensible thing to do." She smiled shyly at Katherine. "I cannot claim so wonderful a thing as foreknowledge."

"I think you will prove a good partner for Persys," Katherine answered thoughtfully, before going off to talk with her husband.

Persys had paused near the drawing room door, close enough so she happened to overhear a few words exchanged between the duke and his beautiful young cousin.

"She thinks that because she is cousin to the Marchioness of Torrington she can claim special privileges, as though that adds to her consequence," Charlotte complained in the manner of one much put upon.

"In the view of some people, it does," the duke replied absently. "I believe, dear cousin, that it is time you followed George."

Not wanting to hear another word, Persys drifted across the room to sit close to Laura on the sofa near the fireplace. Opposite her the duchess perched with Katherine coming to join her at once.

Persys poured tea and dispensed tiny ratafia biscuits while wondering what went on in the entry hall. Did Charlotte plead prettily to remain at Eddington Park? Did she cast herself at the duke, batting long-fringed lashes over those remarkable green eyes while beseeching him to let her stay?

The duchess placed an empty cup on its saucer, then looked about her. "I trust we shall all be happier once Charlotte has gone."

"She is leaving?" Katherine wondered aloud. "I had not heard. It *was* an accident, was it not?" Katherine searched the duchess's face with concerned eyes.

"I could not prove anything, having had my back turned at the moment. Regardless, she has overstayed her welcome. Perhaps her temper will improve when she joins her brother?"

When the duke and Charlotte entered the room not a word was said about the incident in the little office. Ninian Hervey strolled over to take a somewhat protective stance behind Persys, which Charlotte immediately noticed.

"Well, Mr. Hervey, coming to the rescue so quickly? I promise I shan't harm a hair of your ewe lamb."

"Miss Timothy is not what you think, Charlotte. But then, you make a practice of jumping to erroneous conclusions."

Charlotte sauntered across the room to stare out the window at the avenue that passed Russell House and led to the main house one mile hence. "What if I do not choose to leave, dear cousin? It is not convenient to join George at the moment. He has gone to the races at Newmarket. It is not a place I wish to visit."

"Then I suggest you return to your home," the duchess interposed. "Your aunt will doubtless welcome you."

That Charlotte was angry at being so summarily dismissed was obvious. However, there was not a thing she could do to alter the situation; she had caused it all on her own.

"Once the letters are ready, bring them up to the house and I shall frank them for you, Persys," the duke said as the group prepared to leave after the uneasy call.

Persys glanced at Laura and receiving a nod from her, agreed.

"When will the students arrive?" Katherine wanted to know as she settled in the landau, tended by her solicitous husband.

"We hoped to begin classes in two or three weeks. There is much to accomplish before we can send off a clutch of schoolroom misses to a Season in London."

"Do teach them that it is acceptable to utter something besides giggles and inanities while at a ball or party," Lord Burfield exclaimed. "I weary so of the talk of gowns and gossip."

"We shall do our best," Laura said, speaking out for the first time.

"I believe I shall have a musical evening soon. There ought to be enough talent around these parts to make it tolerable. Do join us, Persys and Mrs. Woodhall. I shall let you know the date," the duchess said before ordering the driver to return to the main house.

The two women watched their guests drive off up the avenue until they were lost to view.

"What a blessing you copied all those names and addresses, Laura," Persys said with relief when they reentered the house. She shut the door with a thud, leaning against it for a moment before crossing the room to survey the desk in the little office.

"I only hope that the ink did no great damage to the desk. Why does she hate you so?" Laura wondered.

"I do not have the vaguest idea, unless she somehow believes the duke to have an interest in me. She always maintained that she would marry him and reign at the house. I would not get any invitations to musicals or anything else were she installed there."

"I did not receive the impression that the duke was even mildly interested in his cousin. She had better train her gaze elsewhere, unless I very much miss my guess."

"The duke must marry one of these days. I am certain he knows what is expected of him, that he must do his duty to his family and lineage," Persys said while gathering up the ink-stained papers. "What a dreadful mess this is." She examined each sheet, tossing the ones beyond hope into the fireplace to be burned later.

Persys continued, "Do you know that while I was yet at the house I read two novels to the duchess and a few others. One was *Pride and Prejudice* and the other was *Mansfield Park*. In both of those stories the fathers ended up blaming themselves for much of the ills their children perpetrated. While Charlotte's parents neglected her sadly, from all I have learned, I believe *she* must bear some responsibility on her own shoulders. One does not have to become a victim of circumstances, does one?"

Laura paused in scrubbing the desk in hopes of removing most of the ink and looked at Persys. "I think it is possible to rise above controlling factors. I believe you have and so have I. I might have sunk into a decline when my husband died so shortly after we were wed. I decided I was too young to die and so I proceeded to make my way in the world. Is that much as you did? When your aunt pushed you out?"

"It was odd, for the very day I was told to leave, the duke was at the wedding. The following day I met him in the park and he suggested I attend his mother until her knee healed." At Laura's quizzical look, Persys added, "She had tripped on a stone while in the garden. She is an avid gardener."

"One does not think of a duchess as an avid gardener, does one?" Laura smiled, then stood back to gauge her efforts. "Well, we can only hope that we can locate a substantial blotter. Otherwise, the carpenter will have to refinish the top of this desk and at the moment we have need of it."

They completed rearranging the office to their liking, then left, passing through the entryway when the knocker was again given a thwack.

"A man," Laura surmised, standing still, a hand on Persys's arm, as Rose went to answer the door. "Only a man makes so forceful a statement when he desires to enter a house."

Rose spun around to say softly, " 'Tis the squire, ma'am."

"Show him to the drawing room," Laura urged quietly. "Persys, I best scrub the ink from my hands. You entertain the squire until I return. I suspect it is well to present a united front, as it were."

So Persys stepped forward to greet the rotund and graying squire when he entered the house. She was most aware he looked her over from top to toe and gave thanks for her suitable attire.

In Katherine's eyes, Persys must have looked a dowd. To the squire, she hoped she looked fit to teach his daughters.

"Miss Timothy?" the squire said, looking out from beneath heavy, dark brows. Disapproving brows, Persys thought.

"Indeed, Squire Mallet. Mrs. Woodhall will be with us directly. Will you not sit down and have a glass of wine? The duke sent down a small but nice selection for us to offer parents when they come," Persys said with resourcefulness. She led the squire to one of the sofas while wondering precisely why the man was here. They'd not had time to accept or reject his application.

"I've come about the girls, you see," he said while seating himself, arranging his coat as though he wasn't quite certain what to do or say.

Knowing Rose would be assisting Laura, Persys poured a glass of canary for the squire, then offered it to him before taking a place on the opposite sofa.

"We shall accept them in the school, you may be sure," Persys said, settling uneasily.

"Thing of it is, they needs come here at once. The younger ones are invited to my sister's place and the older girls—Mary and Jane—cannot be left alone with naught but the housekeeper."

Laura had entered at his last words to join Persys on the sofa, signaling the squire not to rise. "I do not see why they should stay at home. By all means, bring them over," Laura said kindly. "You are going away for some time?" she gently inquired. In short order, and scarcely aware of it, the squire had emptied not only his glass of canary but his budget of all his intentions. He planned a trip to Newmarket, then on to London to visit a brother with the ambition of persuading his brother's wife to launch the girls on a modest Season. The squire was wealthy and he made it plain both girls had generous dowries.

"Well, that is that," Laura said when he concluded his tale. "Bring them here whenever you please. We will be ready for them."

The squire was not anxious to depart and lingered as long as he dared, enjoying the company of two charming and single women.

At last Laura rose, which meant he must as well, and said, "We will not detain you, sir. You have shared your wisdom and company with us to our advantage, but it would be improper for us to think of preventing you from rejoining your children."

He looked a trifle disgruntled, but bid them both a polite goodbye. The house fell into utter silence until Persys began to giggle, followed by Laura.

"Oh, dear, I hope I shan't go into whoops when he comes again. Will we likely face such a parent another time, do you think?" Laura asked when able to speak.

"Well, the rest are safely married. I do believe he studied you with more than expected interest, Laura," Persys said with glee.

"But *I* am only the daughter of a baronet. *You* are the daughter of a baron, thus far more worthy of being Mrs. Squire Mallet number three."

At last their laughter subsided and they went about the rest of their day without hindrance.

The next morning found Ninian Hervey on the doorstep and Persys wondered what had brought him out at such an early hour.

He shook off a few drops of mist from his hat, then set it on the hall table, a gesture meant to let her know he intended to spend some time with them. "Charlotte has gone. Left as early as did George, as though the duchess had given orders to be gone with no delay tolerated. Didn't think Charlotte had it in her to meekly obey. I cannot deny I am happy to see her departed. Shocking temper!"

"Perhaps she had an unhappy childhood, sir?" Persys suggested. "Come join me in a stroll in the garden," she offered, thinking it likely he had come to see her and not Laura. Judging by the smile on his face, she was correct. She picked up an umbrella as protection against the slight mist while he retrieved his hat.

"Foxglove and lupine, cranes-bill geraniums and campanula, what a pretty garden the duchess designed," Persys said. "It is amazing what can be done with transplanting and not a one of them droops nor dies." She bent over to examine a clump of lady's mantle with blooms that glowed a peculiar greenish-yellow.

"Miss Timothy—" Mr. Hervey began only to be forestalled with Persys pointing out the herb bed Her Grace had ordered planted.

"We have everything from feverfew to yarrow. There are some herbs for healing, some for dyeing, and some for flavoring foods. She is very comprehensive in her planning."

"I am aware of Her Grace's propensity for herbs. I want to discuss something else entirely."

"Not gardens?" Persys said with a twinkle in her eyes.

"Not gardens," he agreed with a wry smile. "Have you no inkling what is in my mind?"

"None, sir," Persys said, confused.

"It is too soon to hope you might admire me, even a little, but I should like to pay my addresses, as they say."

"Pay your . . ." Persys sank down on a blessedly convenient bench to contemplate his words. While a tempting offer to most young women who would appreciate a nice-looking and respectable gentleman, it held no appeal for Persys.

"I see my words surprise you," he added dryly. "I had hoped you had possibly begun to nurture an interest in my humble self. Is your regard elsewhere?"

"Regardless of my favor possibly being elsewhere, I am truly impressed with your intentions, Mr. Hervey. Thank you, for it is lovely to know the esteem of such a distinguished and kind gentleman. I decline and desire not to receive your addresses, sir, as you may anticipate I must." Persys looked at her lap, where her fingers nervously pleated her skirt.

"I see. Can't say I'm surprised." He sighed and sat down beside her, quite as dejected as one might expect. He cleared his throat, then said, "The duchess sent me to tell you that she has decided to hold her musicale a week Friday. Both you and Mrs. Woodhall are invited."

"That presents a problem as at least two of the students will be here by then." At his questioning look, she added, "The squire's daughters, Mary and Jane. He does not wish to leave them with the housekeeper and the younger children are off elsewhere while he jaunts to Newmarket and London."

Moggy chose to explore the garden where Persys sat at that moment. He stared up at Ninian Hervey, then jumped up at Persys where he curled in her lap.

Persys stroked the cat, cuddling it against her while she sought the right words. At last she said, "I am sorry, Mr. Hervey. I like you very well, just not enough to consider—"

"Please, spare my blushes," Ninian said lightly.

"Kindly tell the duchess I shall discuss what might be done in regard to the musicale, will you?" Persys clutched Moggy to her and got up from the bench, the umbrella forgotten in her confusion.

Taking this as a cue for his departure Ninian rose, then walked at her side to the front door. Here he bowed over her hand, gave her a rueful smile, then mounted his horse and rode toward the main house.

"You had a caller, I perceive," Laura said, when Persys entered the house, not questioning but looking as though she would listen if Persys wished to talk.

"Mr. Hervey brought us a message. It seems Her Grace will hold the musical evening a week Friday. That presents a complication as the Mallet girls will be here by then and I cannot ask the duchess to bring them along. However, I told Mr. Hervey the circumstances and doubtless he will convey them to the duchess. Should it be deemed acceptable for the girls to come, we can all attend."

"I see. That took some time to relay," Laura said, wisely not saying anything more.

"I was caught by surprise," Persys admitted quietly. "It seems Mr. Hervey wished to pay his addresses to me. I told him it would not do," she concluded with a sad smile.

"Not because of the school?"

"No. The school has nothing to do with my decision. Now, where were we before I was interrupted?"

The subject was not mentioned again.

By the time of the musicale, the Mallet girls had settled into the room they had elected to share. They were thrilled when informed of the musicale at the main house to which they had also been invited.

Persys and Laura had agreed on a rota of duties, sharing some, dividing others as they pleased.

Persys had seen little of the duke which was just as well, she knew. While it was very difficult, she must steel herself to a life without him. What utter folly, to fall head over heels with a duke!

Laura supervised the Mallet girls as to what was appropriate dress for a musical evening. "It is good experience for them, for Her Grace is of the highest *ton*," she explained to Persys with enthusiasm.

The Russell House party entered the awe-inspiring entry of the main house with appropriate hesitancy. Only Persys looked to feel somewhat at ease and she worried about meeting the duke after all these days.

At that moment, as though sprung from her thoughts, the duke ran lightly down the stairs. He murmured something to Portman, then came forward to greet Mrs. Woodhall and the Mallet girls. He turned to Persys at last. Somehow she found her arm tucked in his and within moments deep in conversation, quite as though she had never left. Mrs. Woodhall took one look and ushered the girls in Portman's wake.

"How do things progress?" he inquired with a nod at the Mallet girls who couldn't contain their awe at the magnificence around them.

"Mary and Jane are dear girls and as good as may be. Which is an excellent thing, you may guess, what with Araminta Caswel due to arrive next week. Drusilla Thorpe is coming as well. After that I anticipate a veritable flood of young beauties on our doorstep."

"You are happy?"

How did she answer such a question? If she said no, he'd demand the reason. If she said yes, it would be a lie. She sidestepped instead. "I am content at Russell House, Your Grace."

"That is not what I asked, but I fancy you'd not give me a direct reply no matter what. Am I right?" He slowly led her into the great drawing room where a considerable number of people were assembled.

"I cannot think why it should be important," Persys insisted, quite unable to deal with his teasing.

"Ninian returned from Russell House not long ago with a hangdog expression on his face. When I demanded to know the source of his distress, he said you had declined his wish to pay you his addresses. You would rather be a schoolmistress than wed?" The duke lingered near the door and such was his demeanor that none dared intrude where he and Persys stood in quiet conversation.

"That is an unfair question but I shall attempt to answer it anyway. Of course I would like to wed, but not the very nice Mr. Hervey, who surely deserves something more than lukewarm affection at best."

"I see. Have you perhaps given your heart to another? Or is that question beyond the pale?" He smiled down at her, and Persys wanted nothing so much as to fling herself into his arms, never mind there was a gathering of people present.

"Assuredly beyond the pale. A gentleman does not ask such a question of a lady, Your Grace." She probably looked as flustered as she felt. She had not anticipated he would probe into her feelings to this extent.

"You blush, delightfully so I must say," he said, definitely teasing now.

"Harry, what are you saying to Persys to put such color in her cheeks?" the duchess demanded in a loud whisper.

"Nothing uncivil, Mother. Persys is too sheltered from gentlemen and their teasing, I fancy."

"Well, come to the front and settle into your favorite chair, Harry, for I would have the music begin. What a pity you cannot read to us, Persys, for I suspect a good many people would rather hear you dramatize Miss Austen than my assortment of musicians." The duchess bestowed a look on her son before swishing off to the far end of the room where a small raised platform had been set up.

"We had best do as she says or she will keep us from the supper later on," the duke said, keeping Persys close to his side as he politely wound his way through the assemblage of guests until he reached a splendid armchair in the front row. There were several others. He motioned Persys into the one next to him and when she had settled, he sat beside her quite as though it was a thing of no importance.

Persys found her brain in a whirl. Why had he singled her out for such attention? Did he think to promote the school in this manner? Or what?

The harpist who performed first was likely talented, although you couldn't have proved it by Persys. Her thoughts chased each other around like a puppy after its tail.

By the time supper was announced she was no closer to a solution but had managed to listen to bits and snippets of the music offered.

"How did you like that Corrette piece for harpsichord, violin, and flute?" the duke inquired as he guided Persys in the vague direction of where the supper was to be found.

"Charming," Persys said, wondering which piece it was and if she had paid the slightest attention.

"As I thought, you were elsewhere. And where were you, Miss Timothy? Or am I unfair in asking?"

And all Persys could do was blush and pray that someone would distract his attention so she could join Mrs. Woodhall.

Chapter Fifteen

*H*er salvation arrived in the form of Lady Caswel, who bustled up to Persys with a self-important air. She totally ignored the duke, launching a verbal attack, as it were, on Persys without any round-aboutation. "I must speak with you at once," the lady declared.

Although Persys was sorry to lose the duke's company, she did not regret the change. He had unsettled her to the point where she scarce knew what she did. "Of course, Lady Caswel." With a politely serene smile at the duke, Persys veered away from his side, taking Lady Caswel with her.

"It is Araminta," her ladyship declared in aggrieved tones. "She insists she has no need of schooling and can do well enough without any guidance. And, Miss Timothy, I know very well she is wrong. She has become a headstrong girl and nothing I say seems to reach her. What shall I do?"

Surprised at the admission from one she considered a stern parent, Persys thought for a moment, then suggested, "Why do you not bring Araminta for tea this coming week? The Mallet girls are with us and Drusilla Thorpe should arrive any day now. Without Araminta knowing it, we shall test her on the social graces she will be expected to have polished. If she is as she insists, you will be spared the expense of her schooling. I should hope the other girls will not be cruel, but even a few giggles can embarrass one."

Lady Caswell sank down on a hall chair—one of the many lining the wall and possessing the sole value of being convenient. They were hard and uncomfortable, but Lady Caswel appeared not to notice.

"That might do very well," the lady said thoughtfully. "I will bring her to tea—shall we say Wednesday next?"

"We will be ready, Lady Caswel," Persys replied, an inner smile lighting her remarkable eyes.

"What a blessing you elected to open a school. You would never get a job as a governess with your looks." Lady Caswel patted Persys on the hand, then rose to sail down the corridor.

"You look rather bemused, cousin. An encounter with a prospective parent?" Katherine inquired, giving Persys a cautious smile.

"Indeed," Persys replied, "a minor problem which will be sorted out in no time at all." At her cousin's look of inquiry, Persys added, "Miss Araminta Caswel is of the opinion that she needs no instruction, that she is quite ready to take on the *ton* just as she is."

Katherine said, "Isn't she the little horror who was flirting so outrageously?" The two women exchanged knowing looks.

"Precisely the one," Persys said with a dry smile.

"What shall you do?" Katherine said as they slowly walked toward the supper room.

"Have her to tea. And invite Mr. Hervey and Lord Burfield as well as the Mallet girls. If she is as I suspect, she will reveal her deficiencies soon enough."

"What a wicked thing to do," Katherine said with a giggle. "But so necessary. When I think of those poor girls who descend upon London with no notion of proper behavior I could weep."

"Not as much as their despairing parents."

Lord Torrington joined them and Persys drifted away from them in a few moments.

"I thought it did not disturb you to see your cousin with her husband?" the duke gently probed, coming up behind her when Persys had believed herself quite removed from him.

"It does not in the least, Your Grace, but"—Persys glanced at her cousin happily smiling at her beloved—"I did feel a bit superfluous. They have no need for company, I think."

"Lady Caswel had a problem?" he questioned while again guiding her toward the supper room as though they had not been interrupted.

"Araminta thinks she has no need for schooling prior to London and Society."

"Good heaven, that chit? And what do you propose?"

Persys explained her plan, and wondered how it was that the duke had again gravitated to her side. Surely there ought to be someone else with whom he could converse? He really had no need to turn her insides into confusion—not that he was aware of her feelings. She caught sight of Laura and was inspired to say, "Excuse me, Your Grace. I must confer with Mrs. Woodhall regarding Araminta."

He murmured acceptance of her withdrawal, then watched as Persys wound her way through the clusters of people to Laura's side. Persys could feel his gaze on her; it nearly was her undoing.

It took but minutes to explain the situation with Araminta Caswel to Laura, who happily agreed with the plan that Persys had devised.

"With any luck at all we shall contrive to make Araminta realize precisely how lacking in social graces she is," Laura said in conclusion.

"I think Mr. Hervey and Lord Burfield will go along with us on this."

"Just what will Burfield do, fair lady?" his lordship inquired, the kind expression on his face making a fiction of his stern tone.

"Perhaps you could explain?" Persys begged Laura.

Curiosity flared briefly in Laura's eyes but she nodded, turning to Lord Burfield to garner support for the needed lesson.

Persys looked about her as she walked to the far end of the corridor, hoping to evade the duke. She could see no sign of him anywhere. She had just breathed a sigh of relief when she heard his voice and froze in place, shrinking against the wall as he continued to speak to someone in the adjacent room.

"You are right, Mother. I must marry—as you have often pointed out to me. You will be pleased to know I agree and have selected my bride."

"I will approve your choice?" the duchess asked, her voice arch.

"I believe you will."

"It is time for me to remove to the dower house in that event," she responded at once. "It will take a little time to make it just as I like. By the time it is ready, you will be bringing your bride home to Eddington Park. I gather she likes the country?"

"Indeed, I believe she does."

"And you tease me with her identity. Can I guess?" the duchess said with a hint of laughter in her voice.

"It will do you no good. I'll not put a jinx on my choice."

"I see," the duchess said slowly. "Well, I wish you the very best. She will have you, of course. Who could resist you?"

"As to that, I doubt my title is all that important to her. I fancy she wants something more."

"Wise girl."

Persys didn't wait to hear beyond those words; they were quite enough. She inched away from her spot, then hurried in the opposite direction as fast as she dared. It would not do to call attention to her flight. At last she sidled up to Laura, hoping it would appear she had been there longer than she had.

"Persys," Laura said quietly, "are you unwell? You seem rather pale. Where did you go?"

"I need something to drink. The heat, you know," Persys responded vaguely. She failed to tell where she had been, for that involved more explaining than she cared to do at the moment. She was in shock: her worst fears were to be realized. The duke would marry and not her.

Laura provided the required beverage by plucking a glass of lemonade from the tray of a passing footman. "Here."

Persys downed the lemonade, then helped herself to a glass of champagne from another convenient tray. Ignoring Laura's raised brows she drank that down as well.

"At least you have some color now. The heat can be dreadful in these affairs," Laura murmured, maintaining the fiction that Persys suffered from such a thing.

"I shall join you for the rest of the evening. I would not presume to intrude upon His Grace again. Indeed, I cannot think why he wished to talk to me, other than to inquire how the school proceeds."

"I had not thought you intruded on him *before*," Laura

protested. "It rather seemed to me that he plucked you from our sides and swept you off with him."

"He was being kind, I believe," Persys said after mulling over the various possibilities for his actions. "He wants the assembled guests to know that the school has his mother's patronage and his as well. He is very thoughtful," she concluded softly.

"How fortunate you have not fallen in love with the man. I should think heartbreak would follow such foolishness," Laura observed, while nudging Persys back to the large drawing room where the little musical evening was to conclude with a harp, flute, and pianoforte trio.

The Mallet girls had not said a word to this point and now an awed Mary whispered, "The duke is extremely elegant, as is the duchess. Will we have to mix with people of that stature while in London?"

"Perhaps not dukes and duchesses, but you will be among the highest in the land, yes. That is why it is so important to know what is proper." Persys dropped a curtsy to Lady Thorpe as she spoke while Mary watched with care, prepared to attempt a duplication if required.

Jane sighed. "I wonder if we shall ever be ready?"

"Half the battle is knowing you have much to learn . . . unlike a few others who think they know everything," Persys said, ushering the girls to their chairs.

She supposed the music was lovely; certainly Laura wore an enraptured expression on her face. Persys could only hear those remembered words over and over again. He had selected a bride. Soon she and the world would learn of his choice. She could only be grateful the school would occupy her every minute; she'd not have time to dwell on the matter.

They drove home in the landau that had been sent for them earlier. Laura leaned back against the squabs and sighed with pleasure. "This is truly like dying and going to heaven; I've not heard such heavenly music in years. Not to mention all those delectable tidbits offered in the supper room. And to have the use of this landau, well . . . we are most favored."

"It is nice," Persys murmured, then encouraged the Mallet girls to talk of their impressions. They had done far better than she had expected and so she told them.

It took a little time to get the excited girls to bed. When done, Persys went to her own room where Moggy awaited her. She closed her door and whispered into the quiet of the room, "I will be a spinster and teach school forever." She gathered Moggy in her arms. "I shall be happy here with you," she informed her cat. Then, to disprove her claim, she threw herself in a heap on the bed pillow and cried her eyes out, snuffling into Moggy's fur and in general letting all her misery pour forth.

In the morning, after smoothing her skin with marshmallow ointment, putting a few drops of eyebright in her eyes, and a careful application of the lotion the duchess had made her for her skin, she braved the breakfast room. Laura appeared to notice nothing amiss. She murmured something about work in the office and left Persys to sip her tea and nibble a piece of toast while sighing over what she couldn't have.

Over her tea Persys came to a conclusion regarding the duke's prospective bride. When she joined Laura in the office after setting the Mallet girls to practicing their curtsy, she said, "I understand the duke will marry before long. I believe he would never marry Charlotte. I suspect it is a case of selecting a name from the suitable list."

"The suitable list? . . . ah, yes. I see what you mean. It would save him so much trouble—courting and all that. Although in fairness I should think a duke could ask just about anyone he wishes. Who would say no?" Laura asked, with a penetrating stare at Persys.

"I cannot imagine," she said absently. "Do you know what day Drusilla Thorpe is to arrive? Tuesday or Wednesday?"

"Tuesday, which will have her here for the tea, will it not?"

"We ought to have more men," Persys said with a sigh. "Pity George Russell was such a nodcock. He would have done nicely. He may be obnoxious, but he is good *ton*—unfortunately."

"His Grace?" Laura suggested, not commenting on Mr. Russell one way or the other.

"I imagine he will be busy if he intends to pursue the matter of a bride. It sounded to me as though he had about made up his mind and was ready to proceed. I doubt we will see much of him these next weeks."

"Are you pleased at the thought?" Laura speculated.

"I am," Persys replied instantly, then wondered she wasn't struck down on the spot for lying.

Drusilla Thorpe arrived Tuesday afternoon as did the recalcitrant Araminta Caswel. On Wednesday the tea was to be held. Persys had found the planning kept her mind fairly well occupied and she blessed the rebellious Araminta for that.

On Wednesday following nuncheon Persys sought out a sullen Araminta and said, "I thought perhaps you would enjoy meeting a few of your fellow students and perhaps displaying to Mrs. Woodhall and me your Society manners."

"I have no need to polish my manners," the girl said rudely. "I will show you all how well I do—that stupid Jane and her prissy sister Mary, and that wretched Drusilla Thorpe—who is too good to be real." She flounced off toward her room, leaving Persys wanting to paddle her.

"Mind you are down in time," she said.

The girl came downstairs just before the others were due to gather. She was garbed all wrong in bright cerise sarcenet, but there was no telling her that. Her dress was more suitable for an evening party, her cheeks had been touched with rouge, and her hair was a confection of feathers and curls more proper for a married woman than a girl of eighteen. Persys compressed her lips and said nothing. Wherever Araminta had found such a dress was beyond Persys's imagination.

Jane and Mary were standing near the fireplace when Persys entered the drawing room with Araminta in tow. Drusilla sat gracefully on the sofa. All three girls were appropriately dressed in pastel muslins with simple hairstyles and not a smudge of rouge among them.

Araminta gave them a sullen greeting, then flounced to a chair.

Rose carried in a tea tray laden with all the delicacies to be found in a London drawing room.

"Mary and Jane, do join us. Perhaps Araminta will pour?"

Before the girl could pick up the teapot, the thwack of the brass door-knocker was heard, followed by bass murmurs in the entry hall.

Rose entered the room, followed by several gentlemen. "Callers, ma'am," she said to Laura. "His Grace, the Duke of Eddington, the Marquess of Torrington, Lord Burfield, and Mr. Hervey." With that recitation, Rose faded away to the kitchen again for another pot of tea plus wine for the men.

Laura rose to greet the gentlemen, drawing them over to meet the girls, quite as though they were total strangers. All did well save for Araminta, who flirted excessively, even with the very married marquess.

Well-primed on the purpose of the call, the men performed beautifully. When complimented, Drusilla lowered her eyes, then thanked Lord Burfield with proper decorum. Jane and Mary were terribly shy, but neither of the girls spilled nor were they rude.

Araminta did almost everything wrong. If Lady Caswel had taught her a thing, it had been forgotten. She slopped tea when pouring, helped herself to biscuits before offering them to anyone else, and laughed far too loudly at a witticism offered by Mr. Hervey. She was rude to the girls and Laura. Worst of all was a salacious remark better left unsaid that might have come from a fast widow.

There was utter silence in the room after she had tossed off what she thought was a very adult bon mot.

Then Drusilla hid her mouth behind her hand to stifle a giggle. She gazed with pity at Araminta, as did the shocked Mary and Jane, who might be young but were not stupid.

All four gentlemen looked uncomfortable, then made their excuses before abruptly leaving. The duke swept Persys along with him to the front door.

"You had best give up on her: I doubt she will be a credit to the school no matter how hard you try. The chit is worse than I thought. She is a shocking horror." He took Persys's hand in his, though to persuade or give comfort, she wasn't sure which.

"She is a foolish young girl who has gained the wrong impression of what is done in Society. I suspect she has observed some woman she admired behave in the same way and copies her. We have a large task on our hands, but I do not think she is entirely hopeless." Persys extricated her hand from the duke's comforting clasp.

"I think this is too much for you to handle—" he began, then stopped at her look of outrage. "Well, rely on Mrs. Woodhall. She will be a great comfort and help to you."

Persys leaned against the door when it had closed behind him and knew then that the school wasn't far enough away from his house. As long as she could see him, talk to him, she was too close.

"Everything be all right, miss?" Rose asked with a worried frown.

"All is as it ought to be at the moment," Persys assured her. Returning to the drawing room, she found the girls in the middle of an animated argument.

"My mother would have been horrified to hear what you said," Drusilla exclaimed. "And your dress is too elaborate for an afternoon tea."

"I do *not* think it proper to use rouge, or at least quite so much of it," Mary added gently.

Jane walked around a seething Araminta and said, "You talked as though you knew how to go on in Society. I daresay my little sister would do better than you. At least she can pour tea without spilling!"

"It is permissible to flirt, but discreetly, perhaps with the fan or the eyes. It is not proper for an eighteen-year-old girl to practically offer herself on a plate to a gentleman," Laura scolded, quite incensed with the girl's outrageous coquetry.

"I hate you all!" Araminta stormed. "You are just jealous because I am prettier and have more dashing dresses."

"I would say that Miss Caswel needs to learn humility, not to mention what is properly worn to various functions, and what is decent conversation—along with a good many other things," Persys inserted before Laura could explode. "Drusilla, Mary, and Jane, why do you not go for a short walk? Araminta, I think Mrs. Woodhall and I will accompany you to your room to inspect these dashing dresses you mentioned. As a mere beginning, you understand. But understand this, my good girl, you are going to do us credit."

The ensuing inspection brought forth an amazing collection of gowns, all more suitable for one Laura's age than Araminta's. They confiscated the rouge pot, whisked off all the unsuitable gowns to be altered before they could be worn, then—leaving Araminta pouting in her room—took refuge in the office.

"Dear heaven, what are we to do with that girl? 'Tis obvious her mother has no control over her—those gowns! I'll wager her mother didn't see the results of their orders to the dressmaker. That I should hear a tale as scandalous as that from an innocent girl is enough to make me faint," Laura said, pouring a cup of restoring tea that Rose had brought immediately as they returned to the lower floor.

Persys picked up one of the gowns to be altered to inspect the low neckline. "Well, I'll say this for her, she has the bosom to do the gown justice."

"Indeed," Laura said with a sigh. They exchanged looks before both subsided into reflections.

"The duke asked what we would do with Araminta. He thinks the school too much for me," Persys said eventually with a loud sigh. "He seems to have a high regard for you at any rate. Said you would be a great comfort and help to me. I suspect I may be in over my head."

"You cannot allow Araminta Caswel to do you in before we have begun!" Laura cried in dismay. "Where is your backbone? You must see this as a challenge."

Persys mildly agreed, but privately had her doubts.

Several other girls who had applied arrived the following day and Persys was relieved beyond measure that they all appeared pleasant, dutiful girls who had no more than a normal amount of spirit. Perhaps the school would not be as bad as she had begun to fear.

By the weekend Persys felt they had settled into a good routine. She was so busy she scarce had a moment to herself and when she fell into bed come night, if she sniffled and wished her life might be otherwise, no one knew of it. Her supply of eyebright was soon depleted and she needed both marshmallow and the special lotion made from elder flowers and crushed almonds compounded by the duchess. Persys liked the scent and decided she would brave the main house in the hope that the duke would be off with his friends.

She took the gig and when she entered the house she found Katherine crossing the entry, garbed as for a journey.

"You must have read my mind. Christopher says it is time to go home and so we must. There is much to be done and we have been away quite long enough. Now that your school has begun I shan't see you but rarely." She studied Persys, a concerned expression in her eyes.

Persys embraced her cousin, said all that was proper, then begged leave to find the duchess. "I must request some of her wonderful preparations, for they do wonders to my skin," Persys exclaimed. Nothing would do but that Katherine go with her. Persys was grateful for her company. Should she see the duke, she would have a protection of a sort.

The duchess was in her stillroom, compounding a lotion from damask roses.

When Persys explained her mission, the duchess was delighted. "How nice to know you appreciate my little lotions. I am rather good, if I do say so." She searched the shelves, pulled several bottles from them, setting them before Persys and Katherine with the air of a conjurer.

"This will do you both a world of good. Take them," she urged. Then she continued talking while walking with them along the hall. "I was coming to see you soon, Persys. I am planning to remove to the dower house and I would seek your help. You did such a splendid job of Russell House. I admire that ability—to see what needs doing and have it turn out so well. I shall want new curtains, possibly at least one new rug. And I want to take a number of things from here. Harry said I might use what I please. I gather he wants his new bride to select a few things."

Persys felt her heart grow icy within her. "He has proposed and been accepted? I had not heard."

"No, no," the duchess said with an impatient wave of her hand. "He says it takes subtlety and time, whatever he means by that. In my day if a man wanted to marry, he put it to the test at once, not pussyfooting around like some shamus."

"I'd wager your husband did just that," Katherine said with a grin.

"Indeed, he did. Now, as to your assistance, if I send someone to help at the school for a few days, would you please aid me, Persys?"

"Of course I will," Persys said instantly. What else could she say? The duchess had been more than wonderful to her since Persys had arrived at the Park. It was the least she could do to help if asked. "Who will come, so I may tell Mrs. Woodhall?"

"My daughter's retired governess lives on another part of the estate. I asked if she would be willing and she fair leaped to assist us. I suspect she has grown a trifle bored with doing little or nothing."

Persys murmured something suitable, then after hugging Katherine farewell and promising to come for the baptism, left the house. Her mind was not on her driving as she guided the little gig back to Russell House. When she informed Laura of the plan, she was surprised to see an exceedingly thoughtful look settle on Laura's face.

"I find it rather odd nothing was said about the governess before this, but I also can find nothing wrong with the plan. If the dear duchess wants your help, then help you must."

If Persys thought she could avoid meeting the duke because she was at the dower house helping the duchess, she was badly mistaken. It seemed that every time she turned around, there he was doing something or other. If he wasn't making a suggestion regarding a painting, he was offering an opinion on where a piece of furniture ought to go. And nothing would do but that Persys come along to the main house to help select the things for the duchess.

"You have an artistic eye," he explained. "I feel certain that now you know what things are at the dower house you will see what can enhance them." He swept her through the entry along to the yellow drawing room. "Now, what about these chairs? Personally, I am tired of yellow, but I'd never say a thing to my mother. 'Tis her favorite color, after all."

Persys, who had come to feel the same way about the over-whelming use of butter-yellow nodded her agreement. "Why not take this chance to send them to the dower house? Your mother will adore them—perhaps those draperies as well."

"The rug? I would see something other than blue and yellow for a change. What would look nice in here do you think?" he asked casually, examining one of the chairs that was to go.

Persys closed her eyes, mentally picturing the room as it might be. "Well, a multicolored Turkey rug of soft hues and pale rose walls, with furniture covered in muted fern greens and rose, with a dash of ivory . . . But"—she halted in mid-thought—"you ought to permit your bride to select the new arrangements."

"You have a point there," he muttered before requesting the rug be rolled up and taken away along with the chairs. "I do think I'll have the room painted as long as the place is bare, however. The room wants a warm color and pale rose would be a welcome change."

It was scarcely bare, but with much of the furniture gone, it would seem denuded. Persys went home that evening in more of a depressed mood than ever.

To make matters even worse the retired governess, Miss Rachael Smythe, turned out to be a jewel. She and Laura got along famously and the girls obeyed the woman accustomed to giving orders to difficult girls.

Persys felt useless, a supernumerary, and wondered where she might go, what she might do. Perhaps she might set up a little establishment of her own after all.

Chapter Sixteen

There was no escaping it; she would have to leave. Now that Miss Smythe was available, seeming eager to do something productive with her life, there really was nothing keeping Persys at Russell House. Indeed, they could use her room for another student, she thought morosely, hugging Moggy to her bosom. The cat appeared to sense her mood, for he snuggled up to purr his raspy rumble in her ear.

"I wonder where I could go that would accept you as well?" she mused. "I have it," she said suddenly, "I wanted to set up my own household and I shall! Society can be hanged. What does it matter to anyone but me?" She rose from her chair by the window, placed Moggy gently on her bed, and pulled her case from beneath it.

"You going someplace?" Libby inquired in much the same way she had before Persys had departed from London.

"Eventually." Recalling that moment in the past, Persys gave her maid a bleak glance, then set about removing some of her things from the chest. "I want to go elsewhere and I am not truly needed here. Miss Smythe and Laura get along splendidly and the girls mind them very well."

"Always thought this was a harebrained scheme," Libby declared, her voice gruff. "Where do we go from here?"

"There is no hurry. I shall study a map, decide upon a likely village, perhaps make a few inquiries before making a final decision."

"That Mr. Hervey would doubtless help?" Libby said with a curious note in her tone.

"I do not wish Mr. Hervey's assistance, Libby."

Whatever else might have been said was lost when Rose tapped on the door to announce the carriage from the main house had come and was waiting for Miss Timothy.

Giving Libby a puzzled glance, Persys smoothed down her simple lavender-sprig muslin gown, picked up her reticule and a shawl, then went down to the entry hall where a footman awaited her.

A footman stood inside the door, a folded paper held out in his hand. Persys accepted the message, scanning the contents quickly. The duchess begged her to come at once to assist her with the arrangements of the dower house.

Laura entered the hall at that moment. Once Persys had explained the situation, Laura urged her to go immediately. "We can manage nicely without you, dear. Miss Smythe is wonderful with the girls. She even has persuaded Araminta there is more to be learned to achieve perfection!"

"Wonders, indeed," Persys said with a brave smile, then left the house with a downcast expression on her pretty face.

The drive to the dower house was short and when she arrived it was to find the place a hive of activity. Footmen, grooms, and other workmen from the estate had been pressed into moving all the furniture and rugs Her Grace had selected.

"Ah, Persys, my dear," the duchess said with obvious delight. "As you see we are moving today. Once I make up my mind—unlike my dilatory son—I want action at once. I intend to have all in place and sleep here this evening if possible."

"Goodness!" Persys exclaimed, awed by the speed with which the duchess proceeded.

"What I wish you to do is to tell the men where to put things," the duchess announced as though Persys was a mind reader of some skill. "Now, do not look at me like that. You have excellent taste. When Harry told me of your suggestions regarding the yellow drawing room, I knew at once you were the one to assist me in arranging my things here." She took Persys by her arm and led her into the house. The smell of fresh paint still hung in the air, but with the doors wide open ought to fade soon. With all the help, it might be possible for the duchess to move in this day. Persys set aside her curiosity as to the need for such haste and studied the area around them.

Casting her reticule and shawl on a small entry chair Persys threw herself into the task. It would, she reminded herself, be excellent practice for setting up her own establishment. She possessed an artistic nature that guided her in the placement of the furniture for not only best usage but also a pleasing arrangement. The rug was already in place so Persys had but to order a chair put here, a sofa there, and the chaise longue between the window and the elegant fireplace. An elegant bombé chest with delicate inlay work she had set between tall windows, and ordered a simple looking glass hung above it. The carpenter who was still constructing desks for the school had set aside his task for the day and quickly did as bade.

Once the drawing room was precisely as she wished, she turned to the duchess and absently remarked, "I wish I might find a house something like this for myself. Smaller, of course, but with the same feeling of warmth and excellent proportions."

"I thought you were wrapped up in the school?" the duchess softly inquired.

"They really do not require my services. Miss Smythe is so exactly right to help Laura and very eager to work again. She is wonderful with the girls and they will listen to her when they merely mind me without heeding any lesson I attempt. I fear I am not cut out to be a schoolmistress."

"I had wondered about that," the duchess murmured. "What shall you do?"

Hardly aware she spoke her thoughts, Persys gazed out the multipaned window to the tangled garden without. "I am determined to find a pretty little house in some quiet village and set up an establishment there. You have taught me much about herbs; perhaps I can become an herbalist?"

"That is a noble objective," the duchess agreed. "I have a suggestion to offer. Why do you not reside with me for the time being? You can help with a thousand and one things as I settle in here. I can also teach you more about the herbs, perhaps suggest books that might be useful."

Persys immediately noted that the duchess did not attempt to convince her to remain at the school. Indeed, it was almost as though she encouraged Persys to leave the school. Stifling regret that her efforts had turned a failure, Persys nodded. "If you wish my company for a time, I am only too pleased to offer whatever help I can give."

Their private moment was broken when a footman inquired as to where he ought to place a cabinet.

Persys plunged back into the work, satisfied to be occupied and while not content about her future, at least feeling she was at last on her chosen path to independence.

By mid-afternoon most all was in place. The bedrooms lacked new curtains at the windows, the old being faded and worn. But most carpets were in good repair and the bed hangings still usable, if lacking a certain luster.

"I am determined to sleep here this night," the duchess declared in an uncertain manner. "But I shall miss the big house and all those people about. Say you will join me, take over any guest chamber if you please?"

Surprised and touched that the intrepid duchess had a reluctance to be alone—never mind she had her servants in the same house—Persys promptly agreed. "If you like I shall fetch my things at once. Libby may come as well? I fear she'll not wish to be left behind."

"A devoted maid is the very best servant one can have," the duchess declared roundly. "Go at once and bring all you can with you."

The duchess stood in front of the house near the less than perfectly trimmed shrubbery while she watched Persys disappear down the lane. Persys might have wondered at the smug look of satisfaction that settled on Her Grace's lovely face had she seen it.

At Russell House all was quickly explained to Laura. Miss Smythe professed herself thrilled to have such an agreeable future before her with dear Mrs. Woodhall. Upstairs, Persys discovered

Libby had retrieved the trunk from the box room and packed nearly everything Persys owned.

"I know you, miss. Once you decided you'd move, I packed. You were never a one to waste time."

"Indeed, Libby," Persys agreed in faint accents. If she had felt a bit hurried before, now she felt positively rushed. It was like being swept out with a sturdy broom.

In less time than Persys would have believed, she had completed her packing and bid good-bye to Laura and Miss Smythe. "I shall visit again. And come holidays perhaps you will stay with me?" she begged Laura before entering the carriage. At Laura's nod of assurance, Persys waved her farewell and was off. Her head was in a whirl, yet she was certain she did the right thing. The relief and gratitude on Miss Smythe's face proved the woman truly needed an occupation more than did Persys. Even Laura had urged Persys to go forward with her plans, although they were of the vaguest sort.

Failure is a hard thing to accept. It rankles, sits ill on one's shoulders, and in general makes one miserable. Persys was no exception. By the time she had reached the dower house she was truly blue-deviled.

The first person she saw upon leaving the carriage was the duke. The sight of the one person she sought to escape was enough to ruin what was left of her day. Although, to her relief, he didn't scowl at her like he was displeased with her departure from the school that had so enthused his mother. Come to think of it, he had never been enthusiastic about the scheme. But now he stared at her and she shifted uneasily beneath his intense gaze.

"Miss Smythe has settled in for good, I take it?" He continued to examine Persys as though uncertain what he might expect from her. Did he think she was likely to explode?

"It is odd how she was so close by, yet not mentioned regarding the school," Persys said, bringing forth a matter that had puzzled both her and Laura. "Why did you not suggest her for my helper before the letter went off to Mrs. Woodhall?"

"She was, um, on one of my other estates and I'd quite forgotten her existence until Mother happened to mention her later." He looked uneasy and Persys could think of no reason why, but she didn't feel she could pursue the matter, either.

Libby slid past Persys carrying two valises. A groom and one of the footmen who remained at the dower house removed the trunk from the boot and disappeared into the house, leaving Persys and the duke alone save for a curious Moggy.

"You brought the cat?"

"I would never desert a friend," Persys declared firmly. "He is most faithful. Where I go, he goes."

"Admirable." He paused a moment, then continued, "Mother is pleased you will stay with her for a time. She mentioned something about a house you want to locate?" He stepped toward Persys, still appearing oddly hesitant.

Having had quite enough of the interfering duke, Persys wished he would just get on with it and fetch his bride and be done with helping strays. "I shall seek a land agent when I decide where I want to go."

"Land agent, yes, of course," he muttered.

Persys was surprised to see him ill at ease. It was totally unlike his usual autocratic self. Perhaps his suit with his intended bride did not go well? The idea put Persys in a better frame of mind.

"I believe your mother awaits me?" Persys said at last, breaking the growing silence with a strange reluctance.

"Indeed," he said with a sigh, escorting Persys into the house with alacrity. "Mother awaits, as usual."

"You have Moggy," the duchess said with delight. "There are mice in the stillroom and I cannot have that! Put him out there at once."

Startled at such a reception, Persys immediately went to the stillroom and placed a wary Moggy on the slate floor. He sniffed, gave Persys a look that told her he knew very well what he was to do, and began his hunt.

She greeted the cook and noted there were two kitchen maids at work. In the hall she spotted another maid and a footman, the stout elderly one, from the main house. The duchess had made inroads on the servants, it seemed.

"Mother said you have been enormous help in arranging everything and I can see she was right," the duke said when he saw Persys at the doorway to the drawing room. "This looks quite like home."

"All this yellow, I suppose," Persys replied, gesturing to the rug and chairs. "It is an agreeable task when there are such lovely things to be arranged. I wonder there is anything left in what was the yellow drawing room." She gave the duke a quizzical perusal. His usually serene mien was ruffled; it would appear that whatever disturbed him had not been set aside.

"Yes, well, it was time for a change," the duke murmured, giving his mother a look Persys couldn't interpret.

She ventured into speech. "Moggy seems to know what's expected of him. I trust the mouse population will be diminished in short order," she offered, finding conversation heavy weather.

She wished the duke would go away. Why was he not chasing after his bride-to-be? Or, Persys glumly imagined, was he so certain of her there was no need for courting? If he had turned to the list of desirable bride prospects there would be no need. His solicitor would contact her parents' solicitor and the agreements would be drawn up without the couple even seeing one another. Most likely they had danced or possibly conversed at some *ton* party. That was often the case, she knew. What a depressing prospect; she would want courting were her hand sought.

The duchess murmured something indistinct and left the room, promising to be back in a trice.

Persys strolled across to the multipaned window once again to renew her familiarity with the disordered garden. "I trust your mother will have a fine gardener?"

"She stole mine," the duke grumbled.

"I'm sorry," Persys said, spinning about to find the duke right behind her, still looking rather uncomfortable.

"Took my cook, two maids, two footmen—my house is depleted from more than just furniture." He stared out the window, no doubt frowning at his loss of the expert gardener.

Persys thought he sounded like a boy who has been deprived of his favorite toy. "Once you are married, you wife will no doubt be of great help and comfort."

"There is that," he murmured, then gave her a startled look. "What do you mean? What wife?"

She was truly flustered. She was not supposed to have heard his conversation with his mother, nor be aware of his intentions. What could she say now? "It is expected that you must marry, Your Grace. Eventually," Persys added desperately, for he looked like thunder.

"I do wish people would cease speculating about my future or meddling. Particularly meddling. It is not as though I cannot manage for myself, you know."

"You must recall that a duke generates far more interest than— say—a mere baron might. I feel certain that once you establish your bride at the Park, gossip will die down."

"Little chance of that," he said with a sigh. "Then they will speculate on when the first child will arrive. People are that way."

There was little Persys could say to deny the truth of what he said. People *were* that way, like it or not. They stood in total silence, Persys fiddling with a draw chord and the duke fingering his watch fob—a singularly exquisite piece of utter simplicity.

"You have everything from Russell House?" he inquired into the stillness of the room.

"Yes." The silence grew until it threatened to smother her.

"Persys . . ." he began.

"I found it at last!" the duchess exclaimed as she waltzed into the room, carrying a book in one hand. "The very thing for Persys. 'Tis an excellent book on herbals and since she has left being a schoolmistress and wishes to take up as an herbalist, I shall help. Of course, she will have to spend some time here with me, but I will welcome her company!"

The duke sighed as though greatly put upon, but said nothing, merely giving his mother a look that for anyone else would have meant dismissal or worse.

"Persys is to embark on herbals, is she?" he said, removing the book from his mother's hand to look it over. In the end he offered it to Persys.

"Yes, dear. Every woman must have some favorite pursuit in which to engage. I have found herbals to be greatly satisfying. Will you join us for dinner? Cook brought down a lovely joint and it is ready." She gave him an innocent smile, then turned to Persys. "Perhaps you would like to freshen up before dinner? At any rate, I want a word or two with Harry."

Persys had long ceased to consider the airy dismissal from the duchess as anything to regard with concern. It was better she speak plainly than be annoyed

Once Persys had gone to her room, the duchess turned to her adored son. "You are angry with me. I was afraid you might be."

"I wish you would stop meddling, that is all."

"Meddling! If it were left to you nothing would be done." She sniffed with indignation.

"Please, Mother, I would prefer to handle matters myself in my own way and in my own time."

"Then do so! I have moved; you are free! What is keeping you, for heaven's sake!" She picked up the book Persys had placed on the center table to flip through it, then put it aside. She gave her silent son an annoyed look, then strolled about the room. "You would make treacle in January look fast. You are slower than a slug. Heavens, if you want a girl, then go after her!"

"Rest assured that when the moment is right I shall proceed with all due speed. I do not want meddling!" he declared with the tone of one sorely tired.

Whatever the duchess might have said to this statement was not to be learned, as Persys entered the room followed by the stout footman, now promoted to butler of the dower house. He stood at rigid attention while announcing that dinner was served.

The three dined in silence. Her Grace's only comment other than regarding the food was that she wished she might hire a few musicians to entertain them. Silence was so unnerving.

"Do you like Herr Beethoven's music, Persys?" the duchess inquired as the sweet course was set on the table.

Persys glanced from the duke to his mother and wished she were a hundred miles away. Were she not here they could discuss whatever problem existed and solve their difference. "I suppose I prefer Haydn and Bach," Persys said, wondering how soon she might slip away from the table.

The duchess proceeded to discuss music with a surprising amount of knowledge. Persys listened. The duke listened. Little else was said.

When they left the table—the duke insisting he had no desire to sit alone with his glass of port—Persys begged fatigue and a wish to retire early.

Once in her room she paced a path from door to window until she decided to slip down the back stairway, fetch Moggy, and after letting him in the garden return to her lonely room to contemplate where she might settle with the cat for comfort.

There was not a soul about. The communication between the duke and his mother must be very calm, Persys thought. But then, they were not the sort to toss vases and shout.

Freed from duty in the stillroom Moggy explored the garden, sniffing his way about. Persys strolled behind him, debating the relative merits of Kent and Wiltshire from what little she knew about each area.

"I thought you were fatigued? Or did you just wish to escape a boring evening with us?" the duke queried softly.

"I cannot imagine either of you ever being boring," Persys answered with a chuckle. "Maddening, stimulating, entertaining perhaps; never boring."

"You enjoy the country—you expressed a desire to settle in a village."

"It is preferable to London. The air is much sweeter, the grass greener."

"Have you ever known a desire to travel?"

"Of course. It is not easy for a single woman to do much of anything on her own."

"If you were married, you could do as you pleased."

"True." Persys bent to pluck a daisy, then proceeded to pull the petals off in time-honored fashion.

"Does he love you?" the duke said at her elbow, startling her into dropping the remaining stem.

"The daisy says yes, but I don't believe that. Daisies can tell lies, I think," Persys said with a catch in her throat.

"Persys . . ." He turned her to face him and kissed her with a thoroughness she found entrancing, enfolding her in his arms so she felt cherished and precious.

Unable to resist his appeal, Persys melted against him to enjoy the kiss. He was not engaged; there was nothing wrong in accepting a kiss while in his mother's garden. Immodest, perhaps. She could rue that the remainder of her life. Now she wished to revel in his touch, his kiss.

"Harry? Where are you? I have an idea for you." His mother's voice floated across the garden to reach them. It was an insistent sound and within minutes she would likely search this area.

"Something will have to be done about her," he muttered impatiently.

Still under the spell of that wondrous kiss that she had felt in every bone and sinew of her body, Persys leaned against that marvelous masculine chest. "Tell her to go fly a kite," Persys said without thinking. A rumble of laughter brought her to her senses. "Oh, good grief. I do beg your pardon, Your Grace."

"You have said nothing I have not thought," he admitted. "My patience is sorely tested. Tomorrow I would take you for a drive in my curricle—just the two of us. Would you come, my Persian woman?"

"Yes," Persys answered without any delay. She decided she didn't have a proper bone left in her body after that kiss. She gathered Moggy in her arms and slipped up the back stairs to her room, refusing to contemplate what His Grace intended by his invitation. Perhaps he had some advice to offer regarding her move? Whatever it might be, she would treasure his kiss.

Come morning the duchess remained in her room. Persys made her way to the little breakfast room with its cheerful green-and-white trellis wallpaper and lingered over her hot chocolate and rolls, still recalling the kiss.

The duke had likely teased—he seemed to do a fair bit of that. Yet he had appeared truly annoyed when his mother intruded. Or perhaps a gentleman simply did not appreciate being interrupted? He had not been seducing her—she couldn't think that. It was merely a pleasant evening and she had been in the garden and he'd been moved to kiss her. That was all there was to it and she had better not read more into it.

"Your mother is still abed," Persys informed the duke upon entering the curricle when he called for her.

"I rather thought she might be. We had a little chat last evening and she likely is still seething from indignation. She means well, in spite of her meddling, you know. It is just that she has had her way for so long that she forgets she cannot order the universe."

Persys gave him a puzzled look and murmured something suitable. They passed Russell House and went on to the main road leading away from Eddington Park. Persys wondered where they were going. Perhaps he had a cottage to show her?

"If you are going to show me a house you may save your time. I'll not live in the village," she said a trifle belligerently.

"Good grief, I should hope not. That would never do," he replied while skillfully negotiating the curricle around a team of oxen pulling a heavily laden cart.

All of which plunged Persys into the depths of vexation. How could he treat her so! "Then where are we going?"

"Away from my meddling mother, from my servants, from well-meaning friends and relatives! Was ever a man so cursed in courting as I?"

"Courting?" Persys echoed, most intrigued with this turn of conversation.

"Courting," he replied firmly. "Allow me to reach the place I have in mind and we shall talk without interruption."

She subsided, speculation sending all manner of wild thoughts and notions raging in her head.

When they reached a gentle stream, its banks dotted with wildflowers and a few willows, he reined in. He secured the horse, then helped Persys from the carriage. Within moments they were strolling along the water's edge.

"I was almost of the opinion I am jinxed," he began, placing an arm about Persys in a wonderfully protective way. "Everything I tried to do Mother seemed bent upon muddling up in her usual custom."

"She seems very fond of you, and most concerned for your future," Persys said.

He sighed. "True. But a man does not wish to have his mother directing his courtship. I thought when I brought you to the Park I would have time to court you properly. I reckoned without my mother. She would have had me whisk you to the nearest bishop with dispatch."

"Indeed?" Persys asked, her violet eyes alive with speculation.

"I believe I fell in love with you when I saw you standing before the altar at your cousin's wedding, so angelic in your pretty gown with the flowers woven in your hair. When I looked into those violet eyes I knew that you were fated to be my Persian woman. Just as soon as I learned that you had to leave your aunt's home I decided to take matters in hand. So I urged you to come with me to Eddington Park. I thought that given proximity I could persuade you to love me as well. I'd not reckoned with Mother. Besides, at first you thought yourself in love with Torrington, didn't you?"

"How did you know?" Persys wondered. "I never said a word."

"I watched you. The eyes of love see more than others do," he said simply.

"It was naught but an infatuation and that ended some time ago," she admitted, liking the way his arm tightened about her at her words.

The duke halted beneath a willow, turning her to face him. "Could you love me? Do you?" he asked, tracing the line of her jaw with a tender finger. "I tried so to please you, to win your love. When Mother suggested the school, I saw it as a way to keep you here longer. I was so furious with George it's a wonder he survived. As for Charlotte, I doubt if she will ever cross our boundary again. Even Hervey tried my hospitality. But then, I could well understand how he could easily succumb to your charms. After all, I had. Marry me, my dearest Persian woman? I do not think I can stand more of this courting."

"Oh, dearest, I have loved you for what seems like forever. I could ask for nothing more in life than to be yours." Persys gazed up at him with her heart in her eyes.

"My duchess? You know what it involves after being about Mother." He held her lightly in his arms, his eyes intently searching her face.

"If you are close by, I can think of no problem that cannot be faced. Even your adorable meddling mother." She reached up to touch his cheek, a tender, loving touch that elicited another kiss while he held her tightly to him.

"It just took perseverance," he declared softly at last with great satisfaction, sealing that pronouncement with another kiss.

It was some time before the happy couple found their way from beneath the willow to the curricle. Persys snuggled close to the duke, or Harry, as she had promised to call him.

The drive to the Park proved exceedingly slow, with frequent pauses so the duke might convince his Persian woman that she could never change her mind—which of course she didn't. By the time they drew up before the dower house, she was quite prepared to face the bishop she was certain the duchess would summon. That good lady never left anything to chance.